Pick and Mix

New Writing from Bath Spa's MA Writing for Young People

www.pickandmixanthology.com

Pick and Mix

This is an Artswork Book, published by the Bath Spa
University Presses, Newton Park, Bath BA2 9BN,
United Kingdom, in February 2009.

Designed by the Artswork PublishingLab.
Printed and bound in GB by CPI Antony Rowe,
Chippenham, Wiltshire.

Contents

Acknowledgements

We should like to thank all those involved in bringing the Pick and Mix anthology together:

Julia Green, Programme Leader of the MA Writing for Young People, for providing each writer with the opportunity to learn, flourish and create the stories showcased in this anthology.

Tim Middleton, Head of the School of English and Creative Studies, for his directional and financial support.

Manuscript tutors Nicola Davies, Julia Green, Marie-Louise Jensen, Steve Voake and Mimi Thebo, for the guidance, support and encouragement they each gave to their students.

Nicola Davies, for an enticing introduction to the writing that makes this anthology.

Gemma Matthews, for her hard work, patience and creativity, in designing the Pick and Mix anthology and her work on the accompanying website: www.pickandmixanthology.com.

Nikky Twyman, our proofreader, for casting an expert eye over the text of the anthology.

And last but not least course tutor John McLay, for sharing his industry knowledge and preparing the writers in this anthology to enter the world of children's publishing.

Prose

Foreword

Get ready. You are about to enter more than a dozen different worlds. Some are versions of the world we live in, others are most definitely not. You'll be passing from one to another, with nothing between them but the turn of a page. Don't get me wrong, this is a good thing; a very good thing.

All the same, I feel you need some kind of preparation.

One of the first things you'll notice, when you make a transition from one world to another, is the difference in light levels. You might go from blazing desert sunlight in one story, to dim seaside drizzle in the next. You'll experience different kinds of darkness, too: the simple dark of an ordinary night; the dark of dimension-crossing storms; the kind of dark that sticks round the edge of the page, like used gum.

Don't avoid that dark. It's where you'll find a lot of the most interesting stuff – dead parents, plagues, assassins, gladiators, goblins, doppelgängers. What's there in the half-light isn't all bad, of course. Imaginary babies, dragons and lunatic travelling companions – you'll find these in the shadows too, but don't make any assumptions about that. And don't imagine that sunshine keeps you safe; you'll find that the sunniest school day or Saturday shopping spree can turn sinister, and that, when you are in the grip of unwanted trouser commotion, daylight is the last thing you need.

You're going to meet a lot of different characters. Not the kind that are cut out of cardboard and coloured in by numbers. These characters are real people, even the ones with ears like streamers or occasional furry skins. They are lovable, hateable, unpredictable, recognisable. You'll meet people in these pages you won't want to leave behind, and some you wish you could.

One last thing: I have to warn you that once you've sampled snippets of these worlds, you'll be hooked, filled with a hunger to know how each story turns out.

I could tell you, but I'm not going to.

Just get ready. Relax. You are in the hands of master storytellers.

Nicola Davies

Alison Killeen | Gomorrah

Chapter One

More dead as the new strain of the Gomorrah virus tears through Liverpool.

Twenty more confirmed dead and still no nearer a cure.

This hacked Jake off because it meant the Liverpool match would be cancelled again. Why couldn't it be happening in Manchester? Folding the paper over, he stuffed it through Mrs Kent's letterbox at number three.

Cycling past some shops he saw an old man rummaging through a bin. It was disgusting – no matter how hungry Jake got there was no way he'd resort to bin diving.

"You're gross, you hobo," Jake shouted.

The old guy raised his fist and barked something that Jake couldn't hear.

"Yeah, same to you," he called back.

In his kitchen, Jake was met with silence. He went over to the sink and turned on the tap. It gave a gurgling rumble and a splutter but nothing came out.

"Great."

Using a tea towel, he cleaned his hands. Emptying a load of Chocolly Crocklies into a bowl a couple of the chocolate-covered balls rolled onto the table. Picking one up Jake ate it. It was stale and tasted of cardboard. He tipped them into the bin. His mum walked in.

"What are you doing?" she asked.

"Chucking them."

"Yeah, but why?"

"They're off."

"Oh, what?" she said. "I only bought them yesterday. People are selling any old rubbish."

Jake watched her walk over to the tap and waited for her to turn it on before saying, "There's no water."

She gave him an irritated look. "Thanks for telling me." She took some bottled water and filled the kettle. Sitting down she rested her head on the table, "I'm exhausted."

"You should try getting up for a paper round," he said.

"Life's so hard." She gave a yawn.

He had to admit she didn't look that great. Her hair hung lank around her shoulders and looked like it needed a wash. There were red rims around her eyes.

It had just been him and his mum for years. His dad had left when he was four to go and be an eco-warrior somewhere in Scotland. It used to bother Jake, not having a dad around. Especially when he'd play football, but then his mum started coming. She'd be so embarrassing, screaming and shouting like some mad woman. One time she was given a yellow card for arguing with the ref. His mate, Mattie, calls her their "groupie" and said that she is fit for a mum. Jake thought that was totally sick.

She picked up their paper and read the headline. Her face clouded over. "Nothing seems to be stopping this Gomorrah virus." She looked up at him. "Jake, we need to talk about things."

Jake could feel a lecture coming on. About washing his hands and being careful about who he kissed, like that was going to happen. He nodded towards the clock.

"It's eight. Shouldn't you have left?"

"Oh, damn! I'm so late." She went into the hall hunting for her handbag. "We'll talk tonight," she called over her shoulder.

"Whatever."

She came hobbling back into the kitchen. "Have you seen my other boot?"

Jake looked under the table. It was there flopped over. "It's under here."

"Thanks." She did a wobbly dance as she put it on. "You want a lift?"

"It's okay, I'm meeting Mattie."

"Well, don't be late. See you tonight," and with that she was gone.

Mattie was never on time. Mr Roberts, their tutor, said that "he would be late for his own funeral". Mattie's response was to wait till Roberts' back was turned, then he'd flick him the Vs. So, when he wasn't waiting for Jake, it didn't surprise him and he walked to school on his own.

It was weirdly quiet, like a Sunday. Since the virus had begun spreading more, and more people had left the country. Jake couldn't see the point; it hadn't spread to Wiltshire yet. The silence was interrupted by the sound of hammering. There was a man boarding up the windows of his house using planks from his fence. The boards were all crooked and the bloke was doing a crap job. A woman came out of the front door carrying boxes full of tins and packets. She went over to a car and tried squeezing the boxes into the already full back seat. It looked like it was crammed with everything she owned. Two kids were squashed amongst the clutter. They were hitting each other. The boy grabbed handfuls of his sister's hair and he was pulling it really hard and shouting.

"You're on my side. Get over to your own side!"

The girl screamed, "Let go, let go. Mum!"

The woman dropped one of the boxes on the pavement. Tins of beans rolled under the car.

"Will you two just pack it in?" She bent down and started groping around under the wheels. "I've had just about all I can take of you two today."

Jake went over to help the woman, but when she saw him she looked really petrified.

"No! Leave it," she said.

"I was just going to get the tin for you."

"I don't want your help." She stood up and backed off. "Just get away."

"It's okay. I don't want your stupid beans." It wound Jake up that everyone treated him like a thug just because he was a teenager. "Get your own sodding tin," he mumbled.

The man from the window came over.

"What's going on?" He looked at his wife. "Has he touched you?" he asked.

"No!" said Jake. "I was trying to help."

"We don't want your help." The man raised his hammer. "Get away from my family."

Jake began to panic, convinced that the man was going to hit him. "Calm down, I'm going."

His heart raced as he moved back and crossed over the road. Jake walked quickly away. Once he was at a safe distance he turned to look.

The man had gone.

"Bloody nutter," Jake muttered to himself.

The two kids watched him from the back window of the car, teddy bears and blankets squished around their faces.

Chapter Two

There was a steady flow of kids all heading the same way as Jake. He passed a group of girls all huddled together. One of them looked up at him and laughed. This made him give his fly a quick check, which sent them into a giggling fit. Jake could feel heat rise in his cheeks as he blushed – girls could be so pathetic.

The school gates were closed, which was odd because they were supposed to be at registration. There was a man wearing a paper mask standing in front holding a walkie-talkie. Through the gate Jake could see the car park, which was full of white vans; masked men in white overalls milled about. He wondered if they were painting the school or something.

Jake went over to walkie-talkie man.

"What's going on?" Jake asked.

He handed Jake a piece of paper. "Read the leaflet," he said, voice muffled by the mask.

Jake looked down at the paper.

Symptoms of the Gomorrah Virus

- *Red eyes*
- *Fatigue*
- *Weak limbs*
- *Difficulty swallowing*
- *Respiratory problems*
- *Paralysis in arms, legs, respiratory muscles*

If you experience any of these symptoms, seek immediate medical advice.

"They've missed out one thing."

Jake turned to see Ollie standing behind him. They had a love–hate relationship. Ollie loved himself and Jake hated him.

"What are you going on about?" Jake asked.

"Death."

"What?"

"Death is a pretty major symptom of the virus."

"Whatever." Jake tried to move away but Ollie blocked him.

"You end up completely paralysed, and then slowly and painfully all your organs stop working, but you can't scream because your mouth's frozen."

Jake knew he was enjoying telling him.

"Your eyes bleed too." Ollie gave a triumphant smile. "I've seen a clip of it on YouTube."

"Why the hell would you watch something like that?"

"It's good to know." Ollie shrugged. "If I'm going to end up that way, best to be prepared."

"You are seriously sick," Jake said, shaking his head. "Anyway, we haven't got it down here. The virus is all up north."

"That's where you're wrong, Jakey boy."

"Name's Jake, and what are you on about?"

"There have been some cases at school," Ollie said, losing interest in the conversation.

Jake's mouth fell open. "What... who... how many?"

"I don't know." Ollie pointed towards the man with the walkie-talkie. "He wasn't that chatty. That was all I could get out of him."

"What are we supposed to do?"

"Go home." Ollie shrugged. "Wait to see if you get any of the symptoms." Ollie pulled down the bottom of his eyes, showing Jake their pinkish, vein-filled insides. "Can you see the blood?" he asked, making his voice sound like someone from an old-fashioned horror film.

"Sod off, Ollie."

"It's a day off school," he said. "Anyway, you're feeling all right, aren't you? No stiffness anywhere?" He winked.

"You're sick."

"It brings a whole new meaning to a killer stiffy." And with that Ollie walked off laughing at his own feeble joke.

Jake was convinced that there was a mistake. Sure they'd been having power cuts and the water kept going off. Supermarkets were getting emptier because of the restrictions but there was no virus, no Gomorrah.

Jake couldn't take it all in. What he needed was to get away, to go somewhere normal. He decided to go to Mattie's and to drag him out of his pit so they could spend the day together. Jake felt better having a plan, but as he walked along he noticed that things looked different. Shops that he'd thought were just closed now looked abandoned. A police car passed him, followed by an ambulance. Seeing them gave Jake the creeps. He could feel the hairs stand up on the back of his neck.

The nearer to Mattie's house he got, the more activity there was. Jake could see that the police had taped off an area to keep people back. It reminded him of a crime scene in a police show and he kept waiting to hear some cheesy music as a guy came bursting out of the door. But instead there were more men in paper white suits. They were looking at clipboards as if they were trying to decide what to do.

Some people were standing around watching and Jake searched for Mattie. This was the sort of thing he loved; a bit of drama. It was then it hit Jake. The tape was outside Mattie's house. He went over to the paper-suited men.

"What's going on?" he asked.

He looked up, disinterested in Jake. "It's nothing to concern you," he said going back to his paperwork.

"It's my mate's house."

He ignored Jake.

"Did you hear me?"

The man looked up, gave a shrug and walked off. Jake started after him but a policeman came over and blocked his way. All the policeman had to protect him was a mask and surgical gloves.

"You need to move away from the tape," he said.

"What's going on?" Jake asked, pleading in his voice.

"Look, just go home, son." He looked nervously over his shoulder at the suited men as they went into the house.

"This is my mate's house." Jake's voice faltered.

"I'm so sorry but you really need to leave."

"No. I want to know what's going on."

A woman called out, "It's the virus, isn't it? They've got the virus."

Jake looked from her to the policeman. "Is she right?"

The policeman looked down at his feet and gave a small nod, took a step closer to Jake and said, "Go. Just get away from here."

The door opened and a stretcher was wheeled out, covered with a sheet.

The policeman looked over, hesitated and then said more urgently, "Get away."

The crowd began to speak in loud whispers. One woman said, "They're all dead."

Jake felt like his insides were going to explode. He had to know if Mattie was all right. He tried to break through the plastic tape but the policeman stopped him.

"Don't be stupid," he said. "The site is contaminated."

"No. You've got it all wrong. It can't be Mattie." Jake could feel tears stinging his eyes. "He's my age – he can't be…"

The policeman lifted his hand as if he was going to comfort Jake, but changed his mind and took a step back.

"I'm sorry," he said in a low voice.

Jake felt a pain deep inside. It was like a fist grabbing him and twisting until he didn't think he could take any more. He watched as the stretcher was lifted into the back of the ambulance. A low wail seemed to come from nowhere and it took Jake a few seconds to realise that it was him making it. Tears rolled down his face and gathered around his chin.

Mattie, his best mate, was gone.

He walked away sobbing, not caring what people thought.

Chapter Three

When Jake walked through the front door, his mum was waiting for him. She gave him a look that was full of concern. He just couldn't face her.

"Jake, I heard about school. Are you okay?"

He shook his head and tried to get past, but she took hold of his arm.

"What's wrong?" she asked.

Talk was the last thing he wanted to do. Jake needed to get away from her, to shut himself in his room and block everything out. He shrugged her off.

"Jake, talk to me." Her eyes were red.

Jake wondered what she had to cry about.

He shook his head. "I don't want to talk about it."

She went to touch his face but he pulled away. "Love, I know you're upset. Tell me what's wrong."

He could feel all the sadness begin to bubble up inside him and thought he was going to cry again. Looking down at the ground he said, "I went round Mattie's. He's... dead."

"What?"

Jake shrugged.

"Was there an accident or something?" she asked.

"No it was the..." he broke off.

She gasped. "Not the virus?"

He nodded and she took hold of his hands. Jake had to stop himself from pulling them back.

"But how did he get it?" she asked.

"Don't know," Jake said. "His dad was doing driving jobs up north, but..."

His mum pulled him into a hug. Jake tried to drag himself from her hold. Slowly he gave up the struggle and buried his head in her shoulder. He breathed in her perfume. It smelled of fresh washing and clean sheets, reminding him of being small, of the times his dreams would be full of monsters and her cuddles would chase them away. The image of the stretcher-covered bodies came back to Jake. He let go. Mattie was dead and there was nothing his mum could do.

"I'm going upstairs," Jake said.

His mum's face looked full of sorrow and she tried to catch his hand. "Wait, Jake. I need to talk to you."

"Later."

"But..."

Jake shook his head and turned away.

"Okay, later," she said in a muted voice.

In his room Jake closed the curtains, kicked off his trainers and got into bed. He pulled the duvet over his head, wanting to shut everything out. Escaping to sleep was the only thing he could do.

Chapter Four

Jake woke the next morning. His stomach gave a loud grumble as he untangled himself from his covers. As he sat up, he noticed his mum. She was moving silently around his room.

Jake rubbed his eyes and tried to focus on her. "What are you doing?"

"Packing."

"Packing?"

As his eyes became accustomed to the light, he noticed what his mum was wearing. Wrapped around her mouth was a stripy scarf, and on her hands she had a pair of pink rubber gloves, just like the ones she used to clean the loo.

"What the hell are you wearing?"

She ignored him and rummaged through his chest of drawers. "Have you seen your blue fleece?" Her voice sounded muffled.

Jake sat on the edge of the bed. He was still wearing the clothes from the day before. His head throbbed, and his mum dressed up like a pantomime spy wasn't helping. "What's going on?"

"Have you seen your fleece? I thought it was in here." She carried on looking through the drawers.

"Sod the fleece."

She looked over at Jake. "This is important."

Jake could see her eyes just over the scarf. It looked like she'd being crying. "Tell me what you are doing or get out of my room," he said.

She picked up a pair of his boxer shorts and absent-mindedly she began wringing them. The pink fingers of her gloves twisted with the white of the pants.

He wondered how long it would be before she'd shred them. "You're wrecking my pants."

"I read the leaflet you brought home," she said suddenly.

"What leaflet?"

"The one with the symptoms of the Gomorrah virus on it," she said, putting the boxers into a bag.

"So?"

"You need to go away," she said, and carried on searching for clothes.

"What?"

"You've got to, Jake."

It began to dawn on him, what she was saying. A cold, clammy feeling spread over him. "You think you've got it, the Gomorrah virus?"

She wouldn't turn round but nodded her head slowly. Jake walked over to her but she jumped back; it was like she thought he was going to hit her.

"Don't come near me. I've got some of the symptoms." Her eyes filled with tears. "You need to leave so I don't infect you."

"I'm not going anywhere," Jake said. "Anyway, if you're sick you'll need me to look after you."

"No, I won't."

He shrugged his shoulders. "Well, I'm not going."

"This isn't up for discussion." She slammed the drawers shut, picked up the bag and walked out.

Jake followed her onto the landing. He felt ready for a fight and he could tell this was going to be a big one. He leaned against the door frame. "I'm not going. Anyway, where the hell would I go?"

His mum carried the holdall downstairs and Jake followed.

"Where?" he asked. "I could catch a train maybe, go to the seaside and have a little holiday? I know," he was really getting into his stride now, "I'll jump on a plane and go to Disneyland. Bit of sun and a chat with Mickey, I'll be sorted."

He could tell he was getting to her, but she ignored him and put the bag down next to a rolled-up sleeping bag. His mum went into the kitchen.

Jake added, "If you hadn't noticed, there is a virus going around that's buggering up all the trains and planes."

Her cool lost, she turned to him and snapped, "Yes, Jake. I had noticed." She took a minute to regain her composure and added, "Have you seen your thermal socks?"

"Sod the socks."

She said as matter-of-factly as she could, "You're going to walk and so you'll need warm socks."

It was getting more and more ridiculous.

"Oh, so I'm going on a hike now, am I? Where to – Everest, Great Wall of China? I've heard that the Pyramids are nice this time of year."

His mum turned away and with her back to him she said, "You're going to stay with your dad on his island in Scotland and you're going to have to walk there."

That was beyond ridiculous. That wasn't going to happen.

"No way." Jake hadn't seen his dad for years and he wasn't going to start now.

"Jake, we've no choice."

"You might not, but I do." He sat down at the kitchen table. "There's no way I'm going to be an eco-warrior."

Pulling out a chair opposite his mum, he sat down. She looked anxious, her pale blue eyes surrounded by red. "I've been trying to tell you for days, weeks, but it never seemed the right time."

"Tell me what?"

"Your dad, he's not an eco thingy." Letting out a slow juddering sigh, she said, "He's a scientist and he's been doing research."

Jake felt like he'd just jumped in the deep end of a pool, her voice seemed muffled. Gradually some of her words got through – "scientist" and "research".

"Research – what's he researching?"

"A cure for the Gomorrah virus. He'd…"

BANG! It was as if he'd hit the bottom of the pool. This wasn't happening. She had to be making this up, because if she wasn't, then, then—

"You've lied." His voice was abnormally calm.

"No. I didn't lie. I just didn't…"

"What? Tell me the truth." He spat the words at her. He got up with such force that his chair crashed to the ground, popping the bubble of calm that he had.

"Jake!"

"What? Are you sorry for lying all these years?"

"It's not a—"

"I could cope with Father Christmas being a lie." He was standing over her. "I was never into the tooth fairy – too gay for me."

As he got nearer to her, she moved away and he wondered if she was worried about the risk of infection or if she was afraid of him.

"But this – you not telling me what my dad was really doing. That's got to be the shittiest thing ever."

"It's not like that. I meant to—"

He slammed his hand on the table, making her jump. "You know what? I don't care what it's like." With that he thudded up the stairs and slammed his bedroom door.

Chapter Five

He lay back down on the bed. Everything he knew was falling apart. Mattie was dead, his mum tells him she's ill and oh, by the way, your dad isn't the no-hoper that I always told you he was.

There was a knock on Jake's door.

"Go away."

"Jake, please. You don't remember what it was like."

"I don't care. Get lost."

"Jake, will you stop acting like a child and talk to me." She whacked the door. "We haven't got time for this."

"I'd say we had about eleven years."

She burst through the door, fury oozing from her. "Enough! You don't remember what it was like. You were so little. The hours you'd spend waiting for him." She shook her head. "And then he wouldn't turn up. He'd be off getting arrested because of some protest. He'd spend hours trying to get people to take the virus seriously."

Her words came out in a rush and she stopped for a minute to catch her breath.

"The government thought he was a joke." She looked down at her feet. "To be honest I began to think of him as a bit of a joke, too."

That got a response from Jake. "Yeah, it's all about you."

"Is that what you think?" She closed her eyes. "If he wasn't holding demonstrations about the virus, he'd be flying off to some country where there'd been a report of a new mutation of it."

She'd started to cry and Jake watched as she caught the tears with the back of her hand and wiped them down her trousers.

"No one in power was listening to them. He and his colleagues decided to set up a research unit on Little Cumbrae Island. He wanted us to leave, to go with him." She looked at Jake and, in a whisper, said, "But I just couldn't do it. I couldn't go."

"Why the hell not?" he asked.

"I thought that you were too young to go and live on a wild island. And I began to think that he'd got it wrong. That the epidemic was never going to happen. People, our friends, began to treat him like some mad scientist and I started to think they might be right."

"But he wasn't mad, was he?"

"I know." She sighed. "I really did want to tell you, but it got harder as time passed. I didn't deliberately keep it from you. I just couldn't find the words."

As Jake looked at her in her stripy scarf and gloves, he thought how stupid she looked and how ill. Her eyes were red and he could tell she was struggling to stand. His mum was really ill. He could go to his dad, but that was if he could find him and then there may not even be a cure. So it could be a massive waste of time.

"If I go to him, what makes you think he'll know who I am?"

"He'll know you. You look just like him." She smiled, wobbled a bit then steadied herself.

"Are you okay?" he asked.

"I'll be fine," she said. "I just need a minute. All that packing has taken it out of me."

They both knew that it had nothing to do with the packing.

"I'll go," he said, just above a whisper.

She stepped forward and, for a minute, Jake thought she was going to hug him, but instead she smiled and then left his room. It was only yesterday that he had pushed her away, but now, as he watched her go, all he wanted her to do was hold him just one more time.

Chapter Six

Once the decision was made, Jake's mum was eager for him to leave. She'd done a thorough job packing and the bag was crammed full of clothes, food and bottles of water.

"I've put £30 in the front pocket of the bag. I know it's not much, but it's all I've got," she said.

"Okay."

"Go sparingly with the water, because you won't know when you'll be able to get more." She paced around the sitting room. "But drink regularly. You don't want to get dehydrated."

Jake sighed and nodded.

"Eat regularly. You'll need to keep your energy levels up." She stopped at the mantelpiece and steadied herself against it.

He nodded again.

"Look after your feet." She ran her hands through her hair. "You've got a long way to walk."

Jake nodded again.

"Avoid people. It'll be hard to tell who's ill."

"Okay."

"You must wash. Just because you're on the road doesn't mean you should forget personal hygiene."

That was the final straw for Jake. "Mum! I'm not a kid. Stop stressing."

She sighed. "Sorry." She went and sat down. "I've put a map with the bag. I marked your route on it."

Jake unfolded the map on the hall floor. It curled at the edges as it hit the walls.

"I picked mainly A and B roads," she said. "The minor roads will be better. Fewer people."

The dark pencil line weaved its way up the page.

Jake stared at the map. It seemed hopeless. There was no way he'd be able to walk that far. "Bloody hell, it goes on for ever."

She came to the doorway and looked down at the map. "That's not all of it." She hesitated. "There's more on the other side."

"Oh, what!" He was doomed.

"It's about five hundred miles to Glasgow. Don't go into the city. Go to one of the coastal towns. Get a boat across to the island."

She'd become very businesslike and it reminded Jake of someone giving a spy top-secret instructions.

"Try and do about twenty miles a day. If you can do that, it should take you about twenty-five days to get to Glasgow."

It didn't surprise him that she'd done the maths. "Twenty-five days! That's nearly a month."

"Yes, well done, Jake. But there is no other way."

"But will you be... you know...?" He couldn't bring himself to ask.

She gave him a smile. "I'll be fine."

Jake tried to fold the map back up. It took him two attempts and filled the hall with the sound of rustling paper. How the hell was he going to make it to Scotland if he couldn't even fold the map?

"There's a bit of an art to that," his mum said.

"Yeah, and I haven't got it." He stuffed it into the front pocket of the bag.

Jake picked up the bag. He could feel the strap cut into him. This was ridiculous – it was so heavy, he was going to struggle to get to the end of the road.

"Take a coat."

Jake didn't do coats. He only had one because his mum insisted on buying it, but he'd never worn it. "I'll be okay."

"It's going to get cold at nights, and..."

"All right," he said, grabbing it from the peg. "I'll take it." He tucked it over the bag.

She smiled, her argument won. "Sleeping bag." She pointed at the green caterpillar-shaped object on the floor.

He mumbled under his breath, "Jawohl." He picked it up by the cord.

Jake went to the door.

"Wait!" his mum called.

She couldn't have more bags for him?

Holding on to the door frame, it was as if she was trying to hold herself back. "I... love you."

Jake could feel his face go red. "Yeah... same." He felt such an idiot. Why couldn't he just say it?

As he closed the front door, the reality hit him. He was walking to Scotland. He turned to see his mum watching from the window. She waved at him. It reminded him of when he was a little kid. She'd wait in the playground for him at the end of the day, and when she saw him she'd wave to get his attention.

But he wasn't a little kid any more.

Janine Amos | The Toothgrinder

Chapter One

Daniel ran. Up the alley alongside the park he went, puffing hard in the cold air. Dad ran next to him. Their trainers smacked the pavement and splashed in puddles left by yesterday's rain. It was getting dark. In the yellow glow from the streetlamp, bushes crouched like monsters in the shadows. Bare branches poked through the park railings: witches' fingers, thin and bony. The wind blew and the branch fingers tapped crazily against the bars. Night-time was coming.

When they reached Daniel's house, they stopped.

"See you soon, Danny," said Dad.

Daniel turned and hammered on the front door with his fist.

His sister Chloe opened it. "You're late," she said. "It's nearly your bedtime." She leaned out to wave to Dad.

Daniel elbowed his way in next to her.

"'Night!" they shouted from the doorstep.

"'Night, you two!" Dad called, walking off down the street.

Daniel stood waving goodnight, until Dad was a grey shape in the distance.

That night, in his dream, Daniel ran.

A bright, round moon lit his way. Branches hit his face and clawed his jeans. The ground was wet and his trainers skidded in the mud. Faster and faster he went, deeper and deeper into the wood.

The air smelled bad; mouldy leaves mixed with a sharper stink, like a dead animal rotting. On and on he ran, crashing through the trees. He was panting, his chest hurt, but he knew he couldn't stop.

There was a high, whining sound and a flash of metal. The trees thinned out and Daniel slowed. In front of him, in a clearing, was a small, wizened creature: a goblin. Some kind of machine was spinning, whirling round and round, flicking darts of light into the trees.

Daniel shrank back in the bushes. The creature looked right at him with slit eyes. It came towards him. It stretched out its arms to him. It grinned.

Daniel's tooth sat, large and smooth, in the goblin's cupped hands.

Daniel jerked awake, staring into the blackness. His heart was thumping. Slowly he got used to the dim light of his bedside lamp; there were his shelves stacked high with computer games and Lego. His football kit lay in a pile on the floor.

He heaved himself out of bed and dashed into the cold bathroom to do a wee. Afterwards he tiptoed into Mum's room and slipped into the big bed.

Eyes wide open in the dark, Daniel listened to the steady tick of the wall clock. He knew he should be asleep; school in the morning. But the tick reminded him of something, something in the dream. He shuddered and shrank further under the duvet. He tried to think about Mum's breathing. In, out, in, out – think harder – drown out the click, drown out the tick. Sleep came.

"What are you doing in here again?" she asked the next morning.

Daniel listened for a crossness in her voice – but it wasn't there. She just sounded a bit stuffed up and muffly like she always did first thing.

"Bad dream, that's all," he mumbled, keeping it low so that Chloe wouldn't hear. He began to slink out of the warm space and back into his own room, but he was too late. Chloe leaned against Mum's bedroom door.

"What's up? Dreaming again?" She rolled her eyes and flopped down on the bed, making it groan. "I never woke up as much as you when I was your age."

"Everyone's different," said Mum, throwing back the bedclothes. "Come on, you two. Time to get dressed."

Hurrying to school in the biting wind, Daniel tested his teeth with his tongue. Two new ones were through at the bottom. They were solid; no problems there. A top front one was out, leaving a big gap. He pushed his tongue gently against the wobbly one, bottom right. That was the one to watch, but there were other loose ones too. He swallowed as parts of his other dreams swam into his head – the *click-clicking* sound of the evil machine, the goblin grinning, twisting away at his tooth, yanking it from his mouth, and mopping up the blood with little red rags. Daniel could taste the blood in his mouth now, a salty metal taste.

He zigzagged off down the hill, trying to outrun his thoughts.

That night things were worse. Daniel couldn't get to sleep at all. He read four comics. He listened to Mr Linsky's TV murmuring through the wall. He was tired. He knew he was tired, he wanted to sleep, but he couldn't let go. He lay on his back and heard Chloe going to bed. She clattered about for ages like she always did. *Thump, thump* went her trainers as she kicked them off. She climbed into her high metal bed and the wall between their two rooms shook. Daniel started humming to himself.

Later on came Mum's bedtime sounds. They were the same as Chloe's, only softer, more careful. He heard her sigh and roll over in the darkness. He wiggled his wobbly tooth with his tongue.

Deep, deep in the wood the Toothgrinder sat. In the trees around him hung scraps of cloth, like tattered ribbons. At his feet lay a selection of hooks and knives. They glistened in the moon's pale light. Between the goblin's knees, Daniel's tooth was balanced on a tiny wheel. It glowed in the half-light; glowed and spun. Tiny flakes of tooth were carved off by a whirring metal blade and scattered on the ground. And the noise: the terrible grinding, whining sound of the spinning metal cutter!

"No!" he shouted.

"OK, Daniel. It's OK." Mum was there. "Settle down now."

Daniel shook her away. How could he settle down? He jammed his head against the wooden headboard and pressed hard. Now he was properly awake. He bit down on his bottom lip to stop the tears coming. That taste was back, bloody, in his mouth. He cupped his hand to his lips and his wobbly tooth plopped wetly into his palm.

"Thank goodness that's come out," said Mum. "I expect those dreams will stop now."

Chapter Two

Daniel washed the tooth carefully and rolled it in a tissue. He put it down on the table next to him while he ate his breakfast. Every so often he squeezed the tissue ball to feel the hard knob of tooth buried inside. Chloe eyed him and mouthed, "Disgusting!" so he moved it to his trouser pocket.

All day at school, Daniel kept the tooth with him, safe in the tissues pressed against his thigh.

When school was over, he legged it back up the hill for home. He made for the kitchen and the cupboard where they kept all the odds and ends: rubber bands, used envelopes and boxes which might come in handy one day. He tugged open the cupboard door and yanked out egg cartons, old stubs of candle, string and empty cereal packets. Soon there was a huge pile of junk spread across the kitchen floor.

"What are you looking for?" Mum asked.

"A box." Daniel showed her the size he meant with his fingers.

He was in a hurry. He didn't want to explain; he couldn't explain. It just seemed really important that his tooth was shut up safely before bedtime.

"How about the box my brooch came in at Christmas?" said Mum. "It's on my dressing table."

Daniel jumped up.

"You can have it", she went on, "once you've put all this away – tidily."

Daniel groaned.

He liked the little box. It was covered with black velvety stuff and had a spring lid. There was a solid feel to it; it looked important, too. He placed his tooth gently inside on the silk lining and snapped the lid shut.

Back in his own room, Daniel took four thick rubber bands from his pencil case. He stretched them one by one around the box so they made a firm criss-cross. *That should do it*, he thought. He stuffed the box into the bottom of his sock drawer and ran downstairs for tea.

It was Friday evening, one of Dad's days. Daniel and Chloe's dad didn't live with them any more, but twice a week Daniel met him for football in the park, or swimming. This evening Daniel was glad to be outside, never mind the cold. He hurtled along after the ball, sped across the grass to tackle, and rocketed into the air for headers. The darker the sky grew, the faster he ran and jumped and dodged.

"Hey, Danny, we'll have to finish soon!" called Dad for the third time, puffing to keep up.

Dashing about wildly in the half-light, Daniel didn't answer him. At last Dad grabbed him with both arms in an enormous hug. Daniel could feel the big chest heaving against him as Dad struggled to catch his breath. He pressed his face into his father's tickly jumper and squeezed his eyes shut. It would soon be bedtime and the dreams would start. His tongue darted round his mouth, checking one tooth after another. He poked his tongue hard into the new hole in his gum, trying not to cry.

"Time's up, Danny," Dad said, breathing into his hair, and Daniel twisted away.

Together they wandered back across the grass.

When Daniel got home he dashed to his room and put his hand into the sock drawer. He felt for the box. There it was, just as he'd left it. His fingers followed the protective pattern the rubber bands made. He slid the drawer in again and went for a bath.

Afterwards, he stood on tiptoes to peer into the bathroom mirror. He wiped away the steam to get a good look, and opened wide. He inspected the tiny red dot left in his gum by yesterday's loose tooth. He swallowed. Slowly he squidged a blob of toothpaste on to his brush and carefully cleaned his teeth.

That night his bed was a mountain of pillows. He'd borrowed two from Chloe's room and one from Mum's. He banked them up around him now and lay back against them, upright under the duvet. It was very late. It felt as if the whole world was asleep, except him. His eyelids were getting heavy.

Squeezing through the bushes, clambering over tree roots, the Toothgrinder hunched his shoulders against the rain. Once, he stopped and lifted his head, like a fox scenting the wind. He moved off again, faster and faster. Coming closer. Up through the churchyard he came, climbing over gravestones slippery with moss. In the alley he ran, his breath blowing out tiny white jets into the night air. His tongue flicked across his lips, wetting them, and a little blob of spit settled in the corner of his mouth. He was getting nearer.

Daniel's eyes sprang open. He wriggled up the bed and sat against the pillow mountain, listening hard. All the usual night-time sounds were in place; the rumble of the central heating boiler, the *drip-drop* of the tap in the bathroom. Chloe turned over in bed and the springs creaked. Every so often the rain outside was blown against his window by the wind. But Daniel was reaching beyond these noises, straining his ears for something else. He covered his mouth with his hand.

The Toothgrinder reached the end of the alley. He forced himself between some wire netting and crouched in the darkness. His wet hair hung in tangles around his shoulders. He shook himself and started off again, squinting against the light of the streetlamp. He slipped on the shiny pavement and let out a hiss, but he carried on. He only stopped when he was outside Daniel's house. He squatted down on the wet kerb, like a toad.

E.C. Newman | Korrigan

Chapter One

I wanted to fit in. To blend into the background.

But I've always been different.

I have this one vivid memory in those early years before the brain actually can remember. Before I trotted off to kindergarten and finger-painted. Before birthday parties and dolls and recess.

I was two years old. Mom, Dad and I lived in Cordova, Tennessee. Nice residential area of Memphis.

One sunny afternoon I was in an inflatable wading pool with a neighbor kid. Tommy. We must have been friends. Tommy's mother was my mom's best friend when we lived in Cordova. She wasn't after that day.

Tommy and I were having a fine old time when he went and splashed me. Got water in my eyes and it stung. Stung so much that I hollered. He laughed at me.

I remember getting so angry at him. I've never liked being laughed at. No matter the age. No matter when my parents said they were laughing "with" me years later. It was something I've never responded well to.

I stared at his scrunched-up laughing face and felt this deep roaring anger in the pit of my stomach. I wished I could splash him back. Make him cry.

In my limited imagination, I saw this huge tidal wave of pool water knock him over. Nowhere to run. Nowhere to hide.

I glared at him and, just like in my head, a huge (well, huge to a two year old) wave of water rose up and splashed him, getting into his open eyes and up his nose.

Tommy started crying.

But I never moved my hands. I didn't really have the strength to do more than a ripple in the water. But he was hit with what could have been a wading pool tsunami.

Boy did he wail.

If our mothers hadn't been so observant, nothing would have been made of it, I'm sure. They would have assumed I'd splashed back and now he and I were put out with each other. But they had both seen. Mom shared with me much later that she'd thought it was weird, but didn't pay much attention to it. Not until the incident in the bath.

Apparently whirlpools don't happen in the bathtub.

But that day with the pool, Tommy's mom quickly excused herself and grabbed her son and left. No explanation or anything.

Tommy and I never played again.

I wasn't to find out exactly what I had done until much, much later. After Mom and Dad's divorce when I was fourteen. After Mom got promoted and transferred to Florida right in the middle of my junior year of high school.

Because that's when things really started happening.

. . .

"Have a good day, girls," Mom told us as she got into her car to go to work. She'd been transferred, which brought us from upper-class Germantown, Tennessee to the tiny town of Keystone Heights, Florida. Mom's job was actually not in Keystone, but in Gainesville, which was thirty minutes away. But Florida, state of tourists and retirees, was not cheap to live in, so it was Keystone, in an old one-story house that sat on a lake.

"Maybe," Wendy replied with a smile. Wendy was the good daughter. She screwed up every once in a while, like forgetting to call home when out with friends, but in comparison to me, the freaky one, she was the better child. "Make new friends!" she teased Mom.

Mom was watching me through the windshield. Hoping I would say something.

"Abby?" she called.

"Later, Mom." I appeased her. She smiled, but it didn't reach her eyes. Not that I had any insight into the adult female mind, but at that moment I knew exactly what she was thinking.

"Please, Abby. Don't do anything weird. Just be normal."

The only thing she ever wanted from me.

"How much time?" Wendy asked me after Mom was out of sight.

I looked at my watch. "Ten. To be on the safe side."

"Sweet." She hurried off to the tiny bathroom that she and I shared. To fix her hair, makeup and whatever else she did in there. My sister was girlier than I. Not that I had any issue with looking nice; I just didn't want to look like I tried or cared. I didn't want to stand out. With red hair and five foot nine in height, blending in was an art form. One I was getting better at each year.

I picked up my cup of tea and sat back down at the kitchen table. The tea was lukewarm. The tips of my fingers prickled, like when your foot falls asleep. But this was different.

Wrapping my hands around my cup and without too much thought, I imagined it hot. A few seconds later I watched the steam rise and sipped it, burning my tongue. No one can drink lukewarm tea.

I rubbed my bare feet on the carpet that hadn't been changed since 1975. Brown earthy tone with geometric shapes. The whole house was like that. Seventies earthy. Browns, greens and oranges. Shag carpet in the living room, to boot. Mom had plans to update it to this decade, but I didn't see it happening any time soon. Besides, there was something comforting about it. Like being in our grandparents' house, complete with the popsicles they always keep for when we visit.

"Okay." Wendy stood next to the sink to get my approval. She wore a knee-length maroon skirt and a cream peasant top. Her thick auburn hair was pulled back into a messy ponytail. Her makeup was subtle: some brown eyeliner, shimmery pink eyeshadow and a touch of lip gloss.

She was definitely the pretty sister.

"You look great," I told her with enough enthusiasm to placate. I didn't ask for the favor to be returned. I knew exactly how I looked. Jeans and a T-shirt. Comfortable and perfect to blend in. No amount of expensive clothes or well-executed makeup would change my Irish (red hair), Amazon (stratospheric height) vampire (too pale skin) appearance.

"Thanks. Let's go," she chirped and grabbed her purple messenger bag and headed out to the car. The car was my sixteenth birthday present from Dad. A blue 1976 Seville Cadillac. It was a boat and wasn't much to look at but it drove without breaking down. And the stereo worked. That was all I needed.

I slipped on my shoes and followed her out, grabbing my canvas bag and keys. I locked up the house. I got into the car and started it up as Queen's "I Want To Ride My Bicycle" blasted out of the speakers. I turned it down and started up our circular driveway, passing the large trees draped in Spanish moss. I wondered if Florida would ever feel like home. It seemed too exotic to be home.

Keystone Heights High had no more than four hundred students. Our old school had a thousand.

Hello, culture shock.

"Are you nervous?" Wendy asked me, her eyes drifting from the many passing trees and houses back to me. "Abby?"

I shrugged.

"I am."

"You'll be fine." And she would be. Wendy always made friends. She loved people and people loved her. She looked like a person to be friends with.

"You gonna try to make friends here?" She sounded scarily like Mom.

I shrugged again, humming along to The Who.

"You could be friendly?"

I smiled a little, amused.

"That's a good start." She laughed, leaning back in the seat.

It didn't take more than ten minutes to get to our new school. It was near the center of town. It took that long because of the twenty-mile speed limit. It was an olive green building, two stories high. No fence except for the one around the soccer and football field. I found a parking space further away from the school.

"Why so far?" Wendy said as I checked to make sure I'd gotten between the lines.

"Walking's good for the body," I intoned, turning off the car. Actually, I'd wondered if the students had their own spots. I didn't want to piss someone off involuntarily. Voluntarily, well that was how I dealt with Dad.

"Cause you're so fat," my sister scoffed and got out of the car. Why she was jealous of her straight-as-a-stick sister I would never understand. Wendy was not remotely overweight. She was just curvier than me. Which meant she was "fat" in girl logic.

I locked the car, watching to make sure Wendy locked her side before waiting for her to walk beside me. It was early. Only a few parking spots were filled.

But we had our transcripts with us and had to do the office thing first.

Entering the double doors, I relaxed a little. It smelled like high school: gym socks, cheap cologne, and sharpened pencils. I glanced at Wendy to see her wrinkle her snub nose. I laughed.

"What?" she snapped, not noticing that a few students who were at their lockers were staring at us.

Small school. We were so going to be the talk of the school.

"Nothing," I muttered and turned to the right to enter the office. Wendy followed.

Twenty minutes later, I was even more convinced that new kids were a major event. The secretary, a Mrs. Johnstone, had asked us fifty questions and maybe half had anything to do with registration.

"At least there's honors classes," Wendy commented, looking at her class schedule. "I mean, how many freshman English classes can there be, with only a hundred freshmen?"

I stepped on the back of her sandal.

"What?" She glared at me.

"Can you lower your voice somewhat?" There were a lot more kids milling about now and we definitely attracted attention. I wasn't thrilled, either, that we were in a tiny town in a tiny school, but I didn't want to announce that snobbery to the school. I knew Mom was doing her best.

"I wasn't shouting. Jeez," she huffed, but did lower her voice. Looking at her schedule again, then around the hall, "I think my first class is that way." She pointed down the hall. "See you later?"

"Yeah. Maybe at lunch?" I agreed and watched her walk away. I looked back at my schedule.

AP Lang & Comp – how many would be in the advanced classes?

I turned towards the other end of school. The walls were painted mustard yellow and lined with dented and scratched metal lockers. One of these somewhere was 346, but I'd find that later.

I passed lots of kids who were all deep in conversations until they spotted me, and then the talking ceased. And they stared. Didn't even try to hide it.

I kept my head up, staring straight ahead, even though I really did want to watch the floor. I stopped in front of the classroom door and checked the number with my schedule. Taking a deep confidence-inducing breath, I walked in.

There were seven students and one teacher. That was good odds for such a small school, I guessed.

"Abigail Korrigan?" The teacher had short dark brown hair. She smiled at me.

I nodded, feeling all eyes on me. She waved me over.

"Mrs. Campbell," she said, handing me a stack of stapled papers and a small paperback. "This will get you caught up. We're reading *The Scarlet Letter*. Find yourself a seat. And welcome."

"Thanks." I turned to face the class. They all watched me with varying degrees of interest. I tried not to make eye contact with anyone as I walked to a seat in the back.

"We'll call roll, so Abigail can learn everyone's name," she continued as the bell rang.

The door opened and closed quickly as a latecomer entered. "Shane." Her tone was disapproving.

"Car trouble, Brenda," the boy said as I looked over. He had on this terribly charming grin. Brown shaggy hair that curled at the ends and deep chocolate mischievous eyes.

This had to be the hot guy of the school.

His eyes landed on me as he strutted in. He perused me clinically as I turned to look back at Mrs. Campbell. He slid in the seat two rows over.

She called roll and I tried to match the back of the head with each name, but I wasn't sure how well I'd do tomorrow.

I did remember one.

Hot guy's name was Shane Wilson.

Chapter Two

My classes more or less passed like that until lunch. I'd be pointed out and stared at before class began. Then once the teacher started, I was ignored, which I liked.

Second period: Honors Chemistry.

Third period: Spanish 3.

Fourth period: American History.

At lunch, everyone drifted to the cafeteria, which also had some tables outside for when the weather was good. And it was Florida, so the weather was good ninety percent of the time.

I looked for Wendy and found her with a couple of other girls at a table outside. We made eye contact and without too much indication I knew she didn't want me to crash her party. Bossy older sister and all that.

I found an empty table inside and sat down, pulling out *The Scarlet Letter* and my lunch. As I opened my bottled water, I noticed it was icy like I'd just gotten it out of the freezer and it had thawed only a little. But I'd pulled it out the pantry that morning. It didn't make any sense.

The proverbial red flag waved in my mind, but I dismissed it. Maybe the air-conditioning was colder than I'd realized?

Lame excuse. It was me. It was always me.

But this time I didn't even know I'd done it. Was it my subconscious now?

"Hey." A boy sat down at my table. I blinked at him. He had short spiky hair and a red sweatband on his wrist. "I'm Ben. We have English and Chem together?"

"Oh. Hi."

He grinned, showing his teeth.

"Abigail or Abby?" He had a cafeteria lunch and it was unidentifiable.

"Abby."

"Cool. Welcome to Keystone. Where'd you move from?" he asked, before shoveling some of the grey meat-like substance into his mouth.

"Memphis."

"No way. Like Graceland and the Blues?"

"Yeah." Why was he eating with me? Did he not have any friends to eat with so he chose the new girl?

"Cool. Why the move?"

"Mom's job transferred her to Gainesville." I fiddled with the cap on my bottled water. "My little sister and I had to follow."

"Sucks being a minor." He laughed.

I felt the corners of my lips turn up a bit.

"So, what are you into?" Ben asked.

"Huh?" Had I been joined by a drug dealer? That would be my luck.

"What are you into? Like I'm on the basketball team, but I actually just keep the bench warm."

I smiled. "Is that fun?" I asked him, the tension in my shoulders loosening some.

"Thrilling."

"My sister swims. I'm an expert at the bleacher-sit."

"I can see that. In fact that was the first thing I thought about you. She looks like a bench-sitter. So, is your sister here?"

"Yeah. Outside. The only other newbie."

Ben turned and looked for her. "She kinda looks like you." He turned back to me, the grin still in place. "Freshman?"

"Yep." I waited for some comment about how hot she was or the like, but he didn't.

"So, you never answered. What are you into?" He had this expectant look on his face, like he was really interested in what I had to say. I'd just met the strangest guy ever.

"Well," I hesitated. Actually, Ben, I'm a total freak who can make water move. Wanna hang out? "Homework." Maybe I'd bore him to death and he'd go away.

"Boring." Still with that grin. "For fun?"

"I play piano," I shared timidly.

"Cool. How long?"

"Ten years."

"Very cool. Like Chopin and Gershwin?" Gershwin. Okay, he was definitely not your regular guy.

"Um, I aspire to play Gershwin. But yeah." I smiled again. Two smiles in under five minutes. Pigs were flying somewhere.

"Very cool. There's a talent show in March. To raise money for our band. You should do it." I opened my mouth to protest, but he just kept on going. "I would, but apparently sucking at basketball isn't a talent."

"That's so wrong. They should recognize the pure genius of missing baskets and tripping over your shoelaces." As soon as it was out of my mouth I regretted it. Was that too much?

He laughed. "You've seen me play, then?"

I relaxed a bit more and sipped my water. It wasn't icy anymore.

"Hey, Ben." A girl with short black hair sat next to him. Then looked at me. "New girl. Abigail, right?"

I nodded as I noticed that she had no lunch with her. Either she didn't eat or she'd already eaten and come over to talk to Ben.

"Mel. Nice to meet you." She smiled and it seemed sincere.

"Thanks." I continued eating as Mel turned to Ben.

"Meeting. After school."

"But..."

"No skateboarding or whatever else you do," she cut him off. "Stuff for college applications, remember? Good college, good life? Or something like that."

"Overrated," Ben muttered. "I'll be there." He glanced at me. "Want to come?"

"Uh. To?"

"Yeah, why don't you?" Mel's brown eyes lit up. "We could use the help. It's mostly student council people, but not everyone is dependable." This clearly upset her.

"Oh. I..."

"Please?" Ben pleaded. "Save me from the misery of bureaucracy?"

I chuckled and Mel rolled her eyes good-naturedly.

"It would be nice to have an outside opinion," Mel stated. "Someone who's been outside Florida." She sighed. "I swear, spring break, I'm out of here."

"Where are you going?" I asked easily.

Whoa, proactive Abby.

"Somewhere with no humidity. Like Arizona."

"I say the OC." Ben chewed happily. "Hot girls and no humidity."

Mel smacked him on the back of the head.

"Don't be a typical guy, Ben. I know you better." Mel looked back at me. "We're meeting here. Cafeteria. Please come. Otherwise it's me, Ben, Natalie, and Cassie. We get sick of each other."

"No Shane?" Ben laughed.

Mel sighed heavily.

"Junior class president and can barely make it to his classes. Unbelievable." She got up from the table. "You two. After school." And off she went.

"She's always like that," Ben explained. "She's a nice form of bossy."

"She seems cool." I nodded. "So, she's not class president?"

"Vice president. Nat's secretary. I'm treasurer." He shrugged as if to say he didn't understand why he was. "And Cassie's just around."

"Shane? From English?"

"Yep. That's the one. Late almost every day."

"Right." Like I'd forget him.

"Yeah. Dependable he's not. But everyone loves him." Another shrug. "Anyway, the seniors get senior trip and homecoming. We get fundraisers and prom."

"I see. Look, I have to take my sister home after..."

"Can you come anyway?" He grinned. "Volunteer stuff is good for college apps and for the National Honor Society. And we need new blood."

"I'm not really civic."

"You are now. And if you do this, Patterson won't recruit you for Parent Day duty."

"I don't have the right to say no?" I was smiling by this point. He was not going to let me off the hook.

"Nope. Not to the principal."

"Right. I'll be there."

And now I was involved.

• • •

Fifth period was American Government. Coach Jenkins, the soccer and basketball coach, made me stand in front of the class and introduce myself.

Not even a minute in and I already hated him.

"Abby Korrigan. Moved here from Memphis." I was glad I hadn't stuttered. It helped that Ben was in my class and was watching me with a friendly grin.

"Elvis still there?" Coach asked. He was like a skinny Jabba the Hutt. He had this greasy mustache that he kept licking at the corner of his mouth.

"Never saw him," I answered quickly, hoping he'd let me sit down. No one in the class looked interested.

"And what will you bring to KHHS?"

What kind of question was that?

"World peace?" I said the first thing that popped into my head. There were some scattered chuckles, which only made me blush. Note: blushing as a redhead is neither charming nor cute. Unless you find tomatoes endearing.

"Interesting." Coach licked his mustache again.

Please let me sit. Please!

"Have a seat."

Thank you.

I walked to my seat, thankfully without tripping or any incident. I'd set my stuff in the back, so I felt everyone's eyes on me as I walked. With the other honors classes, I'd recognized some faces, but with this class I was at a loss.

Ben gave me a thumbs-up, super-cheesy like, but I chuckled anyway.

The girl in front of me looked back at my laugh. She looked Floridian. Blonde, tanned flawless skin. Really pretty. Her makeup wasn't too much; just enough to make her look like she belonged on a magazine cover. I immediately didn't like her.

She shot me a dirty look. For what? For laughing? I just raised my eyebrows in question.

I may have wanted to blend in, but I didn't wilt before pretty mean girls.

Which she apparently was.

She rolled her eyes and turned back to Coach Jenkins, who was droning on about checks and balances.

. . .

My schedule ended with Pre-Calculus. An awful way to end the day. After, I stood at my locker, staring at my newly acquired textbooks that I had to make covers for. Like that would protect them after a decade of student handling.

"Abby!" I jumped at my name.

Wendy bounced down the hall towards me, her ponytail swinging.

"Good day?" I asked, stuffing all my books in my bag.

"Really good. Everyone's nice." She fiddled with her bag strap. "Small place, but nice."

I heaved my bag onto my shoulder.

"Oh, and I got special permission to try out for the swim team tomorrow. It's at the pool."

"Where else would it be?"

"I mean, it's not at school," she explained. "It's two blocks that way." She pointed as we walked to the parking lot. "Want to drive me?"

"You can walk that."

"Please?"

"Whatever." Mom would make me, anyway.

"Did you make any friends?"

We got to the car and as I got in I looked across the lot to see Shane, hot guy from English among other classes. He was getting into a beat-up station wagon, but he caught me staring.

He winked.

Or had dust in his eye.

I got into the car and started it.

"Did you?"

"Dunno." I turned up the music.

Chapter Three

"Where are you going?" Wendy asked me when I'd dropped her off. I threw my books on my bed and grabbed my bag and keys.

"Back to school."

"What?" She stood in my doorway. "You like that place already?"

I snorted. "I sorta got volunteered to help out with some fundraiser planning."

"What?" Wendy's mouth dropped open exaggeratedly. "You're kidding?"

"Nah. Tell Mom I'll be home for dinner." I walked past her.

"You're really going? To be with other people?"

"You act like I'm a hermit," I called back, as I walked to the garage.

"You are!"

I turned to look at her, my eyes narrowed. She could get under my skin like nobody else.

"Maybe I don't need my self-worth defined by how many friends I have." And I got in the car and drove off.

So I was not real social. Is that some sort of mental deficiency? Most of my peers were shallow and self-involved. It got old. Talking about boys and clothes had a limit.

I hadn't had a really good friend since I was about seven. And she'd moved away. After that, I never clicked with anyone.

Maybe they could sense my weirdness.

I parked at the school and grabbed my bag. As I walked towards it, my stomach turned. Did they really want me to show up? Was it one of those hazing things? Tell the new kid there's a pool on the roof and then lock them up there.

I hesitated at the door. Did I really want to do this?

I opened it slightly with the plan of just peeking in and then leaving. I got my head in when I heard:

"You came," Ben exclaimed. He was sitting in a chair backwards, a black beanie on his head. He really was a skater boy.

Mel was there with a clipboard. A girl with waist-long brown hair was arranging papers on one of the tables.

And the mean, gorgeous blonde from American Government was there, flipping through a notebook. Great.

I walked all the way in. Can't leave now.

"Hi," I greeted lamely. This was a bad idea.

"Abby's going to join us because, basically, I roped her into it," Mel explained with a smile. "That's Cassie."

The brunette gave me a small smile.

"And Natalie."

The blonde. She looked put out that I was there. Or I was paranoid. That was possible.

"Hi."

"Welcome," Cassie piped up.

"Yeah, welcome." Natalie didn't sound at all convincing.

What had I done to her?

"Thanks." I walked over and dropped my bag on the floor.

"Okay, have a seat, Abby. To raise funds for our marching band, which, despite our size, is pretty good," Mel said, sitting on the table right on a huge sheet of white paper.

Ben pulled up a chair next to him and patted it. I walked over to sit before realizing it. It was strange how it wasn't flirty with him. Normally, I'd steer clear of a guy who treated me so casually so quickly, but with Ben, that was just him. I sat down with my notebook to take notes.

I still wasn't sure how I got involved.

Mel was still talking. "We need a theme and we have to have auditions. The date for the show is set. March 5th."

"Who does the auditions? Us?" This was Cassie, sounding appalled at the idea.

"We do. But there has to be one faculty member present." Mel flipped to a new page on her clipboard. "That's Mrs. Campbell."

"Okay." Natalie leaned back in her chair. "Do we have judges?"

"I'm working on that. We were hoping we could get someone from city council and maybe someone from the University of Florida." Located in Gainesville. Huge, huge school. "That's on my plate. Ben, you're the artsy one, I want you to work on fliers and posters. And, uh, Abby? Do you have good penmanship? Because Ben's awful."

"Um, yeah. I took a calligraphy class once."

Ben gave me a funny look.

"I was having a boring summer," I shrugged.

"You won't here," Ben assured me. He sounded pretty confident.

"That sounds great. You'll help Ben." Mel moved on. "Nat, can you take care of morning announcements for it? And mention that faculty is welcome to be involved."

"Are we sure about that?" Natalie pressed her glossed lips together and ran a hand through her silky hair. She didn't have a hair out of place.

We of the curly hair would never be so lucky.

"I mean, we can't cut a faculty member if they suck," Natalie continued.

Good point. Wouldn't admit that to her.

Ben sniggered. "Like Coach Jenkins on the guitar. I'm sure he was off key in the seventies, too."

"We can leave that to Mrs. Campbell," Mel said. "She's nice and blunt. Nat, I know you dance and sing. Cassie also sings. Ben..." Mel raised one eyebrow. "Any talents?"

"Skate..."

"Other than?"

"Not really," he grumbled, his eyes still happy. "But Abby plays piano – she could help." He held out his hand. I gave him a weird look.

"Huh, what?" I was scribbling out different writing styles.

Ben pointed to my notebook paper. I grinned and ripped out a page for him. I looked back at Mel.

"With the audition process. You can cover instruments." Mel ticked something off on her clipboard. "Ben, will you talk to some drama guys about sound and lights?"

"Shane knows them better." Ben doodled some more.

"I'll try him." Mel sighed heavily. "Okay, when should we have auditions? I mean, how long do we need to polish? A week, two weeks? A month?"

"A month would be good. Just on the safe side," Cassie said. "In case of disaster."

"Very optimistic, Cass." Mel laughed. "Okay, so auditions the first week of February, which is coming up." She jotted something down.

"Themes?"

"Last year's was 'Superhero' or something." Ben told me. "Really lame. Apparently no one on the planning committee has ever read a comic book."

I didn't hide my smile. Ben looked so offended.

"Well, should we do something classic or topical?" I asked, seeing that Natalie was taking notes and shot a dark look at my doing the same. Okay, only the secretary can take notes. Control freak.

"Either. I mean, I would prefer to avoid sparkle and shimmer and go for something classy, but the budget's crap, as it usually is." Mel looked at all of us. "Hit me, guys."

"Marvel comic superheroes?"

"You are kidding, right, Ben?"

"Well, it should be remedied." He huffed. I patted his shoulder in sympathy and he shot me a quick grin. I slipped my hand away immediately, wondering at my comfort with him in just a day. My general rule: don't touch boys.

"We could do something Floridian," Cassie offered. "Beach or lake-like."

"Maybe."

"But that's so done. Especially by schools who never even see a beach," Natalie vetoed mercilessly.

Cassie didn't look annoyed. I would have been.

"What about a decade? Like the twenties?" Natalie said.

"But then wouldn't all our acts have to fit in with that? That would discourage anyone interested in music from the last few decades," I said.

Another glare. I was expecting them from her now.

"Good point, but we'll put it down anyway. So, in general, with a decade theme. Floridian." Mel wrote it down. "Any more?" We were quiet. "You guys suck."

"Do we have to have a theme?" Ben twiddled his pencil. "I mean, can't it just be Keystone High Talent Show, 'Come One, Come all'?"

"That sounds like a circus," I commented.

"Circus. That could be fun. And that could be period, which could also be interesting. Like Carnevale," Mel jabbered on.

"Who?" Natalie asked.

"HBO show..." Ben answered. "Slow as anything, but set at the turn of the century. We could do everything in sepia tone."

"It's an idea." Mel grinned. "Nice, you two."

Ben and I looked at each other.

"We're a team." Ben laughed.

I didn't mind the idea.

· · ·

"Where are you going?" Mom was at the dining-room table, papers strewn across it. It was her workspace till we fixed up the room adjacent to the back patio for her study. At least most of the boxes were gone.

"Out." I stopped at the sliding glass door that led to the back patio. "To the lake."

"It's nearly midnight." She looked up, her short auburn hair weirdly sticking up in several places. The new job must be hectic. "It's not safe."

"I'm not going swimming. Just going to sit on the shore."

"Abby." It was the "tone." The "no weird stuff" tone.

"Just sitting," I repeated, my jaw clenched. I opened the door and slammed it behind me.

I stomped across the grass, avoiding the roots of the trees. The grass ended at a concrete step and I walked down to the sand. I slipped off my sandals and continued till I felt the water touch my toes.

She didn't understand. No one did.

I walked a little further, until my feet were fully immersed in the lake. It was chilly. It was January, after all. I wiggled my toes down deeper into the sand.

And I felt better. The tension of the day, all the nerves and worries of the move, my life, just faded.

By the water.

It wasn't just the lake. I could have put my feet in the bathroom sink and filled it with water and gotten the same reaction. It went way beyond just soaking my feet.

I only knew what I could do. I didn't know why or how I could make my tea hot or cold without microwave. All I knew was that it had to remain a secret. I hated it as much as I ached to do it.

But this was my way to relax. My own form of yoga.

I had a feeling I would be doing this a lot in the next months.

Dawn McNiff | Baby Celeste;
Tiny Troll and his Princess Mummy;
Lottie the Big Junior

Baby Celeste

Chapter One

I don't do crying. Not ever. Full stop. The *END*.

I pressed my thumbs into my eyes to make the tears go back in. The inside of my nose fizzled.

I just didn't get it. Why was Dad being such a pig? No, that wasn't even fair on nice pigs. He was more like one of those boars from the woods. Hairy, ugly and angry.

I stuffed more jelly babies into my mouth and chewed fast.

I thought: it's, like, SO unfair. First, Dad *makes* me spend the summer in Luncing-by-stupid-sea while he does up Nan's mouldy house – even though I'd rather eat worms. Then he's horrible to me non-stop – biting my head off all day long for no reason.

I stomped out of my room to get some bog roll to blow my nose.

That's how long I was out of my room. I swear it. Not even two tiny minutes. But when I got back, there she was.

A baby.

Lying there on my duvet, crying her titchy head off.

A real, true-life baby.

Come from nowhere.

· · ·

I nearly jumped out of my skin when I saw her.

Obviously.

I stood there, staring at her all stupid. Shaking my head. Opening and closing my eyes.

Oh my GOD! Where had she popped up from?

Was she a *ghost*?

But she didn't look like one – she was proper pink and gurgly like a real-life baby. And she wasn't wearing a flowy, ghostie cloak – she had on a normal baby suit with a big red raspberry on the front.

I reached out towards her. *Will my hand go straight through her?* I poked her quickly in the tummy. She felt solid, squidgy and warm. Definitely not made of cold cloud like ghosts.

I got even closer. Bent right over her.

She smelt sort of nice, like vanilla ice-cream.

She looked right back at me, with ginormous eyes full of tears. She stopped wailing the moment she saw me, and made a coo-ee baby noise. That did it – I jumped in the air again and ran backwards out of my room, tripping over the stuff on my floor.

"DAD! DA-A-D!" I yelled.

Then I remembered: Dad had gone out in a strop.

I was on my own. At least I had thought I was...

But babies don't just turn up on their own, do they? Or go shuffling off on their nappy bums into strange people's houses? Had someone brought her in and put her on my bed?

I ran to the front door.

It was locked and bolted, and the chain was still across. Just like Dad told me to do when he was out.

I ran back to the kitchen. The back door was bolted, too – from the inside.

No one could have got in or out without unbolting the doors. And all the windows were shut 'cos of the rain.

Still, I checked in every room. I tiptoed up and down Nan's dusty stairs, peeking round all the doors, hardly breathing, my skin all goosebumpy. It's a small house, so there weren't many hiding places.

There was definitely nobody there.

It was just me and the weirdo baby.

I was kind of scared and not scared at the same time. 'Cos she wasn't really a scary thing, being that titchy and babyish. So I went back to my bedroom door and peered round.

She was sucking her tiny thumb, happy as anything now.

I went in and crept a bit nearer.

"How d'you get in here, little frog?" I whispered. I stroked her face with my little finger, and her skin felt as soft as marshmallows. "Who's your mummy, eh?"

But I just couldn't see how she could be *anyone's* baby. She definitely hadn't been there when we arrived three days ago, and the old place had been empty since Nan died.

It was like she'd just dropped out of the sky on to my duvet from nowhere.

Like magic.

Magic.

I got freaked out again then. It was all too weird. I leapt off the bed away from her.

I had no blinking idea what to do. All I could think of was showing her to Dad when he came in. Even though he was in such a fat mood.

I squeezed my bum on to my windowsill on the other side of my room. I could keep an eye on Babyface from there and watch out for Dad.

He was ages. I sat watching litter blow across the road on to the beach, and ate loads of mint toffees. I made a pile of shiny green foil for my sweetie wrapper mosaic. I'd already covered a big patch of my bedroom wall in just three days.

I kept looking over at her. She'd fallen asleep – I could hear her soft, whispery breaths. Sometimes I tried tricking her – glancing away, and then back really fast to see if she disappeared. But she never budged.

I waited some more.

I waited so long the window got all steamed up, so I rubbed away a peephole with my sleeve to look at the stars. I could see lots of twinkles up above the sea. I drew a picture of the baby on the steamy glass and made two of the stars into her eyes.

Still no Dad.

Not that I knew what I was going to say when he did come home.

Like "Hello. By the way, you know Mum lost the plot and ran away. Well, now I have too, 'cos I think I've got a magic baby on my bed."

It was all double, triple, raspberry-ripple loony.

Chapter Two

When Dad came in, it was nearly ten. I didn't go down to him, straight off. I stayed on the windowsill and drew fast swirls in the steam until the glass squeaked.

The baby was still kipping. I reached for her, holding my breath, and picked her up, dead awkward, like. She felt like a dough dolly, all warm and damp and floppy. Her head lolled forward and I caught it. She stayed asleep.

I carried her down the stairs – like a plate of dinner, all out the front.

Nan's telly was already on.

"Dad," I said loudly. I walked right in front of the small screen, so he had to look at me.

"Dad, lookie what I've got."

It sounded dim, that: "lookie". I said it in a bright, fun voice like I was showing him an interesting beetle or a cake I'd made.

"What?...What you doing?" he said. He tried to look past me at the telly.

"No, Dad... LOOK!" I practically stuffed the baby in his face.

"Look at what? What you on about?"

He was looking straight at her, but he flipping well couldn't see her. He really couldn't see her.

I was well scared then. I got pins and needles all over and just stood there, staring at him.

"For God sakes, Shelley – move it, will you! What you gawping at? I told you to go to bed by nine." The crowd on the telly cheered. He threw his arms up, and fell back on to the sofa. "Ahhh! Now look! You made me miss the flipping goal."

Dad's yelling woke the baby up and she whimpered. I jolted out of my daze and carried her back upstairs, my legs wobbling. I put her down on my bed and sat right on the other end away from her, breathing hard.

Come on, Shells. Pull yourself together, girl.

My head whizzed.

Oh my God! Dad couldn't see the baby. He really couldn't.

I turned on my big light, so I wasn't so scared. I stared at her again. Looked at her really properly this time.

She was so tiny – almost as small as a baby doll. Was it me, or was she way smaller than normal babies? And she had these strange eyes. They were pale purple like lavender flowers. Beautiful. I'd never seen eyes like that before in my whole, entire life. Lavender eyes.

I caught my breath.

Blimey. Maybe she's a fairy baby!

Then I almost laughed my head off at myself. A fairy baby. I was losing it now. But secretly, I kind of hoped it might be true.

I shuffled up the bed nearer her. Gently I unpopped her suit. I slid my hand in, feeling her back for wings. Totally loony tunes, I know.

No wings.

Shame...

Just a dinky baby back. All soft and weeny.

Her ears were normal, too – small, pink and round. Not pointy. If she was a baby fairy or a pixie, they would be a bit pointy, wouldn't they? Maybe...

She started squeaking right then. Her face went all red. One second later, I had to hide my nose in my sleeve. What a right old pong and a half! She'd gone and done a poop in her nappy. She smelt real, alright. I didn't think ghosts and fairies usually went around pooping at people. Or did they? I didn't know.

She arched her back and bleated louder.

Now what am I supposed to do?

Then suddenly I knew.

Brainwave.

I opened the cupboard in my room, and pulled all the tat out on to the floor.

I knew what I was looking for. That doll Nan gave me. I'd seen it in her cupboard yesterday – still in its packaging. She'd given it to me when I was seven – the one and only time I ever saw her. I don't remember much about the visit, except that I had a meringue mouse which tasted like stuck-together icing sugar. Then Dad shouted at Nan, so we had to go before I got to play with the doll.

There it was. I tugged it out of the cardboard. It had a pretend milk bottle and nappies exactly like real ones, but smaller. I could use them to change Little Miss Fairy's bum.

Now for the stinky bit.

I went to the bathroom and got some wet bog roll. Slowly, I took off her suit – it was dead tricky 'cos her fingers stuck out all spiky and got in the way. She got in a right proper paddy. Her rubbery little legs kicked about, her face went red like a squashed raspberry and she screamed her complete head off. I waited, ready for Dad to come up and see what all the racket was about, but he never did.

"Oh well, little frog," I said to her. "Seems like Dad can't see you *or* hear you." It was proper weird.

I cleaned up her bott, and put on the clean nappy and her raspberry suit. I put some of my doll's little booties on her, too – just for cuteness.

I jiggled her in my arms and soon she stopped booing.

"Well done, baby woo," I said to her, kissing her little nose. "Nice clean bott now." I was kind of getting used to her.

Kind of.

When I didn't think about her being a mad, magic baby.

I didn't know what to do with the whiffy nappy, so in the end I stuck it in a Woolies bag and hung it out my window.

I was well proud of myself. I'd done my first nappy. *Look at me, Mini Mum.*

I lay down and cuddled her. She was still gulping a bit, but she gave me a little, wet smile. Like I really *was* her own mum. Then she fell straight to sleep, tucked up with me like a small, fat teddy bear.

"Where did you come from, Fairycake?" I whispered. "I'm dead glad you came."

We stayed there – all snuggled up for hours, listening to faraway seagulls and the rain plink at the windows. We were so cosy, just the two of us. She sucked her thumb and dozed on and off, but course there was no way I could sleep. I was too totally wowed by her. I swear, when she peeped up at me, her lavender eyes glittered like fairy lights in the grey-ness. Like she had real stars for eyes.

Then suddenly I knew her name. It just pinged into my head.

"Celeste," I whispered to her. 'That's what I'm calling you. I think it's a proper angel name, like Gabriel, but for pretty girl angels.'

Chapter Three

In the night it got even weirder. I had a dream. Well, a sort of dream, but I swear I was awake.

I don't know where I was – the edges of my eyes were all blurred.

But in front of me was a *real* baby fairy. She was as tiny and as chubby as a plum, and had tiddly wings on her back – pure white and fluffy like baby birds' feathers, and so delicate even my breath made them tremble. She wore a dress made out of pale pink rose petals, sewn with tiny stitches. She had an incy-wincy silver wand, which she kept chewing.

Celeste.

I knew her by her lavender eyes.

She wanted to be close and hold on to me, but her hand was too small to go round even my littlest finger. So she sat in my palm, smiling and squeaking. She waggled her wings and bopped up and down on her bottom, sending up sparkles of fairy dust, which smelt like lemon meringue. I had quite a job making sure she didn't fall off my hand – I was sure her wings were way too tiny to fly with.

I fed her mashed strawberries and ice-cream from the tip of a teaspoon: somehow I just knew that's what real baby fairies eat, and she loved it.

A purple shadow passed by the background – I blinked and strained my eyes to see what it was. A huge window... An old beige sofa...

I shook my head to make my eyes work. I realised I was in Nan's grotty front room. In my nightie. Celeste was there in my arms. She wasn't a Tinkerbell fairy, but a little baby again.

What am I doing down here?

The loud ticky clock on the mantelpiece said half past two in the morning. *Did I sleepwalk down here?*

The room was lit by the orange streetlamp shining through the big window.

Celeste gazed up at me, thumb stuffed in her mouth.

The dream...

I shivered.

Maybe she WAS a real baby fairy, then. Maybe she COULD do magic and grant wishes.

Shall I test her and see?

I wondered if it was mean. She was only a baby, so she might not know any magic yet.

I tried to think of an easy-peasy wish that would only need a little spell.

"I wish for… um… um…" My brain was concrete.

"I wish for… um… some chocolate peach creams! The posh ones with the orange crinkly wrappers – please.'

I looked at her and waited. Celeste sucked her thumb and looked back at me blankly.

"But it doesn't matter if you can't, though!" I said, quickly.

I was hoping Nan's front room would suddenly be piled high with orange shiny sweets like a tipper truck had just emptied itself through the window. Full of sweets again, like in the old days when it used to be a sweet shop.

But still nothing happened.

I felt dumb then.

"Never mind," I said. I kissed her soft head. "Magic is very hard."

Celeste had fallen asleep in my arms. My eyelids were heavy too, so I carried her carefully back up to my bed.

I went out like a light, zonko.

Chapter Four

When I woke up, she had gone.

I knew it straight off. My room felt different – sort of quiet and sad, like the day after your birthday.

I sat bolt up and stared around. I was alone in my bed, and it was properly morning now – already half nine. All I could hear was the plop of rain on the window, cars and seagulls – no little baby coos or cries.

I leapt up, my head going at a hundred miles an hour. *Oh my God. where is she?* What if I'd, like, rolled on her, squished her or suffocated her or something? I yanked all my covers up. I scrabbled down the side of the bed, and peered behind my bed head. *Can a magic, baby, like, die?* I tipped up bags and searched my whole room until I'd wrecked it.

I stopped suddenly and sniffed the air. Could I smell her lovely vanilla-ish smell?

But where was she?

Not anywhere.

She had totally and completely disappeared. Just gone.

My mouth went dry like I'd been sucking tissues. What was happening? It was too weird for words. All my scaredness crashed in my head and sent sharp prickles down me.

The worst part was wanting her so much – longing to snuggle her again. It was totally loony 'cos she'd only been with me a little while. I held my breath, gritted my teeth, and wished and wished and wished that she'd abracadabra herself back to me. I kept closing my eyes and opening them to see if it worked.

But she didn't come.

It was just me. Alone in Nan's ugly, pointless back bedroom.

I picked at a big, pink flower on the peeling, musty wallpaper.

I wanted to cry so much. I had an achy feeling in my throat from holding my crying in, and my tonsils were nearly exploding. But I never cry. So instead I chewed my pyjama cuff nearly to bits.

I got back into bed and let myself suck my thumb – just a little bit. It's proper babyish, I know, but sometimes I still do it if I'm very upset – and only in real secret so no one knows.

Maybe I really had gone loony and made Celeste up. Perhaps next I would see giant bunnies, and talk to myself in supermarket queues like a proper maddo.

I pulled back my curtains to make sure the world was still the right way up. And yes, Luncing-by-stupid-sea *was* still there, bad luck for me. And there was nothing magic about it out there. It was a faded grey day. Grizzly-drizzly clouds. Ponky car smells from the big road. Seagulls wark-wark-warking in the sky.

Then I saw the nappy bag hanging from the window latch.

It made me jump – like when I'd first seen Celeste. I opened the window and pulled the wet, little bag into the room. I changed my mind straight off, and bunged it back out. What a whiff. But Celeste had been here, alright. She was real.

I felt all funny then; excited *and* scared like before a too-fast, big ride at the fair.

If she's real, then where is she?

I got this bonkers idea that I was going to look for her. I pulled on my clothes in a rush. I didn't know where I would look. Somewhere, any-where...

Dad was in the bathroom.

'Just off out, Dad,' I called. Telling him I was going out, like I was supposed to. But quietly-on-purpose so he wouldn't hear me and ask any questions.

I ran down the stairs.

As I went for the door, I saw something orange and shiny sitting on the windowsill.

I stopped.

It was a sweet. Could it be...?

I unwrapped it and bit into its soft centre. A chocolate peach cream! Exactly like the ones I'd wished for last night.

Weird.

But there was only one. Perhaps Dad dropped it.

Or my wish had come true. Celeste had made it come true...

Oh, Celeste – come back. Please come back!

Chewing on my sweet – my magic sweet? – I ran out into tipping rain.

Chapter Five

In the street. I didn't know which way to go. I suddenly felt like a proper Womble, going nowhere in such a big hurry. Looking for a lost, magic baby...

But it was freezing standing there. The wind was whipping across the main road from the sea. So I just walked any old way, down the road.

The wrong way.

I had to go past a garage block. Some big boys were there – kicking a ball against a wall and showing off like total geeks. One of them shouted something at me and the others laughed. My tummy tensed.

Oh no. Can't face this now.

I turned round to go the other way, but a boy about my age appeared on a bike right behind me. I nearly crashed into him. His bike was blocking my way – a nasty, yellow-stripy-waspy bike.

But he smiled at me.

It's probably a trick. He's probably mates with the garage boys.

I didn't smile back.

His smile changed instantly to a scowl.

"What's your problem, eh?" he said. "Moody cow."

A ball came flying over towards us from the garages followed by a big boy.

"Who's your dumb little friend, Jay?" called the big boy, puffing.

"She's not my friend." He gave me a right evil.

Oh no, here we go. My heart started galloping.

With his poppy-out eyes and his too-long, orange hair all stuck up at the front, he looked like an angry chicken. "The little squirt's got a attitude problem. Can't even crack a smile," he said.

Squirt? Cheek! I hate it when people say stuff about me being small.

"Get lost, Chicken Boy!" I said, pushing past him. "And get a haircut!"

The moment I said it, I wished I hadn't. Me and my ginormous mouth. The big boy laughed his head off and started clucking like a hen.

Chicken Boy swore and lobbed his bike down like he was going to grab me. His sharp eyes stabbed me.

Now I've done it...

I turned and ran across the road. A car beeped me like mad.

I could still hear the big boy calling and laughing. "Chicken Boy!" he cockadoodledooed. "Jay-Jay Chicken Boy!"

"I'm gonna flipping do you for this," Chicken Boy squawked at me over the road.

I ran back towards Nan's house. But I was on the wrong side of the road now, so I kept going past it towards the beach.

The traffic was stopped at the lights, so I charged across the main road and kept running and running. Across the rough grass and on to the shingle, slipping and sliding on the pebbles. The rain was stinging my eyes. My face was boiling hot and my head was bang-banging.

I could still see his evil look. *I'm gonna flipping do you for this.*

I was sure he would come after me – with some of his big mates – and they were going to do me in. I tried to listen as I ran. Were they coming? I couldn't hear a thing; only my own gaspy breaths.

It was high tide and the beach was only a skinny strip, so I got to the edge of the sea in about two seconds flat. Then I realised what a numpty I'd been. There was nowhere to hide down there. Nowhere to go.

I turned round fast, ready to scream my block off, but there was no one there. The beach was empty. No boys. No one at all.

Not yet.

Where could I hide? I ran along the beach and clambered over a big pile of rocks. I crouched down and I peered round the side.

Nothing, nothing, no one. So they hadn't come after me. I'd been running like a crazy loser girl for nothing.

But I waited there for ages just in case, squinting out through the rain. I pulled up my hood, but I was getting soaked.

Everything on the beach looked dim and grey.

Just banks of dull pebbles, litter and washed-up old breeze blocks, half chewed by the waves. I couldn't even see the horizon: it was like the rain had washed the whole sky into the sea. *Lovely blinking summer. Lovely Luncing-by-stupid-sea.*

Dad was being so narky – much worse than usual. And now I'd gone and made a big, fat enemy too, even though I'd only got here about three teatimes ago.

I wanted to cry again – *again*! What was wrong with me?! But I didn't cry. I thought of Celeste, my little magic girl, and wished and wished for her again.

It was ages before I felt brave enough to come out. Then I didn't know what to do or where to go. I wanted to buy some sweets – to cheer myself up. But could I get past those der-brains by the garages and get to the shops?

I peeked round the rocks again dead quick. No one.

I ran until I got to the corner of the garage block, and flattened myself against a garage wall – like one of those detectives on the telly when they're following someone. I peeped round. Still no boys, but their bikes were there, chucked on the ground. I could hear shouting and laughing coming from inside one of the garages. So, fast as I could, I nipped past and legged it down the road to the shops.

I was even colder by the time I got to the Co-op. I rushed through the door. The newspaper rack was right in front of me.

My tummy flipped out.

In big letters across the front of a paper, it said: *"LOCAL COUPLE'S BABY AGONY"*.

Tiny Troll and his Princess Mummy

Trolls love their mummies.

Tiny Troll loved his Mummy a lot. More than puddles. More than earwigs.

But Tiny Troll's Mummy was going out to an Ogre Rave.

"Coming with you!" said Tiny Troll.

"Sorry, Squidge," said his Mummy. "The party's only for grown-ups. Mrs Hag is going to babysit you."

"But I'm NOT a baby," he wailed, "and I don't want to be sat on!" But his Mummy wouldn't listen.

Tiny Troll scowled and cuddled his toy slug.

He sat on his Mummy's lap while she painted her claws and curled her bristles.

He held on to her leg while she waxed her tail and rubbed slime into her scales.

Then she dabbed herself with her bluebottle perfume, put on her high-heel clodhoppers and her pondweed cloak. She was ready.

Tiny Troll took one look at his Mummy and loved her so much he nearly popped. She was the prettiest troll Mummy *ever*. She was a princess Mummy.

He put his arms in the air. His Mummy picked him up. She smelt grown-up and strange. Not really like his Mummy.

Mrs Hag arrived.

Tiny Troll clung tighter round his Mummy's neck.

But his Mummy was firm. She put him back down on the ground.

"Mrs Hag will look after you, Pumpkin," she said. "Give Mummy a kiss goodbye."

But Tiny Troll shook his head. He turned away and pouted.

So his Mummy blew him a kiss and slipped out of the cave door.

Tiny Troll roared and threw himself at the door.

"MUMM-Y-Y-Y!"

"Come on, lovie," said Mrs Hag. "How's about some warm mudmilk and a story?"

He thought about mudmilk. He liked mudmilk. But, no, he loved his

Mummy more.

"NO!" he yelled, "MUMM-Y-Y-Y!" He flung his toy slug against the wall.

"Okay... I'll be in the swamproom if you want me," said Mrs Hag, kindly.

Tiny Troll lay with his face scrinched into the itchy mat. His tears made a big, wet patch.

'Meanie Mummy,' he muttered. He drummed the door hard with his tiny tail. *WHACK! WHACK! WHACK!*

Soon he smelt a creamy, muddy smell coming from the swamproom.

He thought about mudmilk. He liked mudmilk.

He stood up and wiped his eyes. He went to find Mrs Hag.

"Does mudmilk make crying go away?" he asked.

"I think it does," said Mrs Hag.

So Tiny Troll had a huge mugful, and Mrs Hag read him his best story about a little troll scaring a big wolf away. Then Mrs Hag let him have MORE mudmilk. Tiny Troll gave her a big smile. His Mummy *never* let him have more.

Before long, Tiny Troll was sound asleep. Mrs Hag carried him gently to his bog and tucked him in.

Much later when his Mummy got home, she crept in to kiss him goodnight. She'd taken off her make-up. She was wearing her old pyjamas, and her bristles smelt of mould again.

"Mummy – you're back!" whispered Tiny Troll. He hugged her sleepily. "Except now you're even prettier than a princess."

Lottie the Big Junior

Chapter One

"Lottie!" called Mum. "We're meeting Auntie Jen and Bert at the park in ten minutes. Get dressed!"

Lottie looked out her window.

The day was brilliant and still, and the sky was blue and soft with the last of summer. It was her favourite sort of day for going to the playground. The kind of day for playing Bat-Girl, skidding, and running up the slide the wrong way.

But not today.

She stuffed her Bat-Girl costume into the back of her drawer, and dragged out her jeans. She wrinkled her nose at them, but she was firm with herself and put them on. Because tomorrow she was seven – *seven!* – and in just one week and two days, she would be in the Juniors. And Juniors didn't pretend to be superheroes even if it was really, *really* fun.

She was done with babyish stuff. Problem was, she was the youngest in the class by two whole weeks and the youngest in her family by eight whole years. Even worse, she was small for her age. So everyone treated her like a silly baby.

She would have to show them. Yes, she would.

She didn't run ahead on the way to the park. She walked tall and straight. She pointed her toes and held her nose high in the air.

She hoped her mum would notice how sensible and grown-up she was being, but Mum was far too busy chatting to Auntie Jen and little Bert.

She walked slowly into the playground. A few children were already there.

"Go on, then," said Mum, making her way to the bench with Auntie Jen. "Have fun!"

But Lottie hesitated.

Lottie the Infant could think of lots of games. Perhaps Batman-Rescues-the-Puppy-from-the-Baddies. Or Wild-Horse-Escapes-the-Meanie-Cowboys. Or just crawling around with Bert, pretending to be a giant toad.

But Lottie the Junior couldn't do any of that.

She looked over at some big girls, who were making daisy chains in the shade. It was Rosie, Lauren and Maisie, all two years above her at school. Junior girls.

She followed the fence until she was standing near them.

She got ready. And then she coughed.

"Urmmm! Hello," she said.

"Hello, Lottie," said Maisie. The other two smiled.

Lottie felt pleased. It was a good start.

"Can I make a daisy chain with you?" she asked, eagerly.

The girls looked at one another.

"Not really," said Rosie. "This game is only for three people... and we're kind of talking about Class Five things. Sorry."

Lottie felt herself go red. She knew what that meant. It meant she was too babyish to sit with them.

"Okay," she said, standing up as tall as she could. "Never mind." And she spun on her heel and walked a slow, Junior kind of walk to the other side of the playground. Once out of sight, she lay on the ground in the shadows between the toddlers' playhouse and fence. She kicked a fence post.

Worms to them, she thought, *and worms to their dumb daisy chains.*

She lay for a while enjoying the cool shade. The grass behind the toddler house was long and good for wriggling in. She was a caterpillar, she decided, hiding from hungry birds. She twisted and turned, getting all damp and dewy. Then she curled into a tiny ball.

"I'm in one of those cocoons," she whispered to herself, closing her eyes tightly. "... and now I'm a beautiful butterfly!" She leapt up and flew around and around in a spin.

She span until the playground swam around her in a blurry rainbow.

Colours like fireworks, she thought. "Yes, I'm a firework." She span the other way faster and faster. "A catherine wheel!... And a rocket!" She jumped off the playhouse stairs. "WHEEEEE!... BANG BANG!"

A laugh jolted her out of her game.

She opened her eyes to see Rosie, Lauren and Maisie walking away.

They must have seen her game. Oh no! She flopped back down on to the grass.

Bert waddled over, He was covered in yoghurt and smelt of strawberries.

"Lott kitty?" he said, thickly. Lottie knew he wanted to play Naughty Kittens. It was a game they often played, and Lottie loved it as much as Bert.

She peered through her hair at the big girls. They were swinging and chatting, and not taking any notice of Lottie and Bert.

"Come with me," she said quietly. She took his fat, little hand and dragged him inside the playhouse.

"Kittens in here," she told him. "Nice kitten house." She crawled around miaowing, purring and rubbing her head on Bert's tummy, being careful to avoid the yoghurty bits. He giggled and dribbled and patted the kitten a bit too hard. So the kitten changed into a wolf and chased Bert round the playhouse.

"Hello," came a voice from the bright doorway. It was Maisie.

Uh-oh, thought Lottie.

"Hello," she said. She jumped up so quickly she bumped her head on the playhouse roof. "Just playing with Bert. Silly baby stuff. He likes it."

"Can I play?" said Maisie.

"What?" said Lottie. "What, really? What about Rosie and Lauren?"

"They've gone home now," said Maisie. "What you playing?"

Lottie felt her face go even redder. "Um... Wolves-in-a-Cave-Chase-Bert-the-Piglet," she muttered.

"Sounds fun!" said Maisie. "Come on – GRRRRRRR!"

Bert squealed and they all three raced round and round the little playhouse, and out into the playground.

They played Giants-Drive-Fast-Cars-and-Crash next. But then Bert crashed a bit too hard, howled, and had to go and sit on his mummy's lap in the shade.

So Maisie and Lottie ran up the slide the wrong way until it was time to go home.

"See you in the Junior playground," called Lottie to Maisie as she left.

"Yeah," said Maisie. "Probably."

Probably? thought Lottie. But she didn't let it worry her. There was not a cloud in her sky as she walked home. She had made friends with a Junior and tomorrow was her birthday.

Emma Ludlow | Shona

Chapter One

Saturday 5th November

Rides swing across the night sky, the carriages studded with coloured lights. Queues snake from the pay booths dotted about the common. The crowds cast long shadows. Smoke wafts from a refreshment stall carrying an oniony tang. The carousel turns slowly, piped music drifting across the grass. A hook-nosed witch flies above the ghost train. The fireworks scream. The sirens howl...

I am queuing for the Ferris wheel. A girl is standing in the pay booth. I look again. We have the same black hair and blue eyes, the same pale skin. It's not just our colouring, but our features too. The girl is so like me except... look at her clothes. That leather jacket is so cool. I'd love to wear something like that. Her make-up is really glam. Mum would kill me if I wore that much. The girl is counting change, clicking gum between white teeth. Two lads are at the booth. The ginger one speaks first.

"How much for a ride then, babe?"

"Three quid each." The girl has an Irish accent.

"You're cheap at the price, aincha?"

Her eyes flare. "Up your arse."

I like her confidence. I wish I could handle myself like that. The lads shuffle away and the queue inches forward. I'm next.

The girl blinks and shakes her head. She's seen the likeness.

I stare back blankly.

"Is it just yourself?" she says.

"No, two, please. My boyfriend will be over in a second."

"Right so. Six quid."

I pass her a ten pound note.

A voice cuts above the music. "That's it for this one."

"You'll have to wait for the next ride," says the girl, passing me my change. She has sovereign rings on her fingers. Her perfume smells like sherbet. "It'll give your fella a chance to get back."

"OK," I say.

"Where's he gone?"

"Cashpoint."

"Oh right, yeah. Save you paying for stuff all night."

"Yeah, something like that."

"What's your name, then?" she says.

"Janey. What's yours?"

"Shona. You live round here?"

"Not far. A place called Blakelock. It's on the edge of town."

"Yeah? What's it like?"

"S'OK. There's not much there really – just houses and stuff."

Shona nods.

"Where are you from?"

"Dublin."

"That's cool."

The music changes. R&B is pulsing from the speakers.

"This song is deadly," says Shona. "You like it?"

"Yeah, I do." I say. "I really like Mary J. Blige."

Shona sings a line or two.

We burst into giggles.

"It's good to dance to," says Shona. "I'm into dancing."

"Yeah, me too," I say. "That's a cool jacket, by the way."

Shona tugs the hem. "Thanks. I've had it a good while. My pal got it for me. I think she got it about…" she screws up one eye. "Two years ago. Yeah, two years. I always wear it. It's my favourite."

"It's nice."

"Thanks. I was thinking about getting some new stuff, except my boss is dead stingy."

"Maybe you should ask for a raise?"

"Oh, I've asked. I'll get the tight-fisted sod to pay up soon enough."

I laugh. "You should. Not that you need new clothes or anything. You look really good."

The men are lifting the barriers. The ride is over. Shona looks over my shoulder. "Has your fella got brown hair and a blue top on?"

"Yeah." I turn and see Jack striding across the grass. "Well, it was nice to meet you," I say.

"Yeah, you too." Shona grins. "You have a good night now."

"Thanks."

We pause; look at the other's identical features one last time.

"I'll see you later," she says.

I nod. "Goodbye, Shona."

Chapter Two

Monday 14th November

"You're going to be late again, Janey." Mum didn't look up from the paper.

I picked a roll from the kitchen cupboard and sat down. "It's only quarter to eight, isn't it?"

"Ten to, I think you'll find."

Get off my back, I thought. *I've barely been awake half an hour.*

"I'm not paying for your education so you can breeze in late every day," said Mum. "You never used to have trouble getting out of bed. What do you think would happen to me if I was late to the shop all the time? I'd have no job and then where would we be? There'd be no money for your car or nice clothes or an expensive education. Do you think everyone has the advantages you've got? This is an important year. You've got your A levels coming up and you need to put the work in. You need three As for Law."

Whatever. I'd die before I spent all day in a drab lawyer's office shuffling bits of paper.

"Are you coming straight home after school or are you meeting up with Jack again?"

"Don't know."

"You're seeing too much of him, Janey. He's a distraction. It's no coincidence this lack of interest in your work started when you met him. It may be all right for him to do some low-grade college course, but it's not all right for you. You're an intelligent girl, if only you'd put your mind to it. I don't know what you see in Jack, really I don't. He hasn't even got any GCSEs, for goodness sake. Do you think someone like that is good for you?"

Yes, actually. Being with Jack was a damn sight better than being stuck here. I brushed some crumbs from my skirt pleats. "I'm going now."

In the hall, I unhooked my bag and blazer from the hat stand. Mum's voice filtered in from the kitchen. 'And remember the speed limit is seventy down that dual carriageway.'

I closed my eyes and leaned against the wall. *Please God let something happen so my life is different. If you help me now, I promise I will never ask for anything again.*

I was haring up the stone steps when the bell went. I headed straight for History. Another pointless lesson. I took my place at the back and pulled out my chair. The girls were filing in silently, sticking to the rules. They unpacked ringbinders and exercise books. They'd be full of extra research and neatly completed homework. This school was so lame. The day I left, I'd be shouting it from the rooftops. Mrs Beauman entered and slammed the door shut. She took a marker pen and wrote "THE COLLAPSE OF THE WEIMAR REPUBLIC" across the board. Beyond the tall windows, rain fell like scattered pins.

At lunchtime, Carole-Anne and I went to Rhonda's. It's a café round the corner from school. We wandered past a parade of shops arm in arm.

"So have you given in your English coursework yet?" said Carole-Anne.

"No, not yet." I'd barely started. "We've got until Thursday, haven't we?"

"Yeah, but there's loads of other stuff to do before then. I've got a Geography assignment and I've got a French test on Friday. I don't know how I'm going to cope."

"It'll be all right."

"You're always so cool about everything," said Carole-Anne. "I wish I was like you."

She didn't. She knew I'd got bad marks lately.

"I'll get that coursework in so I can spend a couple of days on Geography and then I'll have at least a day for French, and... What?" Carole Anne stopped next to me.

A flyer was flattened to the ground by a lamppost. I'd caught sight of the photo.

"What?" said Carole-Anne again. "What you looking at?"

"It's a Missing poster," I said.

"Yeah? And?"

"It's this girl. I think I might recognise her." My heart was hammering.

"Really?"

"Hang on, let me read it."

MISSING
Can you help?

Shona Lynch

Age at disappearance: 17

Shona has been missing from Fenley since 5th November. She had spent the evening working at a fairground on Fenley Common and left her pitch at 7pm. She has not been seen or heard from since.

Shona is 5 feet 3 inches tall, of slim build with blue eyes and long black hair. She has an Irish accent. At the time of her disappearance, she was wearing a black leather jacket, blue jeans and white trainers.

If you have seen Shona, please call Fenley police station on 812812.

"It's definitely her," I said. "She was taking the money for the Ferris wheel."

"Was she?" Carole-Anne didn't sound bothered.

"Well, what do you reckon I should do?"

"Don't know really. I mean, what can you do?"

"I think I should go to the police."

"I wouldn't bother. Aren't they looking for people who've seen her since the fair?" Carole-Anne grabbed my arm and dragged me towards the café door. "Come on. Let's get some food. I'm starving."

The waitress set our toasted cheese sandwiches on the table.

"Toasties, brilliant." Carole-Anne took a bite and wiped a string of cheese from her lip.

I slid my plate aside. I'd lost my appetite.

"So I saw that film on Saturday," said Carole-Anne. "You know, the one with Ashton Kutcher in it? God, he's so fit. I was, like, drooling the whole time."

I nodded and sipped my tea.

"He's so sweet and funny and he's such a good actor. I so like him." Carole-Anne looked up. "What's the matter? You look weird."

"Do I? Sorry."

"What's up?"

I chewed my thumbnail. "I'm thinking about that girl."

"Why?"

"I think I should go to the police."

"And say what?"

"I don't know... I'll tell them what happened. I did speak to her, you know."

"Yeah, but she wasn't missing then, was she?"

"No, but—'

"You'll only get yourself in trouble," interrupted Carole-Anne. "Didn't your mum tell you not to go to that fair?"

"Yeah."

"So she'll find out and then she'll probably ground you. Why bother?"

"Because it's important," I said. "What if something's happened to her?"

"What? In Fenley? I don't think so."

"I'll feel guilty if I leave it."

"I'd keep out of it if I were you."

"I want to try," I said firmly.

"Well, I think it's a bad plan. What if they ask you to come back and give evidence or something? It's not worth the hassle."

"So there's no chance of you coming with me, then?"

"No way." Carole-Anne twisted her lip. "I can't tonight, anyway. We're out for my grandma's birthday. Give Jack a ring. He'll go with you."

"He will not."

"Course he will. Why wouldn't he?"

"Can you imagine Jack voluntarily entering a police station?"

"He'll want to help you. He's your boyfriend, isn't he?"

"Well yeah..."

"Give him a ring. It'll be fine. Oh, and give me a ring when you've finished, as well. Let me know how it goes. Maybe you're holding the vital clue that'll wrap up the whole case."

Carole-Anne was laughing, but I had butterflies in my stomach. If she knew what I'd seen that night, she wouldn't find it so funny. She hadn't heard the whole story.

. . .

I rubbed my cold hands and glanced at my watch again. Where was Jack? He said he'd be here by five. I looked over my shoulder at the police station. A WPC was moving around a Perspex-screened office. A boy in a baseball cap was sitting with his back to the window. I hated places like this. They gave me the creeps.

Jack dashed across the road. He was wearing a black pilot's jacket and jeans. My heart did a double beat.

"Alright, bird?" He pushed a straggle of hair from his forehead.

"Yeah, fine. How are you?"

"Not so bad. Sorry I'm late. I got a bit held up."

That was nothing new. "It's OK," I said.

"So are you serious about this missing girl thing?"

"Well, yeah. I was talking to her."

"I know. You said."

"Didn't you see her?"

"Nah, I don't think so," said Jack. "I don't suppose I was paying much attention."

I stamped my feet and shivered. "Can we go in now? I'm getting a bit nervous here."

"Yeah, OK." He patted my hand. "Just let me give my dad a bell and we'll get this over with."

A pug-faced man with sandy hair collected us from the waiting area. He led us into an interview room with a desk and a bank of filing cabinets. We sat down. He opened his notebook.

"I'm DI Butler and I'm in charge of the investigation into Shona's disappearance," he said fixing me with piggy eyes. "I need a full name, address and contact number from both of you."

"It's Janey Selway, 37 All Saints Road, Fenley 209367."

DI Butler looked at Jack. "And you?"

"Look, I'm just here to help Janey. I really can't remember anything, so you better..."

"I need to log that you were present at this interview," interrupted the Inspector.

Jack huffed and rested his chin in his hand. "It's Jack Shaw, Flat 5, 133 Elton Road, Fenley 861002. You're not going to ring me or nothing, are you?"

"It's unlikely we'll need to ring you, though it all depends on whether you have anything worthwhile to tell us." DI Butler smiled thinly. "Janey?"

I tried to remember what I could about the night I'd seen Shona. I explained she'd been working in the paybox when those lads started bothering her. It wasn't long before DI Butler was asking questions.

"What did these men look like?"

"They were about 18 or 19. One was tall, like six foot, with bad skin."

"You mean acne?"

"Yes, acne and a ginger crew cut."

"Build?"

"I don't know really."

"Slim? Medium? Stocky?"

"Slim, I suppose."

"And the other?"

"He was shorter, with black hair. He was Greek - or Spanish-looking..."

"Mediterranean?"

"Yeah."

"And how tall was he?"

"Maybe about five feet six."

"Did they seem drunk or intoxicated in any way?"

"A bit drunk, maybe. It was hard to tell."

"And what time was this?"

"About six thirty."

"Did you see where they went afterwards?"

"They just went on the ride."

"You didn't see them again?"

"No." I rubbed my temple. He was stressing me out.

"So how did Shona seem when you spoke to her?"

"Fine."

"She didn't seem anxious or distressed?"

"No."

"What was she wearing?"

"A black leather jacket with a blue jumper underneath it, lots of jewellery."

"Did you see her again after this?"

"Yes."

"When?"

"About two hours later, when we were leaving the fair…"

The crowds move under the floodlights. The music is pounding.

"Come on, let's go on something else," I say.

"I dunno." Jack glances around. "What time is it?"

"It's only nine. What about that?" I point to the Waltzer where two guys in neon jackets are whirling the carriages around.

"You're joking, aincha?" says Jack. "I've just had a burger."

"Well, the dodgems, then."

"I dunno, Janey. I think I've had it for tonight."

"So let's go on somewhere else."

"Like where?"

"We could go to the pub."

"Do we have to?"

"Go on Jack. Please."

"Yeah, all right, but I can't be too late, OK?"

DI Butler was scribbling in his notebook. "Which way were you heading?"

"Away from the fair, towards Woodlands Road," I said.

"What time was this?"

"About nine o'clock."

"And then?"

Jack and I skirt the common. A car loops around the road, flinging our shadows against the trees.

"Blimin' heck, it's freezing," says Jack.

"It's not that bad," I say.

"Not that bad?" Jack shoots me a look. "These are sub-zero temperatures. If it gets any worse, we'll be calling the mountain rescue. They'll find us frozen to death with our limbs rotted off." Jack's so caught up in his rant he nearly walks into a lamppost. "Now, are you starting something?" he says, waving his finger at the lamppost. "If you want a punch-up, let's take this somewhere else."

I'm cracking up.

"Will you give us a loan of your scarf?" says Jack.

"No way," I say. "It's you who's supposed to be lending me your stuff."

"But you're wrapped up like a flippin' Eskimo. I'm half naked compared to you."

"That's not very gentlemanly." I march on ahead.

"What do you mean, not gentlemanly? I'm the perfect gent."

"Yeah, right."

"Let's have it, Janey." Jack tugs the scarf from my neck and runs, letting it trail behind him.

I tear after him. "Come back here," I shout. I'm breathing heavily, my trainers slapping on the sodden ground. "Give it back." I'm gaining on him when I slip and fall to the ground. Shit. "Jack, wait up will you?" I get up slowly, rub flecks of damp grass from my hands and knees. I look across the road. Shona is standing by the trees. She folds her arms and glances up and down the street. She's agitated. I wonder what she's doing.

"Did you speak to her?" said DI Butler.

"No."

"Was there anyone with her?"

"No."

"And did you see which way she was heading?"

I shook my head. "That was the last time I saw her."

Jack and I left the police station. We schlepped down the steps into the icy night.

"That bloke was a complete idiot," said Jack. "Anyone'd think he was cross-examining a serial killer."

"I hope nothing bad happened to Shona," I said. "I mean, what if those lads ended up attacking her?"

"That's jumping to conclusions a bit, innit?" said Jack. We sat down on a low wall. "Just because a few blokes crack on to a bird, it don't mean they're going to rape her or nothing. DI Butler only wants them as witnesses."

"But I should've asked if she was all right."

"I don't think so, bird. You can't go up to every random person you see looking a bit upset and ask if they're OK."

Shona didn't feel like a random person. We'd got on so well. "I still feel bad, Jack."

"Come off it, Janey. Don't be daft. I mean, she probably just ran off. We've been to the police and now you've got to forget about it." He coiled some hair behind my ear. "There's nothing else you can do."

Chapter Three

Friday 18th November

Mystery of missing fairground girl

Police are concerned for the safety of an Irish fairground worker who disappeared from Fenley Common on 5th November.

Shona Lynch, 17, left colleagues at 7.00pm and was last seen by a witness two hours later on the west side of the common near Woodlands Road. Police are anxious to trace two men aged approximately 18–21 who were seen talking to Shona earlier in the night. One is white, around six feet tall with ginger hair. He has a tattoo on his hand and was wearing a hooded top and jeans. The other is five feet six tall with black hair and of Mediterranean appearance.

Shona is originally from Dublin, Ireland, and had been in England only four months at the time of her disappearance. Her family and friends are anxious for news that she is safe and well.

Detective Inspector David Butler, who is leading the investigation, commented: "Shona is a confident and outgoing young woman who has made many friends through her work at the fairground. I would urge Shona, or anyone who knows of her whereabouts, to contact police as soon as possible."

I was sitting in the school library turning the clipping over in my fingers. Shona's familiar face stared back from the photo. Since I went to the police, I'd kept an eye out for news about her. I couldn't forget what'd happened. I knew Jack was right and I probably couldn't have helped, but I still felt guilty. I mean, Shona was really nice to me. I should've asked if she was OK. DI Butler told me I was the last person to see Shona before she went missing. It's hard to explain, but that made me feel involved somehow. I'd started asking myself questions about Shona. Where had she gone? What had made her run away? She'd seemed fine when I spoke to her. None of it made any sense.

Later that night, I was curled up on the sofa flicking channels when the phone rang in the hallway.

"Can you get that, Janey?" Mum called from upstairs. "I'm trying to get ready." She was going to a lot of trouble for a stuffy dinner party. I padded into the hallway and lifted the receiver.

"Hello?"

"All right, bird?" It was Jack.

"Oh, hi, Jack. How's it going?"

"Yeah, yeah, all right."

"What you up to?"

"Not a lot. Just been to the chippie. Do you fancy coming over?"

I pressed the buzzer to Jack's block and the catch was released. The bulb in the stairwell had gone again. Upstairs, Jack was standing by his front door. A square of light shone on to the landing.

"All right? You got here quick."

"Did I?" I didn't want him thinking I'd raced over here. "Yeah, well, the roads were pretty quiet."

"Oh right, yeah."

We shuffled inside.

"Dad! Janey's here."

His dad was slumped in the living room as always, his face lit by the TV.

"Hello, Janey."

"Hi." I mustered a smile. "How are you?"

"Not so bad love, not so bad." His voice was far away.

"We'll probably stay in tonight," said Jack. "Give me a shout if you need anything."

"All right, son." His dad fumbled in his pocket for a cigarette. "No bother."

"What do you mean, we'll stay in?" I plumped down on Jack's bed and glared at him. "I thought we were going to do something."

"What? Go out?" Jack's shadow shifted on the wall as he put on a CD.

"Yes, go out."

"What do you want to do that for? This is where the party's at." He did a comedy sway and I giggled.

"I'm serious," I said. "We could go into town. There's that new bar opened up on King's Street."

"Nah, I don't fancy it. It looks like it's full of twats. Besides, I don't want to leave Dad alone."

Typical. I knew his dad was depressed, but it didn't mean we had to stay in all the time. "I only want to go to the pub."

"Yeah, but I feel bad if I keep leaving him." Jack sat beside me. "He's on his own too much as it is."

"Come on, Jack. We should be getting out there and doing stuff."

"Like what?"

"Something fun. You know, like going raving and getting pissed. All that stuff."

"Yeah, but you can do that with Carole-Anne. No one goes clubbing with their bloke, do they?"

"But you're 18. Whenever me and Carole-Anne go out, we always end up in the same places 'cos we can't get served. It's either the Shaker or the Riverside and I'm fed up with them. I want some excitement."

"Last time we went out, we ended up going to the police about missing girls," said Jack. "Ain't that exciting enough for you?"

I wandered over to the window and lifted the curtain. The road was empty under the streetlights. The parked cars glittered with frost. "I've been thinking about Shona a bit," I said. "I've been looking in the paper for stories about her."

"Why?"

"It was weird being tied up in something like that. I hope she's OK."

"Well so do I, but I don't s'pose we'll ever find out. People go off all the time, don't they?"

I looked back at him and let the curtain fall. "Maybe she went to London? Loads of runaways go there."

"Yeah, maybe."

"I guess she might've found another job at a fair?"

"I guess."

"It's weird when people just up and leave like that. I mean, why would you do that?"

"Dunno."

"I suppose she might've had a row with her boyfriend or her family? She looked sort of upset."

"Yeah, p'raps," said Jack. "Do we have to talk about this? Why don't you come and sit down?" He was looking at me like I was mad.

"Oh, OK." I suddenly felt a bit stupid.

Jack hooked an arm around me. "Do you want to watch a film or something? I've got *Blade Runner* on DVD."

My heart sank, but I didn't argue.

Chapter Four

Monday 21st November

"By now, all of you should've started revising for your mock exams." Mrs Beauman was stalking between the desks, her heels clicking on the polished floor. "I will be running twice-weekly revision classes from tomorrow and I expect everyone to be in attendance. The mock exams are the best indicator of the grade you are likely to receive at A level. It's a general rule that if you get a B in this exam you'll get an A in the June assessment."

I looked at the classroom wall; at the dog-eared notices and stopped clock. This was so boring. Beauman was rambling on like our lives depended on these exams. Why couldn't summer be here so I could do the things I really wanted? I'd get a job, something cool like bar work. It'd be an excuse to stay out late and have drinks bought for me. I deserved some fun after seven years sweating it out in this dump.

"I'm sorry, am I boring you, Jane?"

I was jolted from my daydream. "What?"

"Do you find the topic of your mock exams tedious?" Mrs Beauman arched an eyebrow. "I'm glad you're so confident of your success you can afford not to listen."

The class tittered and my face flamed.

"I don't know what's got into you lately, but this isn't the first time I've caught you staring into space during my lesson," said Mrs Beauman. "Do you have more pressing matters to contemplate than your History A level?"

My blush deepened. The old witch was enjoying this.

"We don't have much teaching time left this term and I suggest you start taking these exams more seriously." Mrs Beauman's lips twitched. "Is that understood?"

After class, I stormed out on to the terrace. Silly cow. Who did she think she was, humiliating me like that? I bet she lay awake at night dreaming up her oh-so-witty put-downs. I huffed down on a bench and folded my arms. A voice startled me.

"What you doing, stranger?" It was Carole-Anne.

"You made me jump."

"Did I? You were miles away." She hunkered down next to me. "How's it going?"

"Not great. Beauman just had a go at me."

Carole-Anne unsnapped a can of Coke. "'Bout what?"

"She reckons I'm not taking the exams seriously."

"Well, you're not, are you?"

"Carole-Anne!" She was supposed to be on my side.

"I'm not being rude. I'm just saying you don't seem as focused on school as you used to be."

"It's just this place." I looked across the playing field. "It gets me down. Don't you ever get fed up with it?"

"Could be worse."

"Could it? Sometimes I just want to get out of here. Tell everyone to get stuffed and go. I mean, there's so much pressure all the time. If it's not Mum on at me, it's teachers. I just want to do my own thing."

"You're applying to uni, aren't you?"

"Yes, but it's just going to be the same old thing, isn't it? More exams, more essays, more pressure."

"I'm looking forward to uni," said Carole-Anne. "I think it'll be a laugh."

"But it'll be full of the same people; stuck-up rich kids. What's such a laugh about that?"

Carole-Anne wrinkled her nose. "What are you talking about, Janey? You're one of the rich kids, in case you'd forgotten. You're acting really weird."

I looked away, embarrassed. She didn't understand at all.

"So you missed a good night, Friday," said Carole-Anne. "I saw Sam in the Riverside."

"Who?"

"You know Sam. He's that lad from the boys school. He's, like, tall with blond hair. He's really gorgeous."

"Oh right, yeah." I'd met him in the Shaker once. He was sweet, though not really my type.

"We were talking for ages – must've been at least twenty minutes. There's definitely chemistry." Carole-Anne took a slug of Coke. "Where were you, anyway?"

"Round at Jack's."

"What did you do?"

"Not much. He's being really boring lately."

"Oh really?"

"Yeah, I don't know. It's his dad. He's worried about leaving him alone."

"What's the thing with him again?"

"He's got depression."

"Oh right, yeah."

"I feel sorry for him and everything, but me and Jack never seem to go out any more."

"You should come out with us lot. I expect we'll go back to the Riverside in a week or two."

"Yeah, maybe." The Riverside again.

"Come on. It'll be cool."

"I'll have to get some new stuff if I'm going clubbing."

"Why? You look all right, don't you?"

I shrugged. "I'm sick of all my clothes lately."

"So get some new stuff. Go on, Janey."

"Yeah, OK. We'll sort something out."

"Cool." Carole-Anne smiled. "It'll give me a chance to hook up with Sam again."

The local paper was wedged in the letterbox when I got home. I unlocked the door and took it upstairs to my bedroom. I put on my Alicia Keys album and sat on the bed to read. There was nothing about Shona again. I wondered why the story hadn't been followed up. Had the police found those lads? I got up and switched on the computer. It bleeped and whirred. I typed "Shona Lynch" into the search engine and a list flashed up: her profile on the Missing Persons helpline, an article from the *Fenley Gazette*. My heart quickened. The last link on the page was called "ALL THE FUN OF THE FAIR". Shona's name was printed in bold and the fragmented sentences below looked like an appeal for information. Hurriedly, I clicked on the link. This was a message forum for people who worked in fairgrounds.

> *I am loking 4 Shona Lynch who went mising on 5 Nov from jennings fair in fenley. It is not like her to runaway and I think somthing hapend 2 her. Shona has blak hair, blu eyes and irish voice. She wheres a lether jaket and smokes B&H. we spent last 2 weeks in Marsdon on sea with the fair and travalled to fenley on nite of 4th. Shona talked to alot of people and if u seen her plese get in toch. i will get back 2 u.*

The message was signed Darragh.

Jack Roberts | Indian Summer

Chapter One

There is something to be said about summer. It's when scars and swearin' are cool, and cruising around on your bikes with the wind blowin' through your hair is livin' as life intended. It's when stories like *Huck Finn* come true, and when danger means 'who's going first'. It's the season of sunscreen, barbecued burgers and ragged tennis shoes that reek like an old bag of Doritos. Yep, there ain't anything much better than summer.

I grew up in a small town on the outskirts of Eastern Oregon called Strawberry. My dad worked for a lumber mill, and did his best to take care of my little brother Tommy and me. My mom had died unexpectedly last fall, and well, you're never ready for something like that. Sometimes I felt sorry for myself, but my self-pity was soon forgotten whenever I thought about Dale.

Dale's dad was a mean curse, especially when he was drunk, which happened to be most of the time. His mom died too, a few years ago. She was a real sweet lady. My dad said that tragedy changes people. I guess it changed Dale's dad for the worst.

Then there was Leroy. His dad ran a cattle ranch, and all the brothers worked the farm to get things done. He was a bit shy, but strong as an ox, Leroy looked more like a sixteen-year-old than a fourteen-year-old. Plus his older sister Summer, holy smokes, was babe-alicious.

It was June, school was out, and we were going to the dirt hills. We were cruising there on our bikes; I rode this Schwinn that was hideously yellow. Dale rode this rusted blue bike that must had been given to him by a neighbor; its brand name had faded years before. Leroy had crashed his bike last summer and was riding his sister's – you know, one of those purple and pink jobs with the colorful streamers dangling from the handle grips. Dale and I laughed when he first rode up on that bike, but one thing was for certain: no other kid in town dared make fun of Leroy, even if he was riding a girl's bike.

We stopped at the base of the dirt hills.

"Hey, Leroy," Dale said. "Dare you to go off Suicide again."

Suicide was the nastiest jump at the dirt hills. It cremated Leroy's bike last summer.

"Why me, you ain't got the guts?" Leroy replied.

"Heck no," Dale said.

We laughed.

"Hey, I'm heading to Dragon's Spit," I said. "Do you guys wanna come?"

"I'm going to Devil's Driveway first," Dale said. "I'll meet you there after."

Leroy looked down at his sister's bike and frowned. "I can't go off any jumps on this. I'll be at the sissy side."

I laughed. "You're gonna be riding a girl's bike on the sissy side? Wait till everyone hears about this."

"Do and die!" Leroy barked.

I loved teasing Leroy. "Come over to the big boys' side when you get bored of the pee-wee hills," I said.

"How about I pee-wee your face!" Leroy hollered back.

Dragon's Spit was a favorite on the dirt hills. It was crazy steep and all about speed. I pedaled over to the edge and peered over. The hill cut straight down like a half-pipe and leveled out to a massive field of tall weeds. I cycled around and gave myself some starting space. I took a deep breath and then went for it. The edge of the hill flew up, and before I knew it I was zooming down the side of the hill. My legs rotated so quickly that they felt like eggbeaters churning on full throttle. My stomach rose into my throat and the rush of the wind flapped my T-shirt against my skin.

I swooshed down the hill and onto the big field of weeds. The tires rumbled over the bumpy ground and the weeds slapped against my legs. I gave the brakes a few soft squeezes and slowed – anything more would've sent me sailing over my handlebars.

I turned my bike around and peered up at Dragon's Spit. Now for the next challenge: going back up. I stood and pumped once again, this time with all my might. I had to get enough speed to carry me to the top. I whizzed up the first part of the hill, but it was so steep that I was quickly losing speed. I pumped my legs like turbines, creeping up the hillside. My knuckles were white tight on my handle grips and my teeth were clenched. *Almost there! Almost there!* My front wheel arched over the top of the hill and I breathed a tired sigh of relief.

A voice startled me. "Hey, butt munch."

I turned. It was DJ-freaking-McAllister. DJ was two years older than me, and was notoriously known as the school bully. During the last week of school I accidentally nailed him in the back of his head with a water balloon. He had been waiting for a perfect time to get me back, you know, mash my head. He was with his butt-head buddy, Tony Reynolds. There they stood, with their biker gloves and grimy smiles.

My heart began pumping so hard, I could feel my pulse pounding in my ears. My legs suddenly felt weak and rubbery. I tried to go around them by turning to the left, but Tony rammed my bike.

Tony squinted. "You thought we would just let you ride by, dim-wit?"

DJ rode up and put his ugly mug right in my face. "You're gonna pay, numb-nuts."

"Yeah, your nuts are numb!" Tony chimed.

They busted out laughing. As DJ laughed in my face, I could see particles of food in his teeth and a thick layer of plaque hung like rafters from off his gums. Yeah, I was going to get pounded, but I wasn't about to go down like a pansy.

"Man, your breath is worse than my farts. Haven't you heard about a new invention called the toothbrush?"

DJ's face turned red and a big vein poked out on his forehead. He swore, then spat.

Right then, Dale rounded the corner. He stopped dead in his tracks when he saw DJ and Tony.

DJ motioned Tony to get Dale. Tony pedaled over and threw down his bike. I knew Dale wasn't scared of Tony; his dad pushing him around was more terrifying than Tony. Tony snorted, then hocked a nasty loogie on Dale. That's when it hit me... DJ's fist.

I tumbled over and off my bike; he was on me instantly. DJ pressed my face into the ground and began hitting me in the back of the head. I was pinned and couldn't breathe. Panicking, I began squirming in every which way I could. I got my head turned and one arm free, then reached up and grabbed at DJ's eyes. He yelled and covered his face. I wiggled free.

Standing, I saw that Tony had put Dale in a headlock and was slugging him like he was a punching bag. I ran at him like a charging bull.

Tony looked up just as my fist was flying towards him like a toma-hawk missile. It came down and smashed the top of his head. He groaned, and his lock loosened enough for Dale to get away.

A feeling of confidence swept through me. I had never been in a fight before and I was standing my ground with these punks. Sure, DJ got me with a cheap shot, but I took it like a man and raked his face like a raging rooster. Now it was Tony's turn to get the smack-down.

Tony held his head and then cussed. I was on my toes, bouncing back and forth, anticipating his next move. He faked right, and then faked left. I didn't anticipate that. In my confusion I kicked. I kicked! Talk about a stupid white dude move. I missed, of course, and Tony slugged me in the stomach.

Ooff! I bent over, wheezing for air.

Tony grabbed my arms and jerked them behind my back. The mus-cles in my shoulders screamed in sharp pain. DJ now approached, with his fists clenched and his eyes red and swollen. Dale ran at him with his arms flailing, but DJ simply grabbed him and tossed him to the ground in one quick motion, as if he were batting away a fly. Dale tumbled to the ground and before he could get up, DJ kicked him.

Tony laughed. "Say, what should we do with this one?"

"I'm gonna break that big mouth of his," DJ ranted. "We'll see how smart he thinks he is when his jaw is wired shut."

Tony pulled my arms back harder. My shoulder muscles felt like they were tearing. "Your jaw is going to be wired shut, dill weed."

A voice boomed. "Touch him again and you die!"

It was Leroy. He tossed his sister's bike to the ground. "Dang it, DJ, am I going to have to dust the ground with your sorry face again?"

My inevitable doom was looking brighter. Leroy had taught DJ a lesson before. He whooped him over good during gym class. It was the first time anyone had stood up to DJ without waking up to black eyes the next morning.

DJ's face hardened. Through clenched teeth he muttered to Tony, "Get rid of the squirt and help me take the beefcake."

Tony kept my hands pulled tightly behind me and pushed me to-wards the edge of Dragon's Spit. With a strong heave, he shoved me over the edge. I hit the hill and began tumbling. Everything became a blurry twirl, with the ground slamming into me every half-second. I reached out to stop but the hill was too steep. I rolled until I reached the bottom, where I laid dizzily, bruised and scraped.

Starring up into the spinning sky, I heard faint screams and groans, then pleas for mercy. I wasn't surprised. Leroy was as tuff as nails. I heard him call out. "Elliott, are you alive down there?"

I looked up and saw Leroy, with Dale by his side.

I didn't have the strength to reply, so I raised my arm. They both made their way carefully down the hill and stopped next to where I lay.

"Are you OK?" Leroy asked.

I sat up. "Did you kick their—"

"Yeah."

"That was fast."

"They aren't nearly as tuff as my older bros, they're more like practice dummies."

Dale piped in. "You should've seen it – he took both of them on at once."

I managed out a smile. "Thanks, man."

"It was my pleasure." Leroy's great grin grew between two deep dimples. "I love pounding those dirt bags."

I went to stand, but a sharp pain jabbed inside my back. I cringed.

"What's wrong?" Dale asked.

I turned over. "I think I landed on a rock."

Dale bent down and looked at my back. "Hey, you're bleeding."

I felt around and found a tear in my shirt. I pulled my hand around and saw blood.

"Is it bad?" I asked.

Dale looked closer. "No, not *real* bad, but it must've been a sharp rock."

I searched between the weeds and the dirt to see if I could find the rock I landed on. That's when I spotted something. It looked like a shark fin sticking up right out of the ground. Pulling at it, it came out with little struggle. It was covered with dirt, but I recognized it immediately. "It's an arrowhead."

Chapter Two

We got to my house and threw our bikes on my back lawn. I kept the arrowhead safely in my front pocket as we walked towards our fort. My annoying little brother Tommy burst out the back door to greet us.

Tommy was eleven and looked nothing like me. He was more like my dad: dark hair, olive skin, and brown eyes. I looked more like my mother, which I was proud of. I had pale skin, light freckles, blond hair and blue eyes. I knew Tommy had been bored out of his mind all afternoon and I saw that he was wearing one of my T-shirts.

"Hi, guys!" Tommy said.

"Hey, what did I say about wearing my clothes?" I barked.

Tommy ignored my comment. "Whatcha up to?"

"Get lost, Tommy," I said.

Tommy pointed at my eye. "Whoa, what happened to you?"

"What?"

"Your eye!"

I felt for my eye. It was tender and swollen. "Oh yeah, that. I... uh... crashed on the bike."

"Where?"

"Get a life, Tommy. We have stuff to do."

Tommy lowered his head. "I just wanted to say hi. You don't have to be so rude."

"I wouldn't have to be if you weren't such a pain in my butt."

"Chill out, Elliott," Leroy remarked.

Leroy was always sticking up for Tommy. "Fine," I muttered. "Tommy, be useful and get us some popsicles."

"You bet. What kind do you guys want?"

"Root beer," I said.

"I want root beer, too," Dale said.

"I'll have banana," Leroy added.

Dale and I looked right over at Leroy disgustedly. "What's the matter with you?"

"What?"

"You don't ask for banana."

"Yeah, unless you're a girl!" Dale chimed.

Tommy interjected. "Banana is my favorite too, Leroy."

"See? I'm not the only one," Leroy said, placing his arm on Tommy's shoulder.

I rolled my eyes. "That girl bike must be getting to you. Come on. Let's go inside the fort."

We built our fort two summers ago in my back yard. We put it in between my dad's red shed and a large tree that splattered us with apricots in July. It was built from scraps we found at the dump. You'd be surprised what you can find there; people toss away some good stuff. It was usually a little rusty, but we always could clean it up and make good use of it. We brought back loads of chicken wire, wooden crates, torn-up tarps, rotten plywood, and rusty sheet metal. Sheet metal was the most useful.

But the best part about the fort was its secret entryway. The only way you could get in was through the shed. Inside, there was a window that faced the apricot tree. So we walled in the fort around the window. You had to climb through the window to get inside the fort. It was pure genius.

Inside the shed, we climbed onto the table and opened the window into the fort. Dale and I jumped through with ease, and after a few grunts and moans Leroy finally squeezed his big body through.

Leroy tumbled through the window. "Maybe it's time we made a door to this fort instead of using the stupid window."

"The window is the best part!" I said.

"It was cool last summer, but it's lame now."

"*You're* lame now! Come on. Let's check out the arrowhead."

I pulled the arrowhead out of my pocket. It was covered with dirt and pieces of pocket lint. I placed it flat on the palm of my hand so all of us could examine it. It was dark grey, like charcoal, and still sharp along its edges (the cut on my back proved that much), and it was shaped like a leaf of an Aspen tree.

I grabbed the bottom of my white T-shirt, now splattered with dirt, blood and grass stains. I spat a white bubbly glob of saliva on it and began to gently clean the arrowhead.

Dale piped up. "Elliott, I'm not so sure you oughtta be using your spit to clean that? It probably should be done by some scientist, you know, with brushes."

"Na, there's nothing that a good spit-shine will harm. My dad taught me that."

I spat out another glob on my shirt and continued cleaning. Turning it over, I washed the dirt off that side, too. But as I did, I noticed there was some kind of design carved in it. I scrubbed the dirt away with my shirt to see it clearer. The carving was right in the middle, and it looked like some bird with huge wings.

"There's something carved in it," I said, showing it to the guys.

"What is it?" Leroy asked.

"It looks like an eagle."

Leroy and Dale leaned in and looked closer. "What is that?" Dale asked.

"I wanna see!" chimed a high-pitched voice.

Cursing, I looked over at Tommy, who had been watching the entire conversation. "Tommy! What have I said about spying on us?"

"I brought over the popsicles is all!" he shouted back defensively.

"Fine. Leave them there and get."

Ignoring my command, Tommy hopped through the window. "Can I hold it?"

"No, you can't!" I said.

"Sure you can!" Leroy boomed, grabbing the arrowhead out of my hands. He handed it to Tommy.

Tommy brought the arrowhead up to eye level. "Wow, is this a *real* Indian arrowhead?"

"Sure is, and it's mine. Now get out!" I said, snatching the arrowhead back. With that I gave Tommy a hard shove. His head jerked back and his legs flew up. He landed square on his back.

"You never listen to me, Tommy. When I say get out, I mean it."

Tommy's lip began quivering, like it always does when he is trying not to cry. "I hate you!"

"Cry me a river, Tommy. You're such a baby."

Leroy grabbed my arm. "Take it easy on him."

I glared at Leroy. "Why are you always sticking up for him?"

"Why are you being such a butt head?" he replied.

"Maybe you should mind your own business, *Lenny*."

Leroy squinted his eyes. "Lenny?"

"*Of Mice and Men,* idiot. The big strong guy with no brains."

"Come on, guys," Dale pleaded.

"Man-child," I muttered, just loud enough for Leroy to hear.

Leroy didn't say anything; he just stared at the ground. He stared there for a while too. Then he lifted his head; his eyes were watery and he was breathing in and out real loud – even his bottom lip quivered. I had never seen Leroy like this, *ever*. Leroy was the toughest of the tough, bravest of the brave, strongest of the strong. Even when he crashed on Suicide and broke both of his wrists, he shrugged it off like it was a sliver or something. "The thing of it is," Leroy said softly, "you were never like this before your mom died." Leroy wiped his tears off his eyes. "You were never like this to me, or to Tommy or Dale."

I didn't know what to say. "I... I..."

Leroy waved me off and walked up to the fort wall. "I ain't using that stupid window anymore," he said out loud. Then, like a bear, he grabbed the tin wall and tore it back, twisting the metal and wire. I cringed at the screeching metal like sharp nails on a blackboard. He ripped the wall down enough to get a leg over, and then he was gone.

"I'm sorry," I whispered.

Chapter Three

I was laying on the couch reading a Gary Paulsen book when I heard Dad's pickup truck drive up the driveway. I had rehearsed the story five times of how I got my shiner. It wasn't even that bad of one anyway: it was only bruised around the outer edge and a little puffy. I wouldn't say anything unless he asked, and when he did ask I'd simply tell him it was a bike crash. Plus, the bruises and cuts on my legs from tumbling down the hill would serve as my alibi.

"Hi, Elliott," Dad said, closing the door behind him.

"Hey, Dad."

Dad sat down next to me on the couch. "Another wild day today, slugger?"

I liked it when my dad called me slugger. "Na, not really."

"Really? So, what's with the black eye?"

"Oh that," I said. "I sorta crashed on my bike today. I just wasn't paying attention."

"DAD!" Tommy yelled as he ran around the corner and jumped on him.

"Hey, buddy!" Dad grabbed Tommy and body-slammed him down on the couch next to me. Tommy kicked and punched, and Dad blocked all his attempts and went in for the tickle. Tommy was the most ticklish kid I knew and would laugh and squirm so hard that the neighbors would hear him screaming. His legs kicked against me as he squealed in laughter.

"Hey, knock it off!" I yelled.

Dad and Tommy ignored my plea and kept on tickling. I tried to push Tommy's legs off me, but it was no use. "Guys! I'm reading here."

Dad stopped and looked over at me with a serious expression. He leaned down and whispered something in Tommy's ear, making him laugh.

"I'm serious. Don't."

Dad looked at me and whispered something else in his ear that made Tommy laugh even harder.

"I said—"

"*Now!*" Dad yelled.

I was ambushed big time. Before I knew it I was pinned and being tickled to death. I resisted at first but, next to Tommy, I was the second most ticklish person I knew. In a matter of moments, they had me laughing so hard tears were streaming down my face and I could barely breathe.

"OK! OK! You win, you *win!*" Their attack finally ended and I lay exhausted with my stomach aching from laughter on the couch. I looked over at Tommy, who was grinning endlessly laying by my dad's side. My dad had both hands underneath his head and was in perfect position.

"Hey, Tommy," I said. "What do you say we *get dad!*"

Tommy shot up like a rocket and immediately began his monkey-like maneuvers to wrestle Dad. I leaped off the couch and onto Dad in a flash and together we pounced, punched and tickled him with all our might. He was roaring in seconds. We all lay breathless on the floor when it was said and done. My head rested on Dad's stomach and Tommy's head rested on mine.

"You Conklin boys have more than just good looks."

I looked down at Tommy. "We make a good team, don't we, little brother?"

Tommy flashed me one of his contagious smiles.

"Now, there's just one thing..." Dad began.

"What?"

"Who's gonna help me make dinner?"

"I will, I will!" Tommy volunteered.

"Alright, then. Elliott, what do you want for dinner?"

"Spaghetti with black olives in meat sauce."

"I didn't even need to ask," Dad said. "I keep thinking one day you'll want something else, but I must admit my sauce is *delicioso*! But you've got to clean up."

"I know, I know," I said as I lay back on the couch. I picked up my book and began reading. I got a page and a half into my chapter when I was hit with a sleeping spell. I was out like a light.

• • •

Tommy woke me up. The smell of cooking spaghetti and toasted garlic bread filled the house. I was starved like a bear coming out of hibernation. I stuffed myself full of warm noodles, fresh salad, buttery garlic bread, and two glasses of cold milk.

After I finished the dishes, we went outside to work on the yard. There were always weeds to pull, lawns to be mowed, and watering to be done. Dad was always working on something when he was home, which meant we were working too.

When we finished, I came in and got showered. I was on my bed when Dad came in the room. "Let's do prayers."

"Come on, Dad. Give it up."

Dad sat down next to me. "Why do you fight me about this, Elliott? You know I promised your mother that I would say prayers with you boys every night."

"Dad, you didn't even say prayers with us when Mom did."

"Well, I should've."

"Well, I don't want to."

"Too bad," Dad said, standing up. "Come on. Tommy's waiting for us."

Dad was never very religious, but he'd been having us pray together before we went to bed, like Mom used to do. It felt so unnatural doing it without Mom, plus Dad didn't pray like Mom did, he would say things differently. Dad suddenly became spiritual since Mom died. I felt like the exact opposite.

Afterwards, I went back into my bedroom. Clothes and baseball cards were scattered all across the carpeted floor. I flopped down on my bed and grabbed the arrowhead from off the nightstand.

I stared at it, pondering how in the world it ended up at the dirt hills. My mind went wild in imagining what story was behind this. Maybe a great warrior once used it in battle to defend his tribe. Or maybe it was used to hunt and slay ferocious beasts. What if the tip was once covered in a poison that paralyzed their enemy?

As I thought about all the wild possibilities, my eyes kept wandering to the eagle that was carefully carved into the stone. There was something mysterious about the design: *Why was there an eagle?* I ran my fingertips over and over the ridges of the carving, feeling its bumpy details. I had a burning desire to know more about it. I couldn't believe I had found it. No, that *it* found me.

Chapter Four

I met up with Dale in the morning. Even though it was early, it was hotter than devil's spit. The bike ride over to Leroy's wasn't that far and already I was getting sweaty. Leroy's mom answered the door and said Leroy was working on chores. She walked us outback.

The Barker ranch was massive. They had acres and acres of land, hundreds of cattle grazing lazily, massive hay stacks and sweaty horses that galloped and whinnied in the wind.

Leroy was in one of the fields, adding some fencing with his older brother, Jimmy. Jimmy was seventeen and, like the entire Barker brothers, was mammoth-like. He was pounding seven-foot T-stakes into the ground while Leroy stretched and pinned the fencing wire around it.

"Hi, Leroy!" Dale called out.

Leroy looked up and squinted to see us against the sun. "Hey, Dale."

I approached with my hands stuffed in my pockets. I felt like a total jerk-face about yesterday. "How's it going, Jimmy?" I glanced over to Leroy. "Hey, man."

They didn't reply.

Dale continued. "We thought we'd drop by."

"You got five minutes to talk to your so-called friend," Jimmy said. "But we got work to do today. So when I get back, *he* better be gone," he said, pointing a finger at me.

I smiled nervously at Jimmy, who was walking towards me. "This is for calling my little bro Lenny." Jimmy slugged me in the shoulder. It felt like a sledgehammer slammed into my arm. I grabbed my now crushed shoulder and moaned.

Dale laughed out loud. Jimmy ruffled his hair as he passed him by. "It's good to see you, Dale."

Leroy seemed pleased at my pain. I handed him a plastic bag I brought from home.

Leroy took the bag. "What's in it?"

I was rubbing my arm. "It's a present, doofus. Look inside."

Leroy pulled out a bag of beef jerky. "Thanks, man."

"Are we cool?"

"Yeah."

I held out a fist. "Stones and bones?"

Leroy hit the top of my fist and I hit the top of his, then we met knuckle to knuckle in the middle. This was our brotherhood handshake, like warriors used to do.

Leroy laughed. "Stones and bones, baby."

It was silent for a bit. I could hear the sounds of cattle groaning.

"So, how long do you have to work today?" I asked.

"Probably till two or three," Leroy said.

"Dang."

"Why, what's up?"

"We gotta figure out this arrowhead."

"I know, I was thinking about it last night."

"Yeah?"

Leroy put a hand over his eyes to block the sun. "Well, I know that Jimmy and his friends take lots of stuff down to the pawnshop and they tell him how much it's worth. Sometimes they give them money for it – good money, too. He got eighty bucks for some of his old tools last month."

"Eighty bucks!" Dale exclaimed.

"Yeah," Leroy said.

"The pawnshop can tell ya' how much stuff's worth?" I asked.

"They can tell you how much anything is worth," Leroy replied.

"Well, we gotta have them look at the arrowhead, then," I said.

"That's what I was thinking,"

"Well, let's go, then," I said.

"I can't go. I've got work to do," Leroy said.

"Come on – can't you do this fence stuff later?"

Leroy laughed. "Yeah, right. Look, you guys go without me."

"We're not going without you," Dale said.

"How much longer is this going to take?" I asked.

"Probably the whole day."

I sighed. "I can't wait the whole day."

Dale spoke up. "We could help you with your chores."

"Really?" Leroy said.

"Why not?" Dale asked. "We got nothing else to do."

"Well, Jimmy and I have this fence about covered, but I am supposed to clean out the horse stalls, and that is something you can help me out with. Then, we can go to the pawnshop."

"You want us to be pooper-scoopers?" I said in disbelief. "Nice try."

Leroy shook his head. "Don't be such a sissy, Elliott."

"Sissy? Who you calling a sissy?"

"You're afraid to get your pretty little hands dirty," Leroy said.

I puffed my chest out. "I'll clean horse crap with my bare freaking hands! Call me a sissy – you're the sissy."

Leroy grinned. "I'm gonna see if my dad has time to show you how to do it, so Jimmy and I can keep working on this fence." Leroy motioned us to follow him.

. . .

We went to a large barn where Mr. Barker was working on a tractor engine. He looked up and smiled when he saw us all standing there. "Well, well. It's good seeing you fellas round these parts. How have y'all been?"

"Dad," Leroy began. "Elliott and Dale volunteered to help me clean out the horse corrals so we can run around this afternoon. Jimmy and I are working on the fence, and I was wondering if you had time to show them how to do it?"

Mr Barker wiped his hands off on a dirty rag. "You guys volunteered to clean the horse corrals?"

"No," I quickly answered. "Leroy is having us do his dirty work."

Mr Barker let out a deep belly laugh. "Well, let's get it started, then."

He took us to a barn, where we put on rubber boots and gloves. He gave us each a wheelbarrow and then rounded up shovels, pitchforks and a shavings fork.

We made our way around to the horse corrals. Once inside, we were instantly hit with a hot, extremely dusty and, need I mention, smelly air. Mr Barker turned on a hose and wetted down the top of the dirt, which cooled things off and helped the dust to settle.

"Here's how we do it, fellas. You use the pitchfork to break up the manure. Then you take the shavings fork and separate the manure from the woodchips. You dump the manure in the wheelbarrow. When the wheelbarrow is full, take it and unload it around back in the compost pile. It's a piece of cake."

"You mean it's a piece of crap," I replied.

Mr Barker laughed and slapped me on the back. Okay, I thought my spine almost snapped. Why don't gigantically strong people realize their own strength?

We got to work carrying load after load of manure. I eventually got used to the horrible stench of the stalls but it was the flies that were making me crazy, buzzing around my head like bees to honey. If only I had some insect spray – oh, I was ready to nuke 'em.

A voice broke the silence. "Howdy, boys."

It was Leroy's sister, Summer. She was saddled on a tall palomino, her strawberry-blonde hair curled down from under a straw cowboy hat. She was so gorgeous. If she were Mexican salsa she would've been so hot they'd name it Fire-Breathing Salsa. I had been in love with her my whole life.

I wiped the sweat from my eyes with my forearm. "Hi, Summer."

"I thought I smelled something foul over here – looks like I found it."

Summer just turned sixteen, and thought I was annoying and lame and puny. She always treated me like an irritating little brother, so I acted like one. "No, that would be your armpits."

Summer's smile turned into a daggering glare. She looked at Dale. "How can you be friends with such a mule?"

Dale was tongue-tied, and just stared back at her.

"Mule?" I laughed. "You must've meant to say *stallion*."

Right then, Summer's horse lifted its tail, leaving behind a steaming pile.

It was Summer who was laughing now. "Even Buttercup agrees. Don't forget to pick up this one... *stallion*." She tightened the leather reins and rode off, leaving a dust cloud for me to cough in.

"What a babe," Dale said.

"Yeah, she's a brat."

"You like her," Dale commented.

"Who doesn't? Come on, let's finish this so we can go to the pawnshop."

C.J. Skuse | The Wonder Twins

Chapter One

Paisley

School counsellor's office, Immaculate Conception Academy for Girls, Lodi, New Jersey

Simpson fumbled getting the tape into the VCR. She was all "Which button is it?" and I was like, "How old are you and you can't even work a friggin' VCR?"

"I'd like you to watch this and tell me how you feel about it," she said, finally getting her fat ass out the way so I could see the screen. The music started over CNN's flashy intro. The words came up: "**CNN BREAKING NEWS: SIX-YEAR-OLD NEW JERSEY TWINS MISSING. MOTHER FOUND DEAD**". Kim Slaughter appeared, devil-red lipstick, concrete bouffant, grey suit, serious face, shuffling her papers.

Hello, I'm Kim Slaughter and this is the news you're waking up to on Monday, March 20th. It's 7:02 am. We can go live now to our NBC affiliate in New Jersey, where Jake Williamson is outside the house where this tragic story is unfolding. Jake, what's going on down there?

Yeah do tell, Jake, I thought. What *is* going on down there?

Thanks, Kim. And tragic is definitely the operative word in this story. I'm here standing outside the Argent family's house in Forest Way, Clifton, a quite unassuming residence where an extraordinary story began to unfold earlier today.

Cue montage of worried faces, woman in the red coat biting her lip, tracker dogs in bushes. Then back to Jake.

This is what we know: at three fifty this afternoon, Fae Wong, who lives next door to the Argents, dropped the twins Beau and Paisley home as she normally does every day after school and went home with her own kids. And then approximately five minutes later a 911 operator received this call. Take a listen...

Cue the blue screen and scratchy tape recording.

OPERATOR: *911 Emergency. What's the problem?*
GIRL: *Hi, um...I think my mom needs an ambulance.*
OPERATOR: *Is your mom sick?*
GIRL: *Uh-huh. She's on the couch.*
OPERATOR: *Is she awake or asleep?*
GIRL: *Asleep. (Background crying) I said, "Mom, wake up," and she didn't say anything.*
OPERATOR: *Okay, are there any grown-ups around?*
GIRL: *No.*
OPERATOR: *What's your name, honey?*
GIRL: *Paisley Jane Argent.*
OPERATOR: *That's a pretty name. Can you tell me where you live?*
GIRL: *1175 Forest Way, Clifton, New Jersey.*
OPERATOR: *(Background crying) Is someone else there with you, Paisley?*
GIRL: *Beau's here.*
OPERATOR: *Who's Beau?*
GIRL: *He's my twin brother.*
OPERATOR: *How old are you, Paisley?*
GIRL: *We're six and four days old.*
OPERATOR: *You're very smart to call 911. Did you learn that at school?*
GIRL: *Mmm-hmm.*
OPERATOR: *Okay, there'll be someone to help you real soon. You just keep talking with me and we'll wait for them. They're coming.*

Jake appeared again. I was kinda glad. I started lip-synching along with him.

Now we know the little girl on the tape there, Paisley Argent, didn't stay on the line. An ambulance showed up to the house around seven minutes later and the body of her mother, Sylvia Argent, was in the living room. But Paisley and twin brother Beau were nowhere to be found...

Simpson stopped the tape. The picture warped into a white sword and disappeared.

Maggie Simpson set the switcher down on the table and put her hands on her lap. Maggie Simpson wasn't her real name. That was just what I called her 'cos she had spiky blonde hair and would sit there in our sessions, pouting and puckering her lips as she listened to me, like she was sucking a pacifier.

"You okay?" she said, eyebrows raised in a loving pyramid.

I looked at her. "What did you expect?"

"I thought maybe that might have brought back some bad memories for you."

All these counsellors had one mission: to get me to cry. And there was no way, even if they pricked my eyeballs with pins or splashed lemon juice into every cut, no way was I gonna cry.

"You rather I started bawling?"

"No. I just want to know how it made you feel, seeing that news item again."

I shrugged. "Hunky-fucking-dory."

Simpson smiled and there was a definite bat-of-eyes. "Can you relate to that little girl any more?"

I sat back in my leather chair and played with my hair. I was running out of boredom indicators. She didn't have a clue how to deal with me. None of them did. It wasn't my choice to have counselling. I was forced to have it. I was one of the school's special cases. Like the piano genius in my music class who only ate orange food. Or the autistic in science who liked banging her head against the fire door.

"Tell me about when you and Beau were in the woods. Were you scared?"

"No, we had the time of our lives. No parents, no peer pressure..."

"Why did you go to the woods?"

"We went looking for our dad to tell him our mom was dead and we got lost," I said, in the same sing-songy way that little kids read out poetry.

"Was your brother scared? Did you look after him?"

I didn't answer.

"Your brother's called Beau, isn't he? Are you close?"

"We're twins."

"Some twins don't get on. Do you?"

"Yes."

"Do you ever experience that strange telepathy with Beau that some twins get? You know, do you feel pain at the same time as him? Have the same dreams?"

"I sometimes get the urge to touch my dick."

"I am trying to help you."

"No shit."

"Would you at least try to open up? Just go with it. No one else can hear."

She had a pock mark on her face that kept catching the light. We're talking crater. The last counsellor was better than her. I called her The Jawbreaker 'cos she had this really large lower face and big donkey teeth that could crush rocks. Then there was Pretty Shitty Blah Blah at Sacred Heart. I called her Pretty for short. Except she wasn't. She was the kind of person who looks pretty to start with but gets uglier the more you learn about them. I could call most people Pretty.

This one, Simpson, was so nervous I only had to sneeze and her coffee cup would rocket up to the ceiling. Such was my reputation, I guess.

"What do you think about your recent behaviour? Do you know why you felt compelled to do that to the piano?"

I shrugged. "I was bored. I'm a fuck-up. That's what fuck-ups do."

I had to meet up with the school counsellor in their office every Tuesday and Thursday after school to talk through my "issues" on pink bean bags with my shoes off – had done long as I could remember. The rooms always stank of coffee and there would be posters up of kids with their heads in their hands, saying things like "We get the blues too" and "Amy didn't like being laughed at". I'd feed them all the usual crap of finding life so tough away from my brother and 'cos Mommy never showed me any affection and they'd look at me sympathetically and give me meditation exercises and stuff. It was all bullshit.

"How do you feel about your mother now?"

"She hated me. It's no biggy."

She looked at me, eyes welling with sympathy. Luckily my bullshit shield kept out such oncoming attacks of sympathy. What's that stuff they froze Han Solo in at the end of *Empire Strikes Back*? Anyway, it was like I had that all around me. No one could get through my shield of that.

Immaculate Conception Academy (ICA) was the best boarding school in New Jersey, highly academic, turning out America's finest girls since 1908. It was also the most expensive. I knew that 'cos I'd been kicked out of all the crappy ones. Our Lady of the Oranges, Rambuteau, Satan's School for Girls (Bayonne High) and Sacred Heart Academy – been there, done that, broken the windows. My grandmother realised that, to keep me out of her way permanently, she had to spend some real money. I had this "volatility" problem. My dad got the blame.

Simpson checked her notes. "Your father's in prison, isn't he?" She was getting confident. "How do you feel about that? Do you miss him?"

I picked my nails. I wasn't gonna answer that. I didn't want to tell her anything about my dad. I only ever talked about him to Beau.

"Your grandmother tells me you're not fighting as much at home."

"That's probably because we're not talking as much at home."

"Oh, you've had a fight?"

"We always fight. So we don't talk to each other."

"Why don't you get along?"

"Uh, because she hates me?"

"She must think a lot of you."

"How do you work that out?"

"Well, she's spending a lot of money to give you a good education."

"No, she's spending a lot of money to keep me as far away as possible."

I remembered the day she dropped me off at Our Lady of the Oranges when I was seven. There was little me, drowning in my huge uniform, standing on the huge mosaic steps with my principal's hands on my shoulders. My grandmother Virginia stood there with Beau. Nowadays I call her The Skankmother. She's too Botoxed to be called Granny. She kept straightening my tie. I hated that.

"You'll make lots of friends. We'll see you at Spring Break."

I looked up at her. "I'll be good, I promise. I won't say any more bad swears and I'll help tidy my room and I won't be mean to Beau..." *I love you, Miss Hannigan.* I'd have said anything to go back to Los Angeles and go to school with my brother.

"We have to catch our plane. You take Mrs Lloyd's hand."

Beau held out his toy owl, Too Wit, to kiss my owl, Two Woo. "Bye, Paisley."

"Please?" I begged Skank one more time.

She looked down at me. "Go with Mrs Lloyd, please."

"We'll keep you informed, Mrs Creed," said Mrs Lloyd. "And we'll take good care of Jane."

Five schools later and they still always called me by my middle name.

"Do you want to talk about those marks yet?" said Simpson, scoping my legs.

I sighed. When were they gonna learn? I decided to throw her a bone. "No. It... it's too painful," I lied, pulling down my skirt hem to hide my cuts. I liked to lie to counsellors. I liked watching them lean forward and get all excited 'cos they thought they were on the brink of something.

"You know, some young people do it because it's the only outlet they allow themselves. Opening their skin becomes a way of leaking out what's troubling them. Do you have any friends that you talk to about it?"

I shook my head. "No. I'm saving up for some of those Harajuku girls. That way I can tell 'em when to get out of my face and they'll listen."

She did the lean-forward thing. "You can talk to me. You can always talk to me. You can think of me as a friend, if you want."

That was a big fat hairy lie. The older I got, the bigger and fatter and hairier the lies got. She was no friend. Just like the counsellor at the hospital when we were six. "Your dad'll be here soon, okay?" she'd said. Yeah, in about ten years maybe. Eight with good behaviour.

I reached into my pocket for my chocolate peanuts.

Simpson took a deep breath, then blew it right out. "You remember in our last session together we spoke about the possibility of you moving to another facility, which might be able to help you..."

"Yeah, a nut house," I said. I popped a blue M&M in my mouth and began flicking it around on my tongue. I liked to suck them until just the peanut was left.

"A behaviour modification facility – quite a different thing. There's one in California as it happens, so you'd be nearer your grandmother..."

I scoffed.

"Well, nearer your brother, then. And I think they'll be able to help you."

I laughed. "Yeah, maybe electric shock treatment is the answer."

"I didn't mean that."

"Knock it off. I know how this works. You just want me outta Jersey. If you can't turn me into a *High School Musical* wannabe, you ship me off to La-La Land where they'll put those little wires on my temples and turn me into a vegetable."

"I can assure you that's not what happens. But it's true that your problems may be a little out of my expertise... Have you tried reading that book I lent you?" She looked down at my legs again.

I looked down at my legs again. "No," I said, bowing my head. *Chicken Soup for the Teenage Soul*. I was using it to balance my nightstand. Simpson breathed a little sigh. Her breath reeked of stale coffee.

I wasn't self-harming. I only liked them to think I was. I was just really bad at shaving, that was all. I have no patience, no interest in doing it right at all. I scrape and scratch away and I'm done in, like, five minutes. I didn't see the point.

My M&M was ready; just the peanut left. I took it out my mouth and split it in two. The little bunny was there. It was always there whenever I opened a peanut. It was something I noticed when I was about eight. I don't think I first discovered it, probably Columbus or somebody. It's the middle bit where the two halves join.

"So, I'm a crackpot. S'that what I put in my next letter home to the folks?"

Simpson sighed. "No, I wouldn't put it like that. But you do seem to be incredibly... tense. You have a lot of frustration and I can completely understand that, after what you have been through. And if we could identify what's causing..."

I popped the nut, crunched down and switched off. I was so fricking fed up of hearing the same old, same old. Yeah, I was tense. Yeah, I needed to make friends. Yeah, I needed help. Sex would have been a great tension reliever, if I could get it. Only problem was, Immaculate Conception Academy for Girls was pretty dry of tension-relievers. No men, just three hundred and sixty-five mechanically engineered lesbians who'd do it with a broom handle if looked at them the right way. I mean, that's fine if that's your thing. I tried it once, back when I was twelve (lesbianism, not broom-molesting) but I just couldn't see the point. There was nothing to go anywhere. What I needed was something with an attachment, if you catch my drift.

But a week after this crunch meeting with Maggie Simpson and the threat of being sent to the cabbage patch, a miracle happened. A blinding light shot down from the August sky and this angel appeared before me in paint-splattered jeans. His name was Jason and he was helping the school gardener. He was twenty-two, had a perfect V-shaped torso and spiky brown hair. I was convinced we were soulmates. I even took more interest in Classics because of Jason and the Argonauts. I imagined that was him, sailing forth to retrieve the Golden Fleece and doing all this heroic shit, when really he was downstairs filling wheelbarrows with weeds.

I was smoking a sneaky one before class when he said his first words to me.

"Who are you?"

"Paisley. Who are you?"

"Jason." He grabbed both handles of his wheelbarrow and checked out my skirt, or rather my belt. "You always dress like that or is it just for me?"

"What's the matter – too long?" I said, hitching it up a little higher.

Pretty soon we were sharing cigarettes behind the pavilion, talking about movies. And then it got physical. I've always seen couples stroking each other and going all cupcakey and texting every five seconds and stuff, but me and Jason weren't like that. We were more your frantic smash-and-grab sessions. Kissing but missing, like magnets. Grappling like wrestlers. Not Elizabeth and Darcy, but romantic all the same. And *then* I understood the point of shaving.

I remember everything about our nights inside the pavilion. The spicy smell of the wood and the stinking rubber of new tennis balls. The candlelight flickering, making our shadows bigger on the wall. His hot breath in my ear. His skin on mine, his hands on my back. Feeling down my glossy, smooth legs. All that kinda crap.

"Tell me you love me," I'd say to him, mid-thrust.

"Of course I do," he'd gasp. "I love you so... MUCH."

"I love you too," I'd whisper into his shoulder and hold him real tight.

How sweet. How heartbreakingly sweet.

We talked. We kissed. He tasted of green apples. He stroked my earlobes. And for a short while at school, I was happy. I lived for our nights in the pavilion. A softer, kinder Paisley was born. Desk lids were scored with "PA Loves JT" instead of "When I Die, Bury Me Upside Down So The Whole World Can Kiss My Ass". My grades rose. I noticed birds and clouds. Tension drained through me like a sieve.

So you can kinda guess what's coming next.

Chapter Two

Beau

9976 Bizcocho Drive, Cahuenga Blvd East, Hollywood, California

I shouldn't have been there, ergo I should never have known about it. What happened was I had to come home from school early to change my clothes. O'Donnell and his merry men had found a new way to humiliate me. They'd dunked me head first into the trash cans by the cafeteria. Despite the walk back in the California sunshine, my Eels T-shirt clung to my skin like food wrap.

I walked in through the back and Concepción, our maid (Connie as we called her), was in the kitchen reading a letter.

"Hey," I said, making her jump about a mile in the air, and she fumbled the letter back into its envelope.

"Ooh, what's that, Connie?" I asked her, thinking it might be from her son, Nando, who'd been sent back to Mexico a few months earlier. I knew she was desperate to hear from him.

"It's nothing. No, don't worry," she said, flapping her arms like she had ants down both sleeves. She noticed my soggy T-shirt. "Oh, you are wet. I will wash..."

"No, I just had an accident at school," I said, trying to sound nonchalant.

She went to put the letter in her apron and I saw the front.

"That's addressed to me and Paisley." That's when my heart started to thump real hard. I asked her who it was from, but she wouldn't tell me, just kept going on about taking my clothes off so she could wash them. She practically had my shirt up over my head before I wriggled away.

"Connie, if that letter's for me, I wanna see it, okay?" I tried my best to be polite, really I did, but I still felt bad for raising my voice to her. She took the letter out of her pocket and placed it quietly on the counter.

She walked from the room and I heard her go upstairs. I looked at the envelope. "Mr Beau and Miss Paisley Argent". It was postmarked Spurina, Nevada. I picked it up and shook out the letter. Words in scrawled blue pen covered one side of a small piece of white paper. And this is what it said:

> To My Wonder Twins, Well, here I am in Spurina like I said. It's not Las Vegas but it's close so maybe when you come visit we can go see the lights. Eddie's putting me up for now in his duplex. It's kinda on the small side, but it has four walls and a shower so it's good enough for me. As I've explained in all my other letters, it's just a stop-gap. I'll get a good job in time and my own place and maybe then you guys could come see me. You're both probably doing so well, you probably don't need your old man back in your lives, sticking his two cents in. But whatever you think, I'll be here waiting, Dad XX.

There was a rush through my whole body and this water-clear release in my head. Dad. He wanted us. He'd always wanted us. He'd gone to jail when we were six, charged with armed robbery. Now he was out of jail. A free man. A free dad! We hadn't seen him, hadn't even heard from him the whole time he'd been inside. I held in my hands the first shred of contact we'd had with him in ten years.

But there were gaps and I didn't understand. When did he say he'd be staying in Spurina? Who was Eddie? Where were these "other letters" and how did he know we were doing "so well"? I didn't think we were doing so well. Who'd told him that?

"Connie?" I couldn't hear her upstairs and I found the lack of floorboard creaks troubling. I heard a distant clatter coming from the far end, near my room. I two-stepped it up the stairs, finding her in the spare bedroom, sitting on the floor in front the bureau, a shoebox of letters on her lap.

"This is all," she said to me. "Miss Virginia made me throw away the presents. This is all yours now. I want no more of this. It is too sad."

I looked down at the letters. There must have been fifty of them. "How long's he been writing to us?"

She smiled, her wide eyes melting like moons. "You and Paisley were seven. Your seventh birthday, a card came. He loves you so much, Beau. So much…"

I started bawling, as is my wont. "You kept them from us?"

She got up and handed the box to me, closing the bureau door behind her. I hated to see her cry. She'd always cuddle us if we cried as children. It had always been her job to feed us, tuck us in, take us shopping and give us cuddles. I tentatively put my arms around her, feeling her tense up, and then go limp and cuddle me back.

"You kept them all this time?" I said, feeling her nod against my head.

"I might lose my job."

"It's all right." '

We released and she tapped the top of the box. "These are yours now. Please, I don't want them. You read them."

And then she left the room and me and the box and disappeared down the stairs. Moments later I heard the vacuum cleaner humming in the den.

And I sat there, all afternoon, reading through every single letter he sent us from prison. Letter after letter that my sister and I had never seen. I held each one like it was some ancient museum document that would spoil beneath my finger grease. Each one took me back ten years in time, back to New Jersey. Back to Paisley and me as children. Back to Dad and how it used to be when he took us out. To the park, to the golf club to eat pancakes on low-lying tables where he had to bend over to eat. When he'd show us coin tricks and we'd play Baby Blackjack for candy.

Then I knew who Eddie was. I wondered back in my mind to the times when Dad used to take us with him on his trips into the city (he was a sales rep for New Jersey Gardenia, who sold toiletries to hotel chains). He'd give us Junior Mints and Mike & Ikes if we behaved. We got to go inside these plush hotels and play on the grand winding staircases, in and out the elevators, slide around on the pristine marble floors in the bathrooms while he did his work. Sometimes Dad'd get someone to watch us, a real old weener who'd keep reminding us how lucky we were and tell us about the crap Christmas presents he used to get as a kid, like oranges and bones. But sometimes we'd get a concierge like Eddie.

Eddie at The Roosevelt was awesome. He'd show us coin tricks like Dad's and make us laugh and tell us stories about the guests, telling us who was super-rich and which ones were just super-weird. "Suits", he called them. Suits with "golden wives". Certain companies would have conferences on and there'd be a horde of suits with matching designer luggage. The men would always do the checking in and the wives would stand around, clicking their heels against the marble. Me and Paisley would take our candy up to the mezzanine and find ourselves a quiet nook where we could look down on the marble lobby and wait for Dad to reappear.

I remember the last time he took us into the city. It was our birthday the next day and as a pre-birthday treat he took us to this diner in Grand Central Station where we had sliders and cheese fries. Dad had a BLT. I was dying to ask him about the fight he and Mom had the night before. Our neighbour Marshall Judd even called over to complain because it was thumping through his walls. Her going all high and screechy. Him being all deep and defensive. And then him all high and defensive and her all deep and judgmental. Paisley and I shared a room above the kitchen, where most of their arguments took place. That night Mom had called us "little shits" and complained that Dad was never home to help, always giving us candy to curry favour. That part is sort of true. Dad did buy us a lot of candy. You want me or my sister to do anything, you give us candy. It's kind of a key to get in with us.

Paisley had ketchup all around her mouth. She asked Dad about the wives at The Roosevelt.

"Are they made of gold, Dad?"

"No, honey. Why d'you say that?"

"'Cos they look gold."

"No, they're not gold. They sure got a lot of it, though. I wouldn't mind a piece of it myself."

"Do they have jobs?"

"No, I don't think so."

"What do they do all day?"

"I don't know, honey."

I couldn't wait any longer. "Are you and Mom going to get a divorce?" I said.

I remember him chewing real hard on his sandwich and frowning. "Why d'you ask, son?"

"'Cos we heard you and Mom shouting again last night."

He took another bite out his sandwich and scrunched up his napkin to wipe his chin. Then he said, "I'm sorry, guys. We thought you were asleep."

"We were," said Paisley. "It woke us up."

Dad shook his head. "We just had a little argument, like you guys do sometimes. We're not gettin' divorced."

"Where does it hurt you, Dad?" Paisley asked him.

"What do you mean, baby?"

"You told Mom you were broke. Where are you broke?"

Dad bowed his head and wiped his chin again with his napkin. When he came back up, he was smiling. He grabbed the menu from the stand. "Who wants cheesecake? Let's see what they got... ooh, strawberry, I think. Or Chocolate Swirl. Y'all want Chocolate Swirl?"

We nodded and dunked our French fries in our joint pot of ketchup.

I remembered it so clearly. On the way home, Dad throwing Peppermint Patties over his shoulder for us in the back seat, them raining down on us like stars. Me and Paisley snuggling down into the blanket.

"Try and get some sleep, okay, guys? Traffic's gonna be bad getting back into Jersey. We got a long drive."

Paisley misses Dad like crazy, even now. She's always talking about him. His on-the-spot bedtime stories where we had starring roles. His BLT subs – the best in Jersey, he always said. The way he always called us his Wonder Twins. I kinda resigned myself years ago to the fact he didn't want us any more. Finding the letters threw me all out of whack. I didn't know how I felt now. I didn't know what to do.

All afternoon spent worrying about it and reading and re-reading the letters brought me to one conclusion: I needed to tell Paisley. That was the next step I had to take. But I didn't know how to do it. She was banned from all the computers at her school, so I couldn't email her and I didn't want to blurt it out on the phone. So I had to write a letter. I spent all evening at it. My attempts all lay beneath me on the carpet in little slowly uncurling balls.

> *Pais, I have to speak to you urgently...*
> *Sis, You are seriously not going to believe...*
> *Dearest Paisley, This is such a hard letter to write, I don't know*

how you're going to take it...

Pais, I don't know how to tell you this...

Paisley, this is really difficult to say so I'll just come right out and say it...

Dear Paisley, Well, look what just turned up on our doorstep...

Dear Sis, You will not believe what happened today. I came home from school and Connie was in the kitchen...

Paisley, I have some really big news, so call me...

P, It's about Dad...

Pais, remember our dad? Well, he hasn't just abandoned us from his prison cell; he's actually been writing to us for ten years and our grandmother didn't think it right to tell us...

However I ended up phrasing it, I knew one thing for sure: she was gonna go ballistic.

Chapter Three

Paisley

Immaculate Conception Academy for Girls, Lodi, New Jersey

I caught Jason screwing a prefect. Not a significant prefect, not Emily-Jane Johnson or Jessica Palmer, the two most popular bitches in school, but Mandy Mackinnon; Paris Hilton in a smashed mirror. Diseased little alley cat, too. She'd once done five St Anthony's boys behind the tennis courts, using an empty potato chips packet for protection. She had those kinda eyes. A slut's eyes.

Seeing those two skanks together became another one of my mind replays. Like the moment we found Mom's body. In those moments between being awake and asleep, my brain has a habit of recalling bad memories of finding her. Being lost in the woods. And from then on this scenario: getting to the sports pavilion twenty minutes early. Taking three tokes of my cigarette. Hearing the floorboards. Hearing a giggle. Rubbing a space on the dusty window. My cigarette dropping to the earth. Them naked. Her lying beneath him like a doll. Him looking up at the window. Smiling. Him carrying on. Harder.

I made out like I'd forgotten about it when I saw him wheeling his barrow up the sports field a few days later. I had this stinging sensation behind my eyes like I wanted to cry, but there was no way I was gonna. There was no way I was gonna punch him, either. Why would I waste my calories on that son of a bitch? No, I would not be conquered, not by a guy. He did not matter. I took my big black boot sole and stamped down hard on any feelings I may have had for him. I consoled myself by writing some sick poetry and this little story about a woman who cut the dicks off her former lovers to make necklaces and then bought a jewellery store and made a fortune. It helped. I concluded Jason was merely a "get-me-through". Like when you're forced to watch a really boring movie and it's numbing your brain, so you develop a little crush on one of the stars, just to get you through it. A get-me-through. That's all Jason had ever been. That's all any man would ever be.

Apart from Beau. And Dad.

But, even though I'm a vegetarian, I still have meat-eater's incisors, so naturally I wanted revenge. And it was while thinking up how to wreak my revenge on this little asshole that I got a letter from Beau. And this letter, this little one-line letter was to open my eyes to just how unimportant the Jason incident had been.

Beau usually emailed me, but since I'd been banned from all computers for making fake IDs, he had to go old-school and write. When the letter was placed in my hands, I immediately thought bad news. A long ramble about a bad beating he'd gotten from the O'Donnell gang at school, written by his nurse. A wordy speech about how he was finally at the end of his infinite tether with our Skankmother and was planning to run away for sure. But it didn't. It said just seven words.

Paisley, I've found Dad. Call me, Beau x

I read it again and again. And it came screaming forward at me like one of those magic-eye posters that your brain has to unscramble before the hidden picture comes into focus. I stopped reading and held it to my chest. Dad. What? He's found Dad? Dad. Dad. I had to say it a couple times before I wrapped my brain around it.

I went from lying in a pit of stinking, slashed-heart despair to being thrust up into the sunlight like a beach ball bursting through the waves. I paced up and down our dorm like some crazy-assed bear in the zoo. I had an open-ended air ticket back to LA so I could easily get a cab to Newark Airport and be on my way back there within twenty-four hours. But I knew the principal, or Super Turbo Bitch as I knew her, wouldn't let me go without my Skankmother's permission. And there was no way Skank was gonna give permission. It meant all the stops would have to come out.

I needed to get myself expelled. ASAFP.

And a week after the traumatic event with Jason, four days after receiving Beau's letter, an occasion presented itself to me.

The whole school lined up for lunch in the long corridor outside the refectory. Jutting off at various intervals along this route were our classrooms and the fiction and reference libraries. Right at the end was the school chapel. This was where we'd meet every morning, give praise for stuff, get scared to death by the tall plastic Jesus figure on the altar and kneel on uncomfortable cushions till the woven imprints of crosses were tattooed on our knees. On the occasion in question, Mandy Mackinnon had the misfortune of standing right outside the chapel, and therefore the end of the lunch line, just as I joined it. The corridor reeked of meat and onions.

"Hey, Mandy," I said. She just looked at me, like I was clowning.

"Oh, hi," she said, turning away. I knew exactly what I would say. I'd played it over and over in my mind to get it right. I took a few breaths before delivering it; I didn't want to stumble or mispronounce anything. I wanted it to be just right.

"Mandy," I said, "I've got this great book if you ever wanna borrow it. I know you're into that kinda stuff."

She looked blank, as she well might. Mandy didn't read. A halogen light flickered above our heads among the wooden eaves and cobwebs. She had so many zits, I could have joined them up and made a shape.

"Kama Sutra, it's called. Yeah, it shows you all these different sexual positions you can get into with your boyfriend. You looked kinda stiff on the floor of the sports pavilion the other day."

Mandy went scarlet. The low mumbles of conversation stopped as the others listened in. I could see some giggling behind their hands. But I wasn't finished. Yet.

"It's okay if that's what the guy likes. But one day you might want to be a bit more adventurous. You know, try opening your legs a little?"

She looked daggers at me. No, not daggers. Swords. Swords with flaming blades and poisoned tips. She lunged at me, pushed me back against the pinboards, grabbing my hair, pulling it any way she could.

"You bitch!" she screamed at the top of her lungs "You were spying. You perv, you complete psycho perv!" Her voice echoed, ricocheting off every wall as we grappled. That's all she could do – grapple and pull hair. She was such a girl. That's how girls fight: they go for the hair. I had never fought like that. That was foreplay to me. I pushed her and swung right back, clocking her across the left side of her face. *Thwak!*

Whomph. Down she went. I can still see her eyes close as my fist caught her cheek, the slow-motion jet of blood shooting from her mouth like a little red fish.

My arms were pinned back.

Cries of "Oh my God." "Is she dead?" "What happened?" "How awful" echoed in my ears as I floated along the corridor, propped up by two teachers, Miss Sutcliffe and Mr Treves. Every pair of eyes was on me, from the prefects right the way down to the tiny ones in their claret and gold lunch overalls, gawking at me as I passed them. Some had their hands on their mouths, others tried to pretend they were suddenly very interested in their shoes. Soon there were no more giggles, no more murmurs of disapproval. Just big eyes. And me, desperately trying to kick and wriggle out of my restraints, screaming at the top of my lungs: "Go on, then. Do it. Do it, you assholes. Put me out of my fucking misery!"

And then *bam*, I was in the principal's office, standing tight-lipped before the massive wooden desk with its row of paperweights and picture frames. Super Turbo Bitch, that day in grey trouser suit and sad new bob cut, glared at me all the way through her lecture.

"I'm not tolerating it any more, Jane Argent," she said finally, in her clipped English tongue, her nose all pointy and high in the air.

"For the past few terms, your behaviour has got progressively worse. Our school motto encourages us to give everyone a fair chance to fit in. But you are an example of everything that is wrong with this school and everything I want to get rid of. I think you'll agree I've given you quite enough chances and you have done nothing, NOTHING, to improve."

Here we go again, I thought. Come on, Baby, give it to me. You know you want to. Come on, rub this dirty little stain out of your clean little school.

She stood up and faced me, leaning over the desk. "Punching a student?" The "p" of "punching" was packed with enough spit to spray my entire face. I motioned to wipe it from my eye.

She huffed. "How am I going to explain to Mandy's parents that she has been punched? That she may have a broken jaw? Hmm?"

I started laughing. I couldn't help it. "What can I say? I made the bitch famous. They'll be talking about it for years." Ooh, I was getting her good.

STB snarled. "Disobedient, arrogant, rude, insolent… I could go on."

"Please do," I scoffed, sucking the tips of my near-frozen fingers in an attempt to give them the warm kiss of life.

"...ruthless, obstinate, rude..."

"You already said rude." I picked at my teeth with the tip of my long purple nail. I'd had enough by this point. I couldn't look at the woman any more, so I concentrated on the William Morris wallpaper and tall dark-wood bookcases all around me. I don't know if it was my near-hypothermic state in that freezing office or the putrid waft of stale coffee I was getting off her breath but it all seemed to be closing in on me. Like the garbage crusher in *Star Wars*. Or was it *Empire Strikes Back*? The one where they rescued the princess, anyway. It used to be Beau's favourite movie, up until he saw that French one with the chick on the bike. Now he likes that one better. Thinks it makes him look more intelligent.

"Look, I get the point," I said finally. "I'm crap. Can I go now?"

"That's what you want, isn't it?" she roared, sitting down on her swivel chair and folding her arms, her too-tight jacket taking the strain at the shoulders. "And that's what you got from all your other schools. They couldn't handle you, so they just let you go. I know you too well."

"You don't know me, at all," I shouted. "Most of the time, you people ignore me. And when you're not ignoring me, you're whining on about me not joining in or not being good enough for this or that... and it's 'waaah, waaah, waaah' in this ear, 'waaah, waaah, waaah' in that ear. Is it any wonder I'm so goddamn ANGRY?"

STB pursed her lips and stood up again, breathing in deeply.

"With a family history like yours, I'd say it was written in the stars."

Mee-ow. Okay, I thought. Let's try this...

"You can't honestly tell me I'm single-handedly... bastardising the entire private school system. I'm a drop in the ocean compared to some of the things that go on here that you don't know about."

"Such as?" she said, hands searching for things to do on the desk – papers to shuffle, pens to put back in the pen holder, a stapler to realign, so it was perpendicular with the edge of the desk. Everything had to be perfect.

I counted them off on my fingers. "Your highly decorated head girl has her own strip show on YouTube, half the eighth-graders are bulimic, and your apprentice gardener has been screwing most of my year."

She looked like she was waiting for a golf ball to drop into her mouth.

Her whole body rose and fell with her breath. She picked up the phone.

"I suppose the piano incident wasn't your fault, either?" she said, dialling.

I thought about it for a second. "No, that was me."

She spoke into the phone. "Morrie, could you send Jason to my office, please... I don't care, it's urgent." She put the phone down.

I leaned in for the kill.

"And, while I'm spilling all these unfortunate beans, I don't suppose you've sat in on any of your husband's German classes recently, have you?"

"Don't you...?"

"...he can suggest things with a long ruler that would make your eyes bleed."

"...DARE. You HORROR of a girl," she bellowed, squinting the words out as though the force was hurting her eyes. "I could have you for slander." Drawn up to her full height, she rounded the desk and marched over to the office door. She opened it, turning to deliver her parting shot.

"Get out of my school."

Mission: accomplished.

"You are a disgrace, Jane Argent. Your future looks *very* bleak to me."

I stepped into the corridor and turned to deliver *my* final blow. "My name is Paisley. And at least I *have* a future. I wouldn't give a bucket of piss for *yours*."

I'd heard that line in a movie once and I'd been dying to use it. Luckily my great brain managed to bring it to my attention at the perfect moment. I was shoved into the long stony hallway on the bang of the door.

"Yeah, thought that'd do it," I said to the echo.

I stood there for a moment, blinking myself firmly into reality. There was a school brochure on the hall table. All the pictures inside were of happy, fresh-faced girls: a shiny blonde in an immaculate tunic lighting a candle in the chapel; a girl sprayed in achievement badges playing the flute in the music room; a circle of cross-legged Girl Scouts sitting around a toadstool, listening intently to a fat woman reading a book. I could never have been the girl in the brochure. I was always the back-of-head in the science lab or the out-of-focus blob on the baseball field. And that suited me fine. I took the brochure in my hands and tore it right down the middle.

As I walked up the staircase to the dorms, the front door opened and Jason lumbered in, taking his boots off, placing them by the door-mat. He looked up and saw me.

"What have you told them?" he glared.

"Everything, darling." I carried on walking.

He came over to the banister and grabbed my hand.

"If you've told them about us sleeping together..."

"Sleeping together, screwing together. Eating Chunky Chips Ahoy together..."

"I'll tell 'em it's all bullshit. You're a kid. And you're a kid with a bad rep. They'll never believe you."

At that moment, Super Turbo Bitch appeared in the doorway to her office, behind Jason. He hadn't seen her.

"But it did happen, Jason," I said, fake-crying, lip quiver and all. "You said you loved me."

His hand felt sweaty on mine. "Give it up, Paisley. It won't work. I got a good rep here. You're not gonna blow this for me."

"That's not what you said before."

"Stop it, all right?!" he whispered, leaning in to the banister. "I'm just gonna tell them you're lying, then you'll be out of here and that will be that."

I stopped fake-crying and looked at him. "But that isn't that, is it? I got proof. I kept our first condom. A souvenir to remind me how much I meant to you."

"Shut up. You know we never used a condom..." He turned and saw Cleeve.

He turned back to me.

I smiled. "Don't that just stick it in and break it off?"

In the dorm, I packed up my stuff and found my plane ticket and passport. I threw off my school shirt and tie, replacing it with my AC/DC "For Those About to Rock" T-shirt, an exact copy of the one Dad wore when we were little. I kept my school skirt on and hitched it up another inch. It was actually kinda cool and went really well with my chunky socks and boots. I kept my stripy tie, too; it made a cool wrist wrap. Everything else – the coat, the yellow sweats, the sewing kit, the white shirt – could go burn for all I cared.

I could hear them all in the refectory as I walked past towards the school entrance. The echo of "For what we are about to receive, may the Lord make us TRULY thankful, Amen." The eager scraping of chair legs and clank of metal kitchen utensils.

I strode on. "Assholes," I said. "All of them, assholes."

Susan Sedgwick | Peregrin Zefyr and
the Alloid Threat

Chapter One

The Windbird

Zeff appeared from nowhere about halfway through the term.

One minute he wasn't there, the next he was. In the yard, in the corridors, most of all in the library. He spent hours on the computers and pulling forgotten books off the shelves.

You could tell just by looking at him that he was different. He looked almost but not quite like a pupil. His uniform didn't look like uniform, for a start. The black really was black, and he kept his blazer buttoned with the collar turned up. He didn't do his tie properly, but none of the teachers seemed to mind. It was as if they didn't notice him at all. His black hair was tied back in a ponytail, and there was a bounce in his walk which suggested that the rules didn't apply.

Like the rest of the school, Benny thought Zeff was in another class, someone else's mate. He didn't think much about him, until the day he found himself sitting next to him in the canteen.

It was lunchtime, a few weeks into the summer term. The air was full of the smell of grease and the sound of high-pitched voices. Benny shoved between the chairs and the bodies, a fistful of cutlery clutched to the side of his tray. He was still too late to get the last seat on the table with his friends.

He slammed his dinner down in the nearest space he could find. The plate left a gluey trail of beans as it slid to the side of the tray. He tucked himself into the table, the chair biting into his back.

Zeff didn't seem to be aware of Benny. He shovelled forkfuls of whatever he was eating into his mouth without looking at it. All his attention was on the shabby book he'd propped up against the plastic water jug. As he turned the pages, he occasionally jotted something down in the notebook open by his plate. Once he tried to write with his knife.

"Benny Jacks!"

Benny swivelled round. Miss Price.

"Benny Jacks, do your tie up properly!"

As he fiddled half-heartedly at his neck, Benny turned back to the table. Zeff was already halfway across the canteen.

Benny nearly missed the book.

Grumbling to herself, a dinner lady bent over the table. "This yours?" she called after Benny, who was weaving his way out.

Thinking she meant the tray left behind by Zeff, he nearly said "No", but then he saw what she had in her hand. It was the notebook Zeff had been writing in.

"I know who it belongs to," he said, and held out his hand. Zeff was still there in the corner of his eye, disappearing out towards the yard. He was going that way anyhow.

Trouble was, when he got there Zeff had vanished. Wondering what to do with it now, Benny looked at what he'd been given by the dinner lady.

He'd just assumed it was a notebook. It was too small for a laptop, and Zeff had it open sideways like a book. But he'd never seen a book like this before. It was a rectangular sliver of black, with a row of pads down the bottom of the right-hand side.

That was the moment when the bell went, and he was hit from behind by three foot nothing of best mate in the form of Sprog Williams. Sprog came flying across the yard and leapt onto Benny's back. Benny was used to it, and carried on walking with his friend hanging off his shoulders.

"Wotcha got, Benno?" asked Sprog.

Benny pressed the bottom pad on the book-like thing, and it sprung open into two halves like pages of black glass. They were covered in silvery snail trails of handwriting.

Benny rubbed the surface with his thumb and then looked at it, expecting the writing to come off. Nothing. Instead, there was a small "pop" and the scrawl of letters sunk through the pages. The surface was left clean and smooth. He tilted the book so it caught the light, and saw layers of writing threaded deep inside.

Benny stopped walking, and Sprog slithered to the floor.

"Uber-doober!" said Sprog. "That is something. I've never seen anything like that before." Which was impressive. Sprog knew everything worth knowing about electronics. "Where'd you get it from?"

"Found it. That boy Zeff, I think he's in the sixth form," Benny looked around, but the older boy was still nowhere to be seen. "He left it in the canteen."

"That has to be imported. What do the other buttons do?"

Sprog was about to press the top one, when a ground-floor window rattled open and Mr Singh leaned out. "Mr Jacks and Mr Williams! An English lesson is about to take place without you! Be here in two, or expect a detention!"

Benny meant to hand the book in after school, but he was in a hurry to get to cricket practice and forgot about it. That night in his room he remembered it again. He flopped onto his bed and rummaged through his bag.

The smelly cricket socks came out first, followed by the rest of his kit. He bundled it up and chucked it against the wall, where it dropped to the floor under his West Indies team poster. Some dog-eared school-books fluttered onto the heap. He pulled the notebook out last.

I can't give it back until after the weekend now, he thought. Might as well take a closer look.

The open pages looked just the same. He could make out the writing under the surface, but couldn't read it. He touched the next button up, there was another "pop" and the writing vanished. It was replaced by a gridwork of symbols that glowed neon red.

That was all he could get it to do. He pressed each of the buttons several times, in combination and in different sequences, and he tried rubbing the surface again. The pages opened and shut, the red characters and the shelves of silver writing disappeared and reappeared. Nothing else happened, and none of it meant anything to him.

In the end, he got fed up. He couldn't be bothered with it any more. He'd take it round to Sprog's in the morning.

Sprog lived in a dead-end street, with a park behind the tall hedge at the bottom.

Benny knocked at his door. The dog barked in the back, but there was no reply. He didn't have anything else to do, so he decided to hang about, see if Sprog turned up.

The rusty park gate squeaked as it opened. The scruffy children's playground was to one side, with a view of the road. He perched on a swing, pushing himself backwards and forwards with the toes of one foot. No one could come into the street without him noticing.

He was expecting Sprog, but it was Zeff who appeared, walking briskly towards his end of the road.

There were no houses there. He walked straight at the tatty line of shrubs and small trees that shielded Benny's view.

Perhaps there was a gate in the hedge he hadn't noticed. Curious, he watched for Zeff to appear on the other side. And waited, until it became obvious he wasn't going to emerge. Where had he gone? Down a rabbit hole?

Benny disentangled himself from the swing and pushed the gate open. He saw straight away where Zeff must be. He just couldn't understand how he hadn't noticed it before.

Tucked away under the shedding branches at the bottom of the cul-de-sac was an ancient vehicle that had been turned into a camper van. Spotted curtains were drawn across the windscreen. On the side, beneath the mould and the birdstains, he could just make out the word "Windbird" in blocky handpainted letters.

It looked about as likely to fly as a hippopotamus. It had the same curved and heavy shape. In fact, it looked as if it was a long time since it had moved at all. It was up on blocks instead of tyres, and the worm-eaten set of steps against the doors at the back could have been there for ever.

Benny approached the steps carefully. They looked rotten and one of them was split. Something damp and twiggy dropped in his hair. He lifted his hand to knock, but the door was slightly ajar. He pulled it open.

Inside, a lot had been crammed into the small space. The bits of fittings he could see were shiny and futuristic, but everything was knee-deep in junk. It looked as if someone had opened the cupboards on the walls, lifted up the lids on the seats and emptied everything out onto the floor.

A layer of clothes tangled up with the insides of something electronic had settled on all the surfaces. A fishing net hung from the light bulb, and the seriously technical panel of instruments by the door had a whoopee cushion on it.

Benny took a cautious step in, crunching a pizza carton underfoot. The roof of the van was higher than he expected, tall enough to stand up straight. There were no windows. He ran his fingers over the instrument panel, then realised that he recognised some of the symbols. They were like the red characters in the notebook.

The muffled sound of something falling came from the cab. "I've looked and it's not in here, either, Snaffler," said Zeff's voice. The door at the end slid aside, and there he stood, looking surprised.

He was still wearing his black jacket, but it no longer looked like part of a uniform. It was unbuttoned, so Benny could see the green waistcoat patterned with constellations underneath. With his hair still tied back, he looked like someone out of the past. At his neck, instead of a school tie in a funny knot, he was wearing what looked like a silvery scarf.

He took a step towards Benny. "Who on Earth are you, and what are you... ?"

"I was sat next to you – remember? And you left this behind." Benny put his hand into his jeans pocket to take out the book, but then everything started to go wrong.

What he thought was a shiny scarf around Zeff's neck had begun to move. It shifted as if rearranging itself, until it didn't look like a scarf any more. Instead, it looked like an animal made out of liquid metal. A very particular type of animal, not Benny's favourite.

Zeff was carrying a metal rat around his neck.

Benny staggered backwards and put out a hand to save himself. His palm landed on one of the knobs on the panel, which depressed under his weight.

A galaxy of coloured lights came on all around him.

Zeff held out his hand, and the rat lifted its head. A pair of green eyes glowed in its sharp-snouted, whiskered face.

Benny took another step backwards. Realising he was about to fall out the door, he went to grab something. As if it was following a script, his other hand reached out and clutched a lever. He carried on falling, while his hand pulled the lever down.

That was when the noise began, the void opened up behind him and he discovered that the Windbird really could fly.

He snatched at the doorframe. He had no idea what was behind him. Whatever it was, it was big and empty and it was sucking him out of the camper van, prying his fingers from the thin metal rim one by one. He clung on, his face frozen in a silent 'O' of disbelief, but there wasn't enough strength in his fingers, in his nails...

His grip loosened and gave way. As he was whipped out into the darkness, the distant spark that had been the Windbird winked into nothingness.

Chapter Two

War Games

Benny carried on falling through space for a long time.

It didn't feel like he was falling. It didn't feel like he had a body at all. And there were no stars, just the darkness.

As he fell, he kept a picture in his mind of the last thing he'd seen: Zeff's unblinking eyes, watching from inside the Windbird. He had time to wonder what was going on, and why Zeff hadn't been sucked out of the van too. He had time to be scared.

Then an icy wind whistled past. He gasped, and his lungs filled with air. Small sounds burst through the silence: snatches of voices, birdsong, the creak of a machine. He began to feel heavy.

The darkness peeled away and he saw it, far, far below.

The ground.

I'm going to die, he thought, and shut his eyes.

Next thing he knew, his back smacked into water in a massive back-flop. As he went under, he opened his eyes to see a fountain of spray around him.

Stinging all over, he sank to the bottom. He was vaguely aware of things in the water with him. He lay waiting for his brain to catch up, watching the light playing on the surface above him.

Which was much closer than it ought to be. He'd just fallen from an unimaginable height, and he still seemed to be alive. But not for long, if he didn't get some oxygen soon. Lungs bursting and arms pumping, he pulled himself up towards the air.

Panting and coughing, he flicked water out of his eyes. He realised just in time that the man half-swimming, half-wading past him was waving a large sword. He ducked.

Some of the things in the water with him were dead bodies, or bits of them. The wooden wall of a ship-side loomed above, cutting out the sunlight.

A pair of men in half-armour wallowed towards him, and he back-paddled frantically out of the way. The man with the red shirt had the man with the blue shirt by the throat, and he was pushing his head under the water. He was trying to drown him.

Benny had just dropped out of the sky, and no one had noticed. That was because they were too busy trying to kill each other.

The water boiled as the man in blue thrashed against the grip that was holding him down. Then his body went still.

A chorus of cheers followed.

Benny turned. On all sides, tiers of stone seats rose high above him, packed with people in fancy dress.

It reminded him of something he'd seen before. What was it?

The people in the stands jumped to their feet with a yell like a crowd at a football match. Benny turned back, but he couldn't work out what they were shouting at. All he knew was that he was in the middle of what looked like a sea battle, but the water was fresh and it was happening in an arena in front of an audience.

Where had he seen this before?

A poster on the wall in primary school.

Ancient Rome.

Not possible, he thought. So, some kind of Ancient Rome theme park, or a film set?

He ducked to avoid a javelin. An arm floated by and he pushed it away. It was still warm and trailing a slick of red.

Too realistic, he thought.

He'd work it out later. What he needed to do now was to get out of the way.

A row of oars cut through the water towards him. As the shadow of a second ship fell on him from the other side, he worked his feet out of his trainers, put his head down and kicked off. It was hard work. He seemed to be splashing a lot and not getting very far.

He'd almost cleared the two galleys, when there was an explosive rattle and a roar of voices above him. One of the ships had fired its grappling hooks, pulling the boats together. The gap between was closing fast, and Benny was in the middle. He took a deep breath and plunged his arms faster, pulling himself towards the free water ahead. He reached the sunlight and turned, to see gladiators clambering across, swords slashing.

He tore his eyes away from the blades and the gore. The arena was huge, large enough to hold a small lake and several fighting ships. Most of the battle was going on at ship level, above his head. Not far away, another pair of galleys grappled closely, with hand-to-hand fighting on deck. Missiles flew through the air and splashed into the lagoon. A body spilled off the nearest ship, turned over and sank.

Benny trod water. He was clear of the action for the moment, in the lee of one of the boats. Perhaps it was safer not to be on board.

This is weird, he thought, like I've gone back in time... Whoa! That can't happen. It has to be some kind of simulation.

That's it. It's a game – a virtual reality game.

He was so excited by the idea, he forgot to paddle with his feet and disappeared under again. He struggled back to the surface, spluttering.

They've done the water well, he thought. I wonder how? Sprog would know.

How did it start? I pressed something in the camper van and that set it off. It must be a projection...

He was interrupted by something hard digging into the back of his neck. A hook lodged in his collar and wrenched him up the side of the boat, the seams of his T-shirt biting into him. He tumbled onto the deck and lay flat on his back like a landed fish.

A dark figure stood over him clutching a boathook. Zeff.

He looked right out of place. He was still wearing his black jacket and green waistcoat. Dropping the boathook, he went down on his knees and leaned close to Benny.

"Where's my Primer?" he hissed.

I suppose this will start to make sense soon, thought Benny. Either that, or it's not a game at all. It's a dream.

He never got a chance to reply. Hardly had Zeff got the words out, when his face pulled away again.

Benny could hear the battle carrying on in the background. Weapons slashed and chopped and whistled past, and voices raged and cursed. The words were coming into focus, like tuning into a foreign radio station and then realising that it's in English. "Which side? Tyrian or Egyptian?" repeated the voice, and this time Benny understood it.

He propped himself up on his elbows. Zeff was being held from behind by a huge man with ginger hair, facing a warrior who didn't look much more than a boy. The lad was slightly built, but he carried a sword stained with red, and he was the one asking the questions. They both wore blue tunics.

Zeff's voice was half strangled by the heavily muscled arm round his throat. "Egyptian," he gulped.

"Wrong side. Get rid of him, Cadmon," said the boy.

That seemed to be too much for Zeff. His body suddenly went limp, like a puppet that's had its strings cut. His breath came out with a sigh and his eyes closed. Cadmon, who'd looked as if he was about to break his neck, tipped him over the side instead.

Benny heard the sploosh as Zeff hit the water, but he was stopped from going to look by a hand in the middle of his chest. The boy warrior fixed him with strikingly blue eyes. At the same time, a heavy, freckled hand fell on his shoulder. The boy repeated his question, but this time he was asking Benny. It was time to pick sides.

Benny remembered what not to say. That only left one choice. His voice came out as a squeak. "Tyrian," he said. "I'm definitely Tyrian."

"It sounded as if he said he was Tyrian," said the boy. "Well, he is wearing blue."

That's lucky, thought Benny.

His sodden jeans and faded T-shirt almost looked like the rough leggings and tunics everyone else was wearing. So long as they didn't notice the zip.

The boy frowned. "Where's your armour?"

That's what I'm missing, thought Benny.

As well as an ill-fitting helmet, the boy was wearing a breastplate that looked too big.

Benny's mind worked fast. No good explaining that he didn't have the right equipment because he'd come from the future, unless he wanted to be locked up as a madman or executed for witchcraft. What could have happened to his armour? "It was dragging me down. I had to get it off."

"Better try to keep out of it, then. See if he can stand, Cadmon, and find him a spare weapon." With that, he was gone.

Brawny hands gripped Benny under the armpits and he was dragged to his feet. He stood reasonably steadily, dripping onto the wooden deck, and faced Cadmon.

He didn't look like the sort of man to take orders from a boy, even one carrying a sword. Benny had to crick his neck back to see the top of his head, which was covered in scars. He studied Benny thoughtfully. So far, he hadn't said a word.

The fighting was mostly on the far side of the ship. They were still eyeing each other suspiciously, when Benny spotted a man in red swinging down from the rigging.

"Behind you!" he gasped.

Cadmon hung motionless for a moment, then swung round like a dancer, his blade slicing through the air. With a wet thud, a head without a body landed at Benny's feet.

Hours on screen playing Warblades had got him to Grand Master level, but it hadn't prepared him for anything so realistic. He clamped his hand over his mouth as the blood spread towards his feet.

Through waves of nausea, he saw Cadmon pull a sword from the grip of the man he'd just killed. He held it towards him. Numbly, Benny wrapped his hand around the hilt. Instructions carried out, Cadmon turned and plunged back into the battle.

Benny was left dangling a heavy blade, dark with blood. Grasping it with both hands, he lifted it like a rounders bat and looked around.

OK, he thought. Blue, on our side. Red, not on our side. What happens now?

He was concentrating so hard on the danger around him, he almost missed the threat coming up from below. A man's head appeared through a hatch at his feet. Benny could see the shoulders of his tunic, and they were red.

He stepped back a pace and hefted his weapon. It was one thing to click on a button, another to swing a blade. The weight felt wrong, and he couldn't help remembering how bad he'd always been at tennis.

Get a grip, he thought. Use the sharp side.

He had to remind himself it wasn't real.

Halfway out of the hatch, the man in red aimed a massive swipe at Benny's middle. Benny reacted without thinking. He jumped.

His attacker was a grown man, and he knew how to use a sword. There was a lot of power behind the cut. Instead of opening up Benny's guts, it connected with his upper thigh and swept his leg from under him.

Before Benny blacked out, he saw his attacker look down in puzzlement at his own chest. A sword point pushed through the red fabric of his tunic. The man's eyes turned up, and he fell to the deck. Behind him stood a slim figure, with a lopsided helmet and blue eyes.

When he came round, Benny had no idea how long he'd been out. It couldn't have been too long, because he was still aboard the galley and he hadn't bled to death yet.

The fighting had stopped and the light was different. He was aware of a slight rocking of the ship as people moved about. Then he heard the quiet. The crowd noise was gone, so the Games must be over.

He was flat on his back on the planked deck again, but this time he was looking up into the blue eyes of the boy warrior.

"He saved you, Cadmon," said the boy. "We can't just leave him. The clean-up squad will be here in a minute."

Benny felt Cadmon's grasp under his armpits and found himself sitting up.

"Are you injured?" The boy crouched down. "Where did they get you?"

"Where do you think?" said Benny.

He looked at his leg. It ached and he expected to see it covered in blood, but there was no sign. He put his hand where it hurt. The wetness was just water. He wiggled his toes and flexed his foot, then bent his knee. There seemed to be no damage.

His spirits lifted. That proved it. No one in the real world could walk away from a chop like that with just a bruise. The whole thing was an illusion. He'd stumbled into a virtual war game, and he might as well enjoy it while he was here. That meant playing it as if it was real, until he could find out the rules. Just a couple of things still bothered him.

Where did Zeff fit into it all?

And what had happened to him?

Chapter Three

Bought and Sold

The boy in the helmet reached down and pulled one of Benny's arms across his shoulders.

"Call me Gwyn," he said. "Let Cadmon support you on the other side."

Lopsided because of their different heights, the mismatched trio lurched awkwardly down the gangplank. On land, guards in Roman uniform waited to herd them into a group with other survivors. They were stripped of their armour and weapons, and marched through a door at the back of the stand. The maze of passages and rooms inside was hot and airless. They were locked in a cell full of smelly bodies, with nothing but rough mats on the floor to sleep on.

Some of the things about this game are a bit too realistic, thought Benny.

Gwyn sat against the bars of the cell. His sweat-streaked hair reflected a reddish glow from the single lamp. He seemed happy to tell his story to Benny: Cadmon still hadn't said a word. The other captives muttered conversations in the background.

"We're prisoners of war," he said. "We're not really from Tyre: that's just a pretend side for the battle. We were captured on an island leagues away from here. It's called Britain. Don't suppose you've ever heard of it."

"Heard of it! I'm from Britain, too," said Benny.

Gwyn looked unconvinced. "I thought you were a Moor, from Afric land," he said. "What's your tribe?"

"The Marleys," replied Benny. It was the first thing that came into his head.

He shifted uncomfortably: his leg still hurt. Then he remembered what he had in his pocket. He slid his hand in, and pulled out Zeff's book.

Its smooth shininess and hard-edged shape contrasted with the grubbiness of the cell. Nothing could have looked more as if it came from another world. Gwyn's eyes opened wide.

"The talisman that protected you!" he exclaimed, holding out his hand. "Can I have a look?" Benny handed it to him.

Gwyn turned it over a couple of times and ran his thumb down the buttons on the side. The leaves sprang open. Startled, he let it slip through his hands before he caught it. The characters glowed in the poor light. He traced the patterns with his finger. Benny guessed that he couldn't read, and wasn't used to books of any kind.

Benny rolled onto his back. He stared up at the dingy rafters, wondering if Zeff's book really had stopped the blade that would have cut off his leg.

What on earth is going on? he thought. This feels real and unreal at the same time. The floor's hard, those people stink and my jeans are damp. My feet are sore because I left my trainers in the lagoon. But why hasn't anyone noticed I'm wearing different clothes? And how come I can talk to them? They're not speaking English, but I understand it.

He remembered what happened to Zeff. He couldn't bring himself to believe he'd drowned.

He's behind all this, thought Benny. If this is a game, I wonder which side he's on? I hope he turns up soon and does some explaining.

The cell was not a restful place, and it took him a long time to go to sleep.

The floor felt even harder when he woke the following morning.

The door opened, letting in a welcome draft. The guard called for their attention, and Benny found that he could understand his Latin as well as he understood Ancient British.

"You're no longer needed for games in the arena. You will be taken to the market and sold. If you're lucky, you'll get bought as slaves. Some of you may even be bought as gladiators."

"I didn't catch what he said would happen to us if we weren't lucky," said Benny to Gwyn.

"He didn't."

Shortly afterwards they were led down a sandy-floored corridor towards daylight. They shuffled along, because there were guards checking each prisoner. Most passed through after a quick inspection, but a few were pushed into a room to the left. Once they'd gone into that room, they didn't reappear.

The closer he got, the more anxious Benny became. He didn't want anyone looking at him that closely. They were bound to notice he didn't belong. Then what would they do?

The other two got to the checkpoint before him.

One guard put his hand on Cadmon's shoulder as if he was about to select him, but the other disagreed.

"Stroppy, that one," he said. "Took three to stop 'im throttlin' Vilius when 'e tried to take the boy. 'E was all lined up for a bit of entertainment with the beasts, but they decided at the last minute 'e'd be better value in the battle."

"So, they'll take 'im for gladiator school."

"Or", the first guard tapped the side of his nose, "back to the pen, ready for the beasts in the next Games. An 'ardworkin' officer what knew 'is form could clean up bettin' on 'ow long 'e'd last."

They winked at each other, then shoved Cadmon down the corridor with the rest.

Benny stiffened with alarm. Was that where they were going, in with the lions? If he warned the others, could they escape? Then the guards started arguing about Gwyn.

The first wanted to pass him through after Cadmon, but the second disagreed again. "Saw that one fight. 'E's 'andy, for a littl'un. And 'e's pretty too."

He gripped Gwyn's face and turned it to the light. Beyond them, Cadmon had stopped and was watching.

"Got any muscle on 'im?" The first guard took hold of Gwyn's tunic at the neck with both hands and ripped it apart. Then a smile spread across his face.

"Well, well... what 'ave we 'ere? This is a turn-up. Clean up room for you, my *boy*," and he shoved Gwyn through the curtain into the side room. Then several things happened in quick succession.

First, Cadmon let out a mighty roar and charged at the two guards. Then a posse of other guards Benny hadn't noticed fell on him out of the shadows. They wrestled him to the floor and dragged him away out of sight.

The guards at the checkpoint didn't give Benny a second look. They nodded him through, and he was carried along the corridor by the press of prisoners before he could see any more.

Then he stood blinking in the light, wondering what was different about Gwyn, and why Cadmon cared so much.

Behind Benny, the colonnaded wall of the stadium radiated heat from the sun. He tipped his head back, and looked at the tall marble buildings that surrounded him.

This is pretty good, he thought. It's just like I'd imagine Ancient Rome would be, only more so.

He was one of the last prisoners to come out. A couple more emerged and they were tied together and ordered into a line, hands behind their backs. A guard barked a command. A tug on the rope, and they set off through the streets.

Benny didn't see much of the city. It was difficult to keep pace with the others, and all his attention was on his feet. Walk too slowly, and he was dragged along by the prisoner in front. Too fast, and he trod on his heels. A man with a whip drove them along, a bit faster than a comfortable walk. He looked as if he'd like an excuse to use it.

Benny knew they'd arrived when the back belonging to the prisoner in front stopped moving.

Still tied together, the captives were penned at one end of a dusty square. The sun beat down and Benny could feel it like fire on the back of his neck. He looked longingly at the shadowed arches around the outside, where he could see stalls selling shady hats, cool drinks and fruits dripping with juice.

Time passed. The sun got higher and his mouth got drier. His wrists chafed under the coarse ropes. The man nearest to him had a wild look in his eye, and no one seemed to feel like talking. They stood with their heads bowed. Benny tried not to think about cold water.

The market got busier. It was full of people shopping, selling, just looking or passing the time. None of them spent much time browsing in the bargain slave pen. Benny wondered again what would happen to him if he didn't get bought, and whether it could be worse than being a slave.

Perhaps I'll get moved to a different level of the game, he thought. I don't think much of this one. If it is a game.

He pushed the idea that it might be anything else firmly to the back of his mind.

Opposite the pen was a platform like a small stage. Around midday, a crowd began to gather as if they were expecting something.

Benny worked it out, when a row of captives lined up at the back of the platform. He recognised a couple that had been chosen earlier, at the same time as Gwyn. They were generally those who appeared stronger, healthier or better-looking (he didn't take it personally). They'd been given a wash and a haircut and dressed in clean robes. A man with greasy hair spoke to the crowd, building up anticipation. He was going to auction them off.

Benny searched the group for Gwyn. He'd been chosen, so why wasn't he there? His gaze met a pair of blue eyes. He'd almost missed him because he'd been dressed like a girl, in a long pale dress with a scarf over his head.

Then Benny realised what it was all about: the fuss when they were being selected, Cadmon's protectiveness. Gwyn was dressed as a girl, because that's what he – or rather she – was.

Some of it still didn't add up. Benny thought women from the past were all long skirts and housework, but Gwyn fought like a man. And what was the link to Cadmon? He was too old to be her boyfriend, so was he her father, or her brother? That still didn't explain why he kept silent, and took orders from her.

The first prisoner to be auctioned was untied and brought forward. He'd been stripped to the waist and oiled, and his chest gleamed. He was made to turn round, so his muscles could be admired. Meanwhile, the auctioneer talked up his strength and his ability to work hard. Then came the rapid gabble of taking bids. The first slave was bought and led away.

It was hard for Benny to keep his interest, as several more were sold while the heat grew stronger. He wondered how much longer he could keep standing. The other prisoners were used to the climate, but yesterday he'd been in England. He might look as if he was wearing the same clothes as everyone else, but he wasn't. His jeans had dried rigid and unbending, and his leg was still painful.

Then it was Gwyn's turn, and his attention sharpened again. The auctioneer described her beauty and her grace, and Benny found himself agreeing.

The spell was broken by a voice from the crowd. "You sure that's a bird? Reckon I saw 'er wearin' armour in the battle, blood up to 'er elbows."

Another voice joined in. "Prove she's a girl!"

Coarse laughter followed.

This is getting ugly, thought Benny.

Then a nudge from one of the other captives drew him back to his own situation. It seemed they had a buyer.

The figure was tall, and wore grey robes that looked almost like the togas all the other shoppers were wearing. It was hooded, and the face was mostly shadowed, except for a pair of pale eyes which slid quickly from one prisoner to another. Benny's wild hope that it was Zeff in disguise died when he saw those eyes. Was it his imagination, or did their gaze rest on him longer than the others? A shiver ran down the back of his neck, in spite of the heat.

The buyer nodded to one of the guards, who came over. They turned their backs so Benny didn't know what was being said, but he heard the chink of coins. He had a nasty feeling it meant he'd been bought by the sinister figure in grey.

As he was being untied from his neighbours, one of them spoke. "Good luck, mate."

"What d'you mean?"

The guard had the end of Benny's rope and was joining him to a couple more prisoners. It looked as if they'd been bought, too.

"Well, let's say I'd hope you're going to be mucking out."

"Mucking out?"

"That woman who bought you, they call her the Beastworker. She's in charge of the animals. If I was you, I'd want to be looking after them, rather than meeting them in the ring."

"You mean, lions?"

"And tigers and mad elephants, and anything else they can get to make a show."

Benny was thinking things couldn't get much worse, when he remembered Gwyn.

She was no longer on the platform, and they were bidding for a tall African man. She'd been sold, and he didn't know who to. He searched the crowds for her, but she was nowhere to be seen.

His new mistress had disappeared too. It seemed she liked her shopping delivered. Benny was about to be led away, and he turned his head frantically, still searching the crowd.

He couldn't find Gwyn, but there was a disturbance growing in the press of people by the auctioneer's platform. A dark head forced its way through, accompanied by loud grumbles and complaints. It was a head he knew. It was Zeff.

I knew he hadn't drowned, thought Benny.

But it didn't make things much better. He was tied up, and Zeff didn't seem to have noticed him.

He was pushing his way through the crowd, and he kept looking over his shoulder as if he was trying to get away from someone. Behind him and moving in the same direction was the hooded figure of the Beastworker. He had to elbow and shove, while the people moved aside to let her pass. She was gaining on him.

Zeff backed up against the platform. His head turned this way and that, but there was only one way out. He clambered onto the stage.

The auctioneer didn't see him climb up because he was finalising a sale. He seemed a little surprised when he turned round to find Zeff on his platform, but he was obviously the sort of man who prided himself on being able to sell anything.

"And what am I bid for this... unique individual with the fine head of hair?"

The Beastworker stopped at the foot of the platform. Zeff's eyes had a hunted look as they searched the crowd, then they met Benny's. Recognition and relief spread across his face.

Benny heard Zeff's voice distinctly. "Let's give you all something that's really worth seeing." Then he did something quite unexpected. He put his hand inside his cuff and twisted his fingers, while looking intently at the auctioneer.

The Roman salesman's voice faltered. He looked down at his legs, watching them as if they were something that didn't belong to him. His knees bent, and he sprang into a somersault.

The crowd gasped. The auctioneer looked as surprised as everyone else.

Zeff made an adjustment at his wrist, still watching the auctioneer. He looked as if he was operating a remote control.

The auctioneer performed a perfect back-flip and started to walk round the stage on his hands.

By now the crowd was shouting with laughter and all the attention was on the acrobatic salesman. But Benny saw what they were not meant to notice. Zeff dropping down off the platform and slipping away, and a streak of metal at ground level, weaving through the legs towards him.

It was Zeff's robot rat, and it was heading for his feet.

He looked up. The Beastworker stood by the stage, and she was no longer looking after Zeff. She was looking straight at Benny.

His mouth clamped shut on the squeal of horror that was trying to get out. He felt the little feet and snaky tail of the rat trickle up his leg. When it reached the waistband, it crawled round under the bottom of his T-shirt and wriggled down into a jeans pocket. Then it went still, its dead weight lying against his leg.

At the same moment, the Beastworker's eyes unfocused and she turned to speak to someone by her side. Perhaps she hadn't been looking at him. Perhaps she hadn't been chasing Zeff. Perhaps he'd imagined it all.

A yank on the rope at his wrists brought Benny back to where he was. The disturbance was over and there was nothing more to look at. They were on their way.

Diana Gittins | Routes

Chapter One

It's Friday the 27th of April and I'm standing here in St Pancras Station with a ticket for Calais in one hand and my passport in the other. It says I'm Elizabeth Clara Hutchinson, though I just get called Liz or Lizzie, except for Dad who calls me Lardy Liz 'cos he says I'm fat. But I don't want to be *any* of them any longer.

I'm starting all over again.

Inside the carriage two blokes with laptops are working down the far end and across the aisle opposite me is a weird woman with spiky hennaed hair and bulging green eyes. I can't help glancing out the window all the time expecting *him* to come running down the platform to drag me back telling me like he always does, *I'll never let you go, we belong together, you and me.* Sweat starts to tingle under my arms when I think about him and if he'll suss what I've done and force me back.

Dead on time the train sets off and there's no sign of him. With any luck he won't realise I've gone till he gets back from work.

Blocks of flats, old warehouses, rows of brick terraced houses with muddy gardens flicker past the window. It's so bloody grey and depressing here, but when I'm in France there'll be sun and beaches and pop stars and I'll find a job and a room all my own with a lock on the door. I close my eyes and see myself sunbathing on the beach and I'm mega-thin and tan and all my spots have gone. A massive bloke kneels beside me and rubs my back with sun cream. He bends over to kiss me.

I wake up with a jolt. Stuff inside the train is reflected on the window and bits of me – one blue eye, a half-moon face and straight black hair – appear all distorted on the glass against a sign outside that says "ASHFORD". Loads of people are on the platform as the train stops. The door behind me opens and I catch a glimpse of a tall bloke in a brown coat — oh my God, I think it's him! I squeeze myself into the corner and press my face against the window and hope he can't see me. What am I going to do? What will I tell him? It's like a hundred hairy spiders are running up and down my skin.

I check out his reflection in the window as he walks past and the train starts again. It isn't him. Phew.

I suck a strand of my hair. My hair reaches down to my bum now 'cos he's never allowed me to cut it. He hates it when I suck on it. Oh shit, the weirdo across the aisle is staring at me, so I pick up the French magazine I bought on the station, 'cos my French is crap and I got 13 per cent on the mock and if I'm going to live in France I guess I need to try and do some work on it. I flip through and look at all the glamorous film stars and slim models. Lucky buggers.

I wake up inside the Channel Tunnel. It gives me the creeps, the thought of all that water overhead, and what if the ceiling collapsed and we'd be trapped and drown?

The train stops. It just stops in the middle of the tunnel. God, I must be psychic or something 'cos it looks like I was right and the tunnel's about to cave in and this is the end. I don't want to drown! I don't want to die!

Two blokes in hoodies run past the window and in the shadowy light it's clear from their faces they're scared witless. What's going on? Maybe they're engineers come to fix the tunnel. Four policemen with guns run after them.

"Shit!" I say out loud, and the next thing I know the weirdo across the aisle is standing beside me staring out the window.

"Refugees," she says. She's well over six feet, with hideous green cords and a purple sweatshirt and puce scarf. "Okay if I join you?"

She sits down before I can even answer.

Bugger, bugger, bugger. I definitely do not want her here *at all,* so I shrug my shoulders and hope she'll go away.

Except she doesn't.

And, as if it wasn't freaky enough already, these spotlights or torches or something start to flash outside the train. Whistles shriek. I'm not sure she's right about them being refugees 'cos they could be terrorists about to blow up the tunnel.

A few minutes later the police march back with the blokes in handcuffs.

"Poor sods," she says. "They're all so desperate to get to England.

They risk their lives all the time. Most of them try and stow in lorries but some idiots still try to get through the train tunnel. Not many get over alive."

"That's gross," I say, which it is. And it strikes me as strange that I can't wait to get out and they can't wait to get in.

She grins at me and says, "By the way, I'm Eve."

I just say, "Oh, hi," and hope she'll give up.

But Eve doesn't give up and stares at me and says, "And you?"

The train starts to move again.

There's no way I can tell her my real name 'cos she might get questioned or something and then I'd be a goner for sure. I stutter and stammer and finally say, "I'm – er – Sophie." And as I say it I realise it was a really cool thing to do. One little lie and I'm somebody else – hey presto, Sophie! Magic. Yeah, I like it. Kind of exotic and foreign. *Je suis Sophie. Je m'appelle Sophie.*

"Where you heading, Sophie?" Why doesn't she bog off back to her own seat and leave me alone?

I wish I'd listened to all those boring French classes and drawn the map of France for homework, but I didn't and all I can think of is Nice, 'cos I know there's a beach there, so I say, "Nice."

"Nice place Nice, ha-ha," she laughs. "So why are you going to Nice?"

I'm getting better at lying. Well, actually I have done quite a bit of it before and it gets easier the more I do. So I say, really casual like, "Oh, you know, work, warm weather – stuff like that."

"Got a job lined up?"

"Sort of," I say, like it didn't matter and this was all really boring.

"You're lucky," she waffles on, "because I'll have to get one."

"Yeah?" Though she's old, she's not *that* old, probably about Dad's age or something, and she looks like she'd already have a job. "What do you do?"

"Whatever I can find," she says with a big smile on her face. "Well, to tell you the truth, I'm on the run."

Is this for real?

"Yeah?" I say.

"Yes, that's right! I slipped out of the hospital this morning. It was definitely time for a change. I hate psychiatrists," she says, and her smile starts to fade, "and most of them hate me too."

Psychiatrists! Shit! I stare at Eve and think, *Hey, I ought to be really scared of this nutter and should pick up my rucksack now and just go,* but actually I'm getting to like her more instead. Maybe she's crazy but she makes sense to me.

"Don't worry," she says. "I'm not a murderer or anything like that. I'm manic depressive – what they call bipolar. You know Stephen Fry? Well, he's bipolar. Lots of creative people are. I'm supposed to take pills to control it, but they spoil all the excitement and make me feel like a cabbage after a while, so I've stopped taking them. I'm going to buy a car in Calais and head south. Want a lift?"

I look at her and in my head hear Dad with his cold razor voice telling me Eve is bad, mad and dangerous to know and don't have anything to do with her. But there's this other voice chirping in – I think it might be Sophie's voice – and it's saying, *Hey, why not? Go for it! You're free now and this crazy lady is kind of awesome.* And anyway it's a free ride and I'm not loaded with cash.

"Er," I say, glancing out the window, "yeah – yeah, why not? Sounds cool!"

Eve claps her hands together like a child and says, "Yee-ha! Thelma and Louise go to Nice!" She laughs with a raucous snorty laugh that sounds like a bunch of crows on ecstasy.

As the train pulls into Calais, all I can see are masses of tracks and overhead wires and a dark grey sky, but I smile at Eve 'cos this is so exciting, and for the first time in ages I feel relieved, 'cos I've done it: I'm here in France and so I say, "Wow! We've made it!"

And Eve says, "Sunshine, we've only just begun."

Chapter Two

If you think France is romantic, think again. Outside the station it's a mass of barbed wire, police and groups of desperate-looking blokes in hoodies. It's more like Guantanamo Bay than what France is supposed to be. I glance round nervously to see if there's any sign of Dad but I can't see him anywhere.

Eve turns to me and says, "Come on, Sophie. Let's get moving. You wait in that café over there while I get a car sorted out."

"Yeah, right," I say, and hurry past three blokes who are peering under a lorry. Two policemen are talking to a girl who's crying, while a group of blokes watch the police from a distance. They're all thin and unshaven. It's started to rain.

Outside the café a load of blokes are smoking and the smell is gross and makes me cough as I push open the door. Inside it's gloomy with just one strip light on a low, greasy ceiling. Groups of miserable-looking people sit hunched round rickety tables and each pair of eyes looks me up and down as I go over to order a coffee.

A dozen or so blokes burst through the café door and come up beside me at the bar. I hate being hemmed in like this and don't know where to look. They're standing way too close and I want to get the hell out, but don't know how or where I could go. Their damp jackets smell long overdue for a wash. They don't say anything and don't look me in the face but I know they're watching me. My body is tight and prickly.

A really short girl with bloodshot blue eyes slips through the crowd of blokes, looks up at me and says, *"Vous êtes française?"*

"Nah," I say in as calm a voice as I can. "I mean, *non*."

The blokes watch and listen.

She tries again, "Engleesh?"

"Yeah." I'm starting to remember some French and say, *"Oui."*

"You buy me a coffee, please?"

I haven't a bloody clue how to handle this 'cos she looks hungry and maybe I should buy all of them something to eat 'cos they all look pretty desperate. But I'll have to be really careful about spending till I get a job, so I say, "Okay. You want a sandwich?"

"You very nice," she tries to smile. "Cheese."

I wish these stupid blokes would piss off. They keep crowding round me, shuffling their feet while I reach in my pocket to find some money. The fat man behind the bar grunts as I pay. When I turn round with the cups, this guy with a moustache bumps right into me and sort of digs against me for no reason at all. The coffees slosh all over the saucers. What a bloody dickhead! I notice then he has a wad of money in his hand, so they can't be all that poor.

The girl follows me and we sit down. She says nothing when the waiter brings her the sandwich, so I try to be polite and say, "Where you from?"

"Ukraine," she says and takes a huge bite of the sandwich. She watches carefully as the blokes dash out and slam the door behind them. "I want to go to England."

"Why?"

"Much work in England. No work in Ukraine."

"What kind of work?"

"I willing do any work – pick the flowers, pick the fruit, pick the fish with shells from the sea. Work English not like doing – you call this black market, I think?"

"Yeah, right," I say. "But how do you get money *here*?"

She shrugs her shoulders, looks away and says, "Different things. Men sometimes. I go now. Thank you."

And she's off.

I stare into the coffee cup. What's it like to be a refugee? Did she mean what I thought she meant when she said "Men sometimes"? That is *so* gross.

"Okay, let's roll!"

I jump like I've been shot, 'cos I didn't see Eve come in at all. "Oh," I say as I stand up. "Yeah, sure."

"I've found a car."

"Brill," I say as I grab my rucksack. "Should I leave a tip?"

Eve shrugs her shoulders and says, "Most people do in France."

I fish in my pocket for some change. But my money isn't there. Where there had been £123.27 changed into euros, now there's only a few coins. I check the other pocket. Nothing. All the notes have gone. My body feels cold and weak. Check again. Shit. This cannot be happening. Bugger. This cannot be real.

"What's the matter?"

"It's... my money. It's, like, not there... it's gone."

Eve looks as wild as a headteacher who's just found a stash of cannabis in the library, and shouts, "WHAT???"

"It's not there. It's... it's gone. I just can't believe this has happened! Oh my God. What am I going to do?"

"JESUS LOUISE, Sophie. ALL of it?"

"Yeah, the whole sodding lot, except for some coins — I just don't understand, I—"

"You don't understand? How can you be so naive? These kids are desperate, their lives are on the line. They've got no homes, no work, no money. They've got absolutely nothing. Nothing whatsoever. SFA. Sweet Fanny Adams. Oh God, Sophie, you fool! Now neither have you!"

"Shit," I say, "and double shit. How could I have been such an idiot to let those foreign bastards take all my money?"

Eve just looks at me.

I stare at the floor and try not to cry. Why did they pick on someone who's got so little? Why *me*? How could they do it! It took me *ages* to save all that! And yet they were desperate and needed it and had nothing to eat and nowhere to sleep, so maybe they needed it more than me. But it was mine and I want it back! My head bumps around trying to make sense of it all and at last I say, 'What am I going to do?'

"Get on the road, that's what. Come on, let's get the hell out of here!"

Chapter Three

"It looks like an overgrown computer mouse," I say, staring at the white car. The bumper's dented and the chrome is rusty.

"It may be old, but it's fast and that's just what we need." Eve clearly thinks it's totally awesome.

The guy with a face like a fox hands her the keys and grins, revealing a crossword puzzle of gold and white teeth as he says, "*Vite, hein?*"

"'*Ah oui!*'" Eve nods vigorously as we chuck our rucksacks in the back seat and climb in the front. The seats are crinkled leather and have holes with stuffing coming out, but it's sort of snug.

"*Bon voyage!*" The man sniggers and walks off while Eve struggles to get the thing going. It splutters and chokes and finally grumbles into action.

"Yee-ha!" Eve bangs her fist on the wooden dashboard, presses the accelerator and we're off into the dusk in a cloud of exhaust fumes.

Driving through Calais everything seems gloomy, with groups of refugees huddled outside shops, and I'm still pissed off at how stupid I was to let those bastards steal my money. But after we've left the town there's fields and farms and a glimmer of pink light on the horizon as the sun goes down.

Eve drives on in silence for twenty minutes or more, then bursts into a deafeningly loud song and her voice is more like a man's than a woman's:

"Once again we must be off
Moving on to El-do-raaaaa-do
la-la-la-la, la-la-la-la."

I've got a headache and wish she'd shut the fuck up, but after a while the headache goes and I think, Hey, this is amazing! *I've made it to France and not only have I got here but I've found someone who's nuts but pretty cool and we're heading south in an ancient car that still seems to work fine. Before long we'll be in Nice! It'll take Dad ages to find where I've gone, if he finds out at all, and by then, well, I'm already Sophie and by the time I get to Nice I'll be starting a whole new life by the sea.*

"There's a hypermarket up ahead," Eve says as we approach the outskirts of a town. "Let's go and get some food and petrol."

"Brill, I'm starving."

She swerves into a crowded car park and screeches to a halt. I'm not sure what's so hyper about it 'cos it looks pretty much like an ordinary supermarket.

Inside, it smells different from Sainsbury's, sort of mixed-up ripe strawberries, bread and posh perfume. A little girl of three or four is pushing a miniature trolley beside her mum and she's talking French and it seems crazy that a kid that young can speak French so well. Almost everyone's dressed in black, like me, except they're small and thin with their hair looking like they've just stepped out of Toni & Guy's. They stare me up and down all the time and I can almost hear them saying, *What a gross girl and why doesn't she lose some weight and do something about those spots?*

I push the trolley as fast as I can, toss in packets of biscuits with labels I don't understand and exotic chocolate bars that I cover up with celery, apples and bread so people don't think I'm greedy. Eve appears with an armful of red sausages tied up with string and dumps them in the trolley, then zooms down another aisle.

I find an enormous display of cheeses that has a sweet, slightly off, smell. They're all different shapes and sizes and some are runny and some are hard, while others are yellow, lots are white and others have holes or blue veins running through them.

I am *so* hungry.

A little woman with beady eyes peers from behind the counter and says, "*Vous en goûtez, mademoiselle?*"

"Er," I say, trying to work out the *goûtez* bit and realising this would be really useful for my French exam next week except I won't be there and, anyway, it doesn't matter 'cos I'd fail it.

She holds out a toothpick loaded with a yellowy cheese oozing in the centre.

"*Merci*," I say, as I take the cheese in my mouth and feel the warm spread of it on my tongue. It tastes like the smell of socks that have been in trainers too long and yet it's kind of cool and reminds me of how my mouth felt the first time (well, the only time) Jason Richards kissed me.

"Mmm," I can't help saying.

"*Vous en voulez?*" She gestures at the huge round cheese with her knife.

"*Oui! Beaucoup!*" I can't believe I'm actually talking to somebody in another language! My mind whizzes around trying to think how I could possibly tell her that I want *all* of that cheese. And then like a miracle it comes to me: "*TOUT!*"

"*Tout le fromage?*" She looks gobsmacked and I'm not sure if it's 'cos of my French or 'cos I want the whole cheese.

It *is* a big cheese.

"*Oui! Tout! J'ai faim!*" It's utterly awesome that I said all that in French.

She hands me another piece on a toothpick and starts to wrap up the rest.

The second piece tastes even better.

I wheel away from the cheese counter just as Eve appears clutching a tangle of clothes, a bottle of whisky, a box of cigars and a large rubber plant. She dumps them into the trolley and I say, "Why the cigars and the tree?"

"Cigars calm my nerves, better than pills, and so does the whisky. Whisky's very medicinal, you know, and the plant, well, it's always seemed to me a home isn't a home without a plant."

"What home? We're in a *car*."

"Exactly! The car's all either of us has got for a home just now, so I thought we need to make it cosy and welcoming. Besides, we're not paying for it!" She lets out her crow laugh and all the shoppers stare at us.

My cheeks burn with embarrassment as I say to her in a really low voice, "What do you mean, we're not paying for it? I thought you said you had a credit card?"

"Oh yes, I do!" She takes the trolley and starts to push it towards the checkout. "It's just that it's not mine."

"WHAAT?" I don't believe this is happening. People her age with posh accents just don't do things like that. "You mean, it's *stolen*?"

"Let's just say I borrowed it from my shrink. She had her fun with it, now it's my turn!"

Oh shit. My body goes all cold as Eve grins and starts to pile the stuff on the conveyor belt. Finally I manage to whisper, "But the police... Won't the police be after you?"

"Probably, yes, almost certainly, but I'm sure we've got a few days before they manage to trace it."

I stand like a statue unable to speak. Oh my God, if the police are after her 'cos she's stolen a credit card and they'll soon be after me when Dad finds out I've gone, what chance have I got then?

Eve chatters away in French to the checkout girl as if nothing was wrong, and when it comes time to pay she sticks the card in the machine and punches in the PIN number like it was the most natural thing in the world.

As we load up the car I ask, "How did you know the PIN number?"

"Oh, I have my ways," she says with a big grin. "If you keep your eyes and ears open, even in the tightest of jams – and I've had a few of those in my life – you can suss most situations out. If you're going to be a survivor, you have to use everything you've got or you won't last long."

It's pitch black now as we head off into the night. Only the occasional car appears on the road and we drive through one little village after another for what seems ages. Eve starts to hum.

I wonder about what madness means, 'cos it seems to me Eve is one clever woman and being mad isn't about being confused or stupid but more about doing things that others don't want you to do or are against the law. So does that make me mad too?

We must have been going for a couple of hours or more when Eve turns on to another, smaller, road. The car has started to smell of cheese, but it doesn't smell so good in the car as it did in the hypermarket. So I open the window to let in some fresh air and that's when I see the lights flash behind us.

Chapter Four

"It's the police!"

Eve looks in the rear-view mirror and gasps, "Oh no!" She hugs the wheel like she was in a Formula One race.

The car lurches ahead.

I stare in the wing mirror and clench my teeth as the car goes faster and faster. It starts to rock from side to side. A load of rattles pitch in.

"They're gaining on us!" I say. The flashing lights are freaky.

"Stop panicking, Sophie." Eve sticks an unlit cigar in her mouth. "They can't be after us already. It just isn't possible."

"But they are!" My voice comes out more like a scream.

The car shudders and picks up speed as we go down a hill.

My eyes are fixed on the mirror as the lights flash nearer and nearer in the darkness, but my vision goes blurry as all these images of angry men with guns and police with batons and *him* with cold fury on his face start to flit through my mind and I struggle to push them away, but still they keep on coming. This is the end, this is it. It was a crap idea to run away. I'm going to be shot or killed in a car crash or arrested and taken back home. All I want to do is open the car door and roll out of this mess before it gets even worse.

"They're getting closer!" I shout.

"I'm going as fast as I can!"

We zoom past a shadowy farm house.

"Oh *shit*, they're right behind us!" Now I can see the front of the van.

And on the front is a big red cross.

"It's an ambulance."

"WHAAAT?" Eve bellows as she stares in the mirror. "Oh, Jesus Louise!"

She slows right down and pulls to one side. As the ambulance shoots past, a man leans out the window with his fist clenched and shouts something vile at us, but I haven't a clue what he actually said. I can imagine it, though.

Eve lets out an enormous groan as she lights her cigar. The stink of it is gross. She reaches into the back seat and gets out the whisky bottle, opens it and drinks with great glugs like it was lemonade or something. She drinks and drinks and says nothing at all.

My stomach's tight and I'm not sure if it's the stink of the cigar or the smell of whisky that reminds me of him or that I'm not too keen on the thought of her driving pissed out of her skull. Or it could be the cheese. Or that I think she's blaming me for what happened.

"God," she finally says, exhaling a thick cloud of smoke. "That was close. I just hope they don't report us to the police."

"Do you think they will?" I'm really taken aback that she hasn't shouted at me or hit me or something by now.

"Who knows? All I know is that I'm really shattered."

"Sorry," I say, staring at my legs, "but all I saw was the lights."

"Yes. You weren't to know." She sighs again.

I keep waiting for her to stop being kind and start laying into me. But it doesn't happen and I just can't believe she's being so cool about it.

Eve takes a final glug of whisky, tosses the bottle into the back seat and says, "We'll take a different road, so they don't find us. Keep an eye out for a place to bed down for the night."

"What, like a B&B?"

"Ha-ha," Eve roars, "that you should be so lucky! A barn, a ditch, whatever. Somewhere the police won't find us."

I peer out the window as Eve drives along dark country lanes. There seems to be nothing but miles and miles of fields and woods and the occasional farm. Not one other car goes past us.

We pass a load of cows lying in a field that look eerie in the moonlight, and just beyond them I spot the silhouette of a shed or little barn or something and say, "How about that?"

Eve slows down and stares out at the field. "Looks okay to me," she says and drives right into the field and parks behind a hedge. Anybody driving along wouldn't notice the car at all.

It's *so* good to get out of the car. It's freezing cold and the air smells of cabbages. Then I see that's what's in the field – rows and rows of cabbages. Hundreds of them.

"God," Eve mutters as she gazes up at the sky. There's an orange glow from the tip of her cigar.

I look up too and can't believe how many stars there are; more than I've ever seen in my life. The sky is littered with them — big ones, little ones, constellations and probably a load of space shuttles and airplanes too. Millions and millions of stars. "Wow," I say. "I've seen stars before, but never like this."

"Isn't it utterly divine?" Eve blows a cigar ring into the night.

"Yeah," I say. "Awesome."

After a few minutes she says, "I guess we should eat something. I'll get some stuff out of the car."

I spot some logs by the shed and set them up on end near the hedge and we sit down and munch a baguette, some very runny cheese and chunks of spicy sausage. Neither of us says anything 'cos there's not a whole lot you can say when there's a sky like that over your head and you're sitting in a field of cabbages and everything is very still except for the distant hooting of an owl.

After we've eaten we explore the shed, which is made of stone and has a dirt floor and an open door. Bits of old farm machinery are in one corner and a big pile of hay in the other.

"It stinks," I say.

"It'll do." says Eve. "It's just musty hay. I bought a couple of rugs in the hypermarket and I reckon if we burrow into the hay we can keep warm enough." She throws a rug in my direction.

"What about rats?"

She shrugs her shoulders.

The hay is damp and smelly as I dig a hole in it, but I'm so tired I don't care all that much and wrap myself in the rug and crawl in. The hay is a bit prickly, but she's right: it's warm.

Eve doesn't lie down, but goes outside, sits on a stone outside the door and lights up a cigar.

"Aren't you going to sleep?"

"Not yet. I don't do much sleeping. 'Night."

Just as I start to drift off, something inside me goes cold and creepy and I start to imagine his face and the rage on it. I shiver, then remember my rucksack and reach out to take the knife I packed, just in case. It's a knife he uses when he goes camping. The handle is comforting in my grasp. Eve's still outside smoking and muttering to herself and it seems okay again – well, more than okay, 'cos here I am in France and I'm Sophie and I'll soon be safe in Nice.

They're after me and they want to get me. They want to kill me. I'm running as fast as I can, sweating and pushing hard, but my legs just won't move. So I push harder and run faster, but my legs have turned to stones that will not move... and my body is wet with sweat and I need to pee and I open my eyes and cannot figure out where I am.

It all comes back when I see shafts of moonlight in the corner of the doorway shining on to the mud floor. Something nearby is making a weird rumbling sound. Is it Eve snoring? I glance over at where she's burrowed into the hay. But it isn't her snoring. It's closer than that. Something is lying beside me. It's warm and soft like a fleece, but I haven't got a fleece with me. It moves.

Oh shit – it must be a rat!

I lurch out of the hole in the hay, and as I do so a small face looks up at me from the shadows of the moonlight.

Kay Leitch | The Other Side of Yesterday

Chapter One

Megan's mother died when the second wave hit the roof of the house. She was swept into the floods trying to claw her way back to her infant daughter. She didn't stand a chance. Sucked down in seconds by a current as swift as it was ferocious.

Megan didn't notice.

The tree that felled her father lay splintered like a twig and was just as easily borne away by the storm as he was, his strong fingers prised from life by merciless elements. Fingers that only yesterday had held hers as she practised walking.

He called her mother's name while he fought the water. But the wind stole his words away.

Megan never heard him.

In the darkness the current carried her wooden cradle past broken cottages and fallen trees. Now and then the lifeless form of a fox or a deer would float by, battered by the rain. After a while the wind dropped, the rain eased and the cradle slowed. Occasionally it snagged on a piece of driftwood.

Megan lay tucked under a woollen coverlet, soothed by the rocking motion of the water. The cradle veered into bushes along an avenue of drowning hawthorns that had once been a road but was now a speeding river. Droplets hung on low branches and shone like diamonds in the light of a cold moon. Distant thunder disturbed the night.

From nowhere two men, dark as shadows, jumped into the torrent. They struggled to keep their heads up, flailing and spitting as muddy water slapped against their faces. Scudding clouds obscured the moon, casting the cradle and its pale coverlet into darkness. One of the shadows gulped for air and adjusted his course. "Over there," he spluttered. "Just push it down. Make sure she stays under."

The shadows swam towards the cradle.

The droplets fell one by one onto Megan's face. She blinked; reached a hand up to catch them. Her calm gaze settled on the dark outline of a hawthorn branch, and a black kitten clinging there. The kitten meowed, then jumped, and landed by her feet. He clung on.

The cradle lurched. The kitten's claws gripped the coverlet, half tipping it into the water. He recovered well, caught his balance, then crept towards Megan's arm and settled beside her. A crystal shard glittered on a chain at his collar. The kitten rubbed his head against the child. She gurgled and smiled. The crystal lay against her palm.

The shadows striving to reach her fought the current, heads bobbing in the rushing water. A break in the clouds bathed them in moonlight and showed the cradle within striking distance. Little by little they gained.

Megan's fingers closed over the black fur and crystal shard. She held tight. The kitten purred and snuggled closer. The cradle gathered momentum in the swell, moving faster into the darkness of drowned meadows. Megan's eyelids closed. The dampness that seeped into the trailing coverlet would chill her through soon enough, but for the moment she was warm in the shawl her mother had laid her in.

The wind died and the night grew silent. The cradle drifted. The shadows were almost upon it.

As Megan slept the kitten took the tip of the crystal in his sharp little teeth and jerked his head. The crystal shard grew bright and cast a glow over them both until it seemed they were lit from within. Around the cradle the air shone like a halo. The halo grew; the light intensified. It sparkled and brightened till it was a miniature sun sitting on dark water. Then the sparkles rose like a veil of fireflies covering the cradle and coverlet, child and kitten alike.

The shadows saw the shimmering light surround the cradle and swam faster, but they could not reach it in time. The halo extinguished like a candle snuffed. The cradle disappeared into the unknown.

And the unknown was waiting.

Chapter Two

Sandor Brightman loved to walk. Especially in the early morning and especially in autumn when the green of the land he loved gave way to red and gold.

There were fine lines on Sandor Brightman's forehead and crinkles round his eyes. His hair curled thick and white round his neck. He had lost his left hand in one of the many wars that had ravaged his country before the Settling. An Elandan warrior had sliced straight through his wrist while he fought off two of them on his other side. Now that King Alfan had ensured peace with Elanda the last few years had been quiet and Sandor had no need to go armed. But he did. It was his nature.

He had a favoured spot on Thorn Rise where a great rock rose out of the crest of the hill. He would often sit there watching the sun rise over the distant walls of the city, while sparrowhawks wheeled above him in the blue.

In fair weather he could see beyond the spires and domes to the bridge on the far side outlined black against the azure mountains. Where the River Thorn reflected the sun and glimmered across the distance, like a mirror with a message.

He was sitting on the rock, on the hill, on just such a day with just such a view when he heard a child's cry.

• • •

Kirrin dreamed he was drowning. In his anguish he thrashed the water only to find it hard and unyielding. Unyielding as a tree.

His eyes opened. He realised his body was slipping from the branch he sprawled on. His arm shot out and he grabbed the knobbly bark just in time. He looked round. He was lying on one of the highest branches, surrounded by red and gold leaves. Below him lay the dark water of the Fringes pool.

He sprang up, the tree rough under his bare feet, and pushed his wet hair back from his face. His head throbbed. His clothes clung to him, sodden. He touched his forehead gingerly and felt the crust of dried blood. A crystal gleamed on a silver chain round his neck.

He remembered the baby he had saved in the floodwater and his heart almost stopped in fright.

Where was she? Where was the baby?

Kirrin clambered over the gnarled limbs of the tree, brushing aside swathes of golden leaves. He leapt into the dip at the centre of the trunk and jumped to the ground. The grass squelched between his toes. A shiver of revulsion shook him; he hated the Fringes pool and the reeds and the way the ground sucked him into its boggy maw.

He scoured the bushes and the dull stagnant water edged with driftwood. He knew how much debris washed down the tributaries of the River Thorn and found its way to the Fringes. Sometimes dead birds and rodents floated down, too.

A sparrowhawk's high call drew Kirrin's eyes across the water. He nodded to his sister as she flew fast and low out of the trees, dipping her wings and swishing close enough to brush his straggling black hair. She settled on the edge of the branch he had almost fallen from and looked down at him, a slash of white on her brow. Her grey-brown feathers fluttered.

Kirrin tipped his head back. "Where is she?" he said.

He heard her voice inside his head, as always. "You was bleeding. I couldn't wake you. They're coming to get her."

Kirrin shook his head violently, droplets of water flying from his hair. The last thing he remembered was the light from the crystal surrounding him and the baby, bringing them from the flooded world to Thorn. He remembered the crib kept tipping in the waves. He remembered the baby; so cold, so small. He was little, but she was littler. He caught his breath.

"She might have drownded," he said. He shook his head again. "Find her, Aquila. Fly!"

"Found her already. So has Sandor."

Oh. Sandor.

Kirrin felt bad. He hadn't told his guardian anything about what he'd been up to. He knew Sandor would have stopped him. But he also knew Sandor would have behaved exactly as Kirrin did, if he had overheard someone plotting to kill a baby: he'd have gone straight into that strange world and stopped them, too.

Kirrin thought, *Where?*

"Beyond the bushes."

Kirrin knew the Fringes pool separated into two parts, almost like the number 8. He'd learnt that number at his lessons. He imagined the trees and bushes curling round it, with water flowing through the centre. He decided to skirt the reeds and stick to the edges, where the ground was more solid. He had only gone a few steps when he saw the familiar white hair and dark waistcoat of his guardian. Sandor was wading into the pool, the water lapping against his thighs, soaking his trousers. Even from this distance Kirrin could see the anger on his face. Kirrin knew there would be questions.

He watched Sandor bend to the cradle and steady it as he flicked aside the sodden coverlet.

Kirrin stretched up to try to see if the baby was all right but the reeds blocked him. He kept sinking; already the cold water had crept past his knees. Sandor's white head came back into view as he straightened. He had unwrapped the wet shawl swaddling the baby and slipped his own woollen waistcoat around her. Then he tucked her into the crook of his arm. Kirrin wondered why Sandor put her in his left arm. That was the one without a hand; it had been cut off in a fight somewhere.

The hair on the back of Kirrin's neck bristled. His ears twitched. He squinted at the trees and bushes behind Sandor. Something was wrong but he couldn't see what. But Aquila could. Kirrin heard her shrill warning call.

Sandor looked up.

Kirrin ducked again as two men parted the bushes down near Sandor. Kirrin's fingers curved as he recognised them from the night before when they'd tried to drown the baby: Ward worked for Gorwyn – everyone knew that. The younger one, with blond hair, was called something like an Assam man.

As Kirrin crept closer he heard Ward call out, "I'll take that." By the time he could see them all Sandor was out of the pool and safely on solid ground. The baby was still under his damaged arm. He held a sword in his right.

Kirrin's eyes widened. Where had that come from? He saw surprise in Ward's face, too. And fear. The other man just looked on, scowling. Kirrin held his breath. It was two against one; how would Sandor manage?

"I don't want any trouble," said Ward. "Just give us the child. She'll be well taken care of."

"Lying scum." Sandor's voice was so soft Kirrin barely heard it.

Ward tried again. "Lady Gorwyn, the Queen's sister..."

"Is a curse on the land." Sandor eyeballed the blond man. "You can report that, if you ever get back to her Stronghold alive."

Kirrin saw Sandor step forward, sword raised. Ward stepped back and tipped his head to look up at him. The blond man looked at them both, seemingly exasperated with Ward's hesitation.

Kirrin realised he was still holding his breath. He let it out slowly. His feet were numb with cold. The year had turned and although the sun was up the air was cool with the promise of winter. He pulled first one foot from the mire, then the other, and tested around him with his toes, trying to find solid ground. There must be some, because Sandor wasn't sinking.

Kirrin heard, "Any time you're ready, old man!" The blond man sprang forward, his sword whipping up towards Sandor's face. Sandor knocked him back. Kirrin worried the baby might fall, but Sandor's hold seemed secure.

The blond man laughed. "You're fast, I'll give you that, for a wet nurse. Let's see how good the brat looks with my sword through its belly."

Kirrin felt a hiss rise in his throat. He quelled it.

He glanced up quickly but couldn't see Aquila anywhere. She always disappeared when there was trouble. The sound of steel clashing reclaimed his attention and he cringed as the blond man slashed down towards Sandor's side. Sandor was too quick for him. Kirrin had never seen him move so fast. It was as if he knew what moves the blond man was going to make before he made them.

A quick flick and Sandor's sword opened the man's shoulder through to the bone. He winced and let out an involuntary cry. Kirrin saw blood drip from his jerkin. Then he caught the movement of Ward's hand as he slipped a dagger from the back of his belt.

Kirrin knew he had to be fast. He felt the familiar surge of heat as he shifted into his Alter. His skin tingled and rippled; his face tightened and his fingers curved. He saw black fur break the surface of his skin and thicken over it, and watched the ground rush towards him as he became a kitten again. He shot across the boggy grass and leapt onto the tree behind Sandor. His claws levered him up to the first set of branches and as he ran to the end he saw Ward stretch his arm up to Sandor's shoulder blades. Ward plunged the dagger down.

Chapter Three

Kirrin meowed loudly.

Sandor twisted and slashed, knocking the dagger and two of Ward's fingers into the grass, then he sprang back and blocked another savage sweep by the blond man.

Ward screamed and clutched his hand.

Kirrin was already in midair. He felt his body crackle and lengthen as his fur blurred and faded back to skin. Arms and legs outstretched, Kirrin crashed down onto the bleeding Ward. He dug his nails deep into Ward's flesh and rolled with him. Ward couldn't shake him off. When they stopped rolling, Kirrin was on top of his chest. He hissed and sank his teeth into his cheek. Ward screamed again.

Kirrin risked a quick look round. The blond man's nose was squashed and spurting blood. He tried twisting his sword in under Sandor's arm but Sandor rammed him on the upward thrust and a slash opened the man's chest. Kirrin had never seen such a look in Sandor's eyes. It was pitiless.

The blond man groaned and folded to his knees. Kirrin felt Ward wriggle and try to heave him off his chest. He grabbed handfuls of Ward's hair and clung on. Ward yelped and swore to break his neck. Kirrin grinned. He looked over at Sandor again and watched as he moved in and slashed down. An arc of blood spurted from the blond man's throat. Kirrin could see from his eyes that he knew it was all over.

Kirrin realised Ward had been watching the swordfight too. Now he tore at Kirrin's shirt trying to snatch the crystal shard swinging at his neck. They wrestled, bucking and rearing on the ground. Kirrin hissed and spat.

He felt his grip loosen as Ward jerked his body round and heaved him off. Kirrin twisted in midair and landed in a crouch. Ward staggered to his feet. He held his scalp where his hair had been torn out. Kirrin bared his teeth and leapt onto his back, hissing. He bit into Ward's ear and ripped it from his head. Ward screamed and twisted again.

Kirrin was just opening his mouth to bite again when he saw Sandor in front of him, sword raised. Sandor flicked the tip under Ward's chin.

Ward froze.

"Kirrin. Come down." Sandor's voice was calm.

Kirrin retracted his nails from Ward's scalp and jumped to the grass. He sprang upright and spat out a piece of torn flesh; it tasted salty. He smiled. If Sandor was angry with Ward, then perhaps he wouldn't blame Kirrin for the baby being wet.

Kirrin looked at the limp bundle in Sandor's arm. She didn't look just wet. Her skin was like wax. Her fingers didn't clench, as they had when he jumped on her cradle last night. She didn't move at all.

Kirrin felt as if a hand had grabbed his throat and squeezed. A terrible heat filled his body. His eyes burned. Tears spilled down his cheeks. He couldn't breathe.

"But she was alive," he said. "She was alive!"

Sandor's voice was ice. He looked at Ward. "Not any more," he said.

Kirrin wiped his eyes and looked at the tip of Sandor's sword as it flexed against Ward's dirty neck.

"What were your orders concerning this child?" Sandor asked.

"I don't know what you mean." Ward cowered like a trapped animal.

Kirrin saw a speck of blood appear at Ward's throat as Sandor pressed his sword home just enough to break the skin. Blood trickled.

Sandor sighed. "Listen to me. That pool can hide two bodies as easily as one. Or I can let you go, to make up whatever tale you please to pacify your master. It's your choice. What were your orders concerning this child?"

Kirrin saw Ward's eyes flick to the trees. But they all knew no one was coming. No one was even within shouting distance up here, especially this early in the day.

"She wants the child dead," Ward said. "So the work is done. No need for any more killing. She just wanted her dead."

Sandor frowned. "She?"

"Lady Gorwyn, the Queen's sister." Ward's tone grew threatening, but if he hoped for fear or regret from Sandor Brightman, Kirrin knew he would be disappointed.

Kirrin looked at Sandor. Sandor's face betrayed nothing.

"Did the Queen approve her sister's intentions?"

Ward shook his head. "She knows nothing about it."

"King Alfan, then?"

"No. No. He's too ill to know anything. The Lady Gorwyn ordered it."

"Why?"

"I don't kn—"

Another trickle of blood.

"I swear! I don't know! Something about augury. Something about, about Elandan prophecy. Ask Skorce. He knows. I don't. I swear I don't know!"

Kirrin sniffed and wiped his nose with the back of his hand. He looked at the baby again. Her pretty lips were tinged with blue.

Kirrin watched Sandor ease the sword back from Ward's throat. Ward cringed and clutched his hand. He folded his thumb and remaining two fingers into a tight fist to stem the blood. Kirrin was pleased to see his face covered in deep weals.

"She said it was easier to get to her when she was an infant. She told us to kill her," Ward babbled. "So, no great harm has been done. The job is finished. She'll be happy."

A different kind of heat filled Kirrin's head now. He had braved that horrible world to save the baby and he'd failed her. He felt a roar rise in him, blocking out everything except his fury. He knocked Sandor's sword aside and leapt back onto Ward's chest. "No great harm!" He clawed and bit Ward's face. "No harm! I saved her and you killed her!"

Ward fell to the ground kicking and screaming. "Get him off me! Get him off!"

Kirrin clawed deeper into Ward's flesh. He could hear high-pitched howling and knew it came from his own mouth. He spat and hissed and tore.

"Kirrin, stop."

Sandor's calm voice cut through the red mist in Kirrin's head. He stopped and caught his breath. Then he sprang off Ward, rolled and stood.

Ward crawled onto all fours, cursing and bleeding. He wobbled to his feet, his face streaming blood.

Kirrin looked at Sandor, expecting a stern telling off and not really caring. But Sandor seemed preoccupied. "What did you mean, 'She said it was easier to get to her when she was an infant'?"

Kirrin saw that Ward looked stricken. Sandor said, "Tell me everything or get ready to bleed to death."

Ward started snivelling. "She made us. Skorce didn't want to use one, we didn't want to use it either, but..."

"Use what?"

Ward flinched, as though he expected Sandor to strike him. "A TimeStone."

Kirrin didn't know what that was. But he saw Sandor's face freeze.

"Using TimeStones has been forbidden for centuries. The penalty is death."

"You tell Gorwyn that. She wasn't going to let anything stop her."

"You'd risk death for this?"

"She'd have killed me anyway, if I hadn't done it. Gorwyn wants that child dead and she'll do whatever it takes, even if it means slipping into her past. We had to force Skorce, but he knew how to do it. We cast the TimeStone and it opened a way into her world. Only problem was the storm it made."

A horrible thought jumped into Kirrin's head. So horrible he had to interrupt. "Does that mean anyone who goes into that world, where the baby was... Does that mean they'll...?"

Sandor kept his eyes on Ward. "They'll be executed. Most likely hanged. The law is clear: playing with TimeStones is forbidden."

Kirrin blinked. He thought he was going to be sick. He had only been trying to help the baby.

He heard Sandor say, "Skorce was involved?" Kirrin knew the old sorcerer was Sandor's friend.

"They hit him," Kirrin said, "They made his head bleed. He kept saying no, but they kept hitting him till he said yes. You can't blame Skorce."

Kirrin couldn't believe they would hang him for trying to help a baby. He wondered what it felt like; how much it would hurt.

Ward had turned to look at him. Kirrin realised he should have kept quiet – they didn't know what he had heard and seen. He was relieved when Ward carried on. "Gorwyn told him he could obey her or lose his eyes. He made his choice."

Kirrin saw a muscle flex in Sandor's jaw.

"What about the child's parents – they must have protected her."

Ward lowered his eyes.

Kirrin wished he could tell Sandor about the storm and how Ward and the Assam man had made sure the baby's parents didn't survive it once they were in the water. But Sandor already knew. "You killed them." His eyes betrayed his outrage. "You killed her parents."

Ward mumbled, "The storm killed them. We just—"

Sandor's sword fell to the grass. Before Kirrin knew what was happening, Sandor had made a fist and punched Ward so hard in the face his cheek cracked. He tumbled onto his backside, stunned, his face split and bleeding. Sandor bent swiftly and retrieved his sword.

Kirrin gave a whoop and did a quick back-flip. It was times like this, he thought, that he loved Sandor Brightman. All the same, he decided he wouldn't mention that he had overheard Ward's murderous plans and followed him and the Assam man into the baby's world. No one need ever know.

"What age was this child in her own world?" Sandor asked.

Ward tried to sit up. His good hand reached to cover his shattered face. He was trembling.

Sandor flicked his sword back under Ward's throat. "What age? Tell me or I'll skewer you where you sit."

"About five, I think." Ward spat out a broken tooth and wiped blood from his split lip. "And I don't know why Gorwyn wants her dead, either. But she does. She really does."

"Get up!" Sandor hauled Ward to his feet. "Tell Gorwyn whatever you want," he said. "For my part, I won't spread the tale that you were bested by a seven-year-old boy. Tell her you fell in a bramble bush, or hit your face on a wall. But if you mention my name, or his, I will cut out your tongue and nail it to your corpse. Understand?"

Kirrin glared at Ward. He felt good standing side by side with Sandor Brightman.

He saw Ward flinch, as though he feared Sandor might not wait to carry out his threat. "But what can I tell her? She wants proof the child's dead. And she'll want to know where *he* is—" Ward jerked his head at his comrade sinking slowly into the reeds.

Kirrin tried to sneak a look at the baby, still secure in the crook of Sandor's arm. He wondered sadly why Sandor didn't just put her down, since she was dead.

Sandor's voice cut into his thoughts. "Kirrin, bring me the child's cover. You, tell your mistress her assassin got caught in the undercurrents and died drowning the child. Tell her they're both at the bottom of the Fringes. Take the lower pathways through Blackbear's Walk straight to her Stronghold. Don't deviate from the path. If you do, I'll know."

Kirrin gritted his teeth and forced himself to wade into the pool to retrieve the baby's cover. He had to swim the last part because it was so deep. Water made his skin crawl. He knew Sandor was aware of that, but he also knew there was no one else here to help. Aquila would stay on the wing as long as there was trouble.

When he returned Kirrin looked over at the blond man's body, already half submerged in the reeds. A dark stain spread round it at the water's edge.

Ward was still snivelling. "What about him?" He nodded to his friend.

"Leave him," Sandor said. "I'll bury him with the child."

Ward took the coverlet and bent to pick up his dagger where it had fallen. Kirrin raised his eyebrows at such foolishness. He could have told him it was a bad idea. He heard the warning noise in Sandor's throat and saw Ward reconsider, then straighten and head for the path leading to Blackbear's Walk. Kirrin looked after him all the way. He didn't look back.

A few moments later, Kirrin heard familiar birdsong.

Aquila flew out of the trees and settled on the edge of a branch above them. Kirrin looked up. "It's safe now," he said. "You can come down." He watched her wings tilt as she alighted on the grass beside him and shifted from her Alter form into the skinny sister he was used to.

She cocked her head to one side and looked at Sandor with her golden eyes. Her tawny hair slipped over her shoulder, her face expressionless as ever.

"Save your brother another torture, Aquila, and bring me the cradle from the water," Sandor said.

Kirrin nodded. That was more like it; it was time she did something useful. Aquila walked into the waterlogged grass with small delicate movements. Her bare feet sank into the mire.

Then came the moment Kirrin had been dreading. The tell-me-what-you've-been-up-to moment. There seemed to be one at the end of every adventure. Sandor had looked after him and Aquila for most of their seven years and had always been kind to them. Loved them, even. But Kirrin knew wise people did not provoke Sandor Brightman. Nor lie to him.

Kirrin tried to find the words to explain what he had done, without actually explaining. For a second he thought he was going to cry again. He stared at the wisps of red hair just visible in Sandor's arm and felt his face crumple in misery.

It had all been for nothing, he thought. The baby was dead and they were going to hang him for going into her world to help her.

"Right," Sandor growled. Kirrin watched him sheathe his sword in a worn leather scabbard that matched his trousers. Then he hunched his great frame down so he could look right at Kirrin. He held the baby securely in his arm. Kirrin wondered again why he didn't just put her down. But he knew he wouldn't have been able to, either; he would keep holding her, just in case there was any hope. Maybe that's what Sandor was doing. Hoping.

He looked into Sandor's blue eyes and sighed. He just hoped they let him say goodbye to Aquila. He quite liked her really.

He pulled himself up straight. "Go ahead. Hang me. I don't care."

Chapter Four

"What?"

"You were away," Kirrin said. "They were going to kill her. You can hang me if you want but I had to help her. I'd do it again."

Kirrin saw Sandor frown.

"What are you talking about?" Sandor said. "No one is going to hang you."

"But you said. You said I'd be secuted. Hanged..." Kirrin looked at the ground. He knew Sandor was smart; he would figure it out. He was surprised Sandor didn't scowl and demand an explanation, as he had last week when Kirrin finished off that pitcher of cream.

"Whatever happens, you are not going to be executed," Sandor shook his head in exasperation and turned his attention to the bundle in his arms. A tiny sound rose from it. Sandor opened the waistcoat, touching his fingers to the infant's cheek, still kneeling on the uneven ground so Kirrin could see.

Kirrin peered at the bundle. "I thought you said...?"

Sandor held the child next to his heart. As Kirrin leaned in to look, her eyes opened slowly. Midnight blue.

"Lesson one," said Sandor. "Don't believe everything you hear." He smiled. Kirrin thought he looked mesmerised by the child.

Relief and joy flooded Kirrin. He clenched his fists and jumped into the air. In his excitement his Alter image began to assert itself and he felt the rising heat that warned him his body was about to change. His form began to shift. He hated when this happened. Whenever he lost control of his emotions he also lost control of his shifting ability. Heat flared inside him, his human shape shrunk and the cat inside him took over. He felt his skin prickle as his fur broke through it and spread over him. His tail swished slowly as he sat in the grass at Sandor's feet, purring. Deep contentment filled him. The crystal shard at his collar glittered as he sprang into the air again and somersaulted.

Sandor waited patiently. Kirrin's body lengthened. His black paws reverted to hands, his fur to olive skin. He wriggled as he shifted back into a boy. "I was hoping she would stay quiet till they'd gone," said Sandor. "Her silence saved her."

"No, I saved her!" Kirrin grinned with delight. "I got her out of that storm and brought her here."

Aquila returned with the cradle and dripping shawl and placed them at Sandor's feet.

"I saved her," Kirrin said again, for Aquila's benefit. He began to walk round her, his head low, pacing. He felt invincible. He watched Aquila's eyes follow him.

"Me," he said. "From killers, and a storm in a horrible world. I brought her here to Thorn. You couldn't have done it. You fly away whenever there's trouble."

"Be still," Sandor chided, still resting one knee on the ground as he rocked the baby. "We're not done yet. Tell me what happened. *Everything* that happened."

Kirrin tried to remember. "They were with Skorce. In his room – you know, the big one, with the books and the shiny stones?"

"I know it."

"I heard them fighting with him, and then..." he lowered his voice. "Skorce said he would never use a sacred TimeStone. They hit him. His face was bleeding." Thinking about it made Kirrin angry and sad at the same time. "You were away." This was an accusation.

"I had to go. I was summoned to the King before he grew too ill." Sandor's patient voice soothed him. "Do you know what a TimeStone is?"

Kirrin shook his head. "No. But they said it would help them find her. They said Lady Gorgon—"

"Lady Gorwyn? The Queen's sister?"

Kirrin nodded. "Yes, her. They said she ordered it. She ordered Skorce. He didn't want to do it." Kirrin remembered something else. "What's a rooned world?"

Sandor groaned.

"Ruined," he said. "They're worlds we used to explore before they grew too dangerous. Tell me, how do you know all this? Where were you?"

Kirrin grinned. "I was Me. I was behind the books. No one saw me. I like being Me."

Kirrin knew Sandor understood. "Me" meant his Alter state. As a kitten, he could hide in the smallest of places.

"And what did you do?" Sandor prompted.

"I decided to help the baby. Skorce held a shiny stone and said something I couldn't hear. Then a moving picture came on the floor. On the floor! Ward and him – the dead one – they kept telling Skorce to make it more worser. I could see a lot of rain and a river and trees falling. They said she hadn't drownded yet so they'd have to go in and make sure she did..." Kirrin frowned at the memory. "And to make sure her mum and dad died too. That was bad. I didn't want them to do that."

Sandor nodded. "Good lad." He laid his hand on Kirrin's shoulder. "Then what?"

"They told Skorce to give them the keys." Kirrin shrugged. It was hard to explain what he didn't understand. "I couldn't see any keys. But you know his big silver cup? The one with the shiny stones in it, like these?" Kirrin held up the silver chain round his neck; the crystal shimmered. "He gave them one each. Said to keep them safe or they'd never get back. They sat on the great big stone on the floor, with the picture in the middle and they just did this—"

"No!" Sandor grabbed his hand as it reached towards the crystal. "Don't twist that, Kirrin. There's a chance you might activate it again. Just leave it. The crystal is a Key. It opens a way into another world. Never, ever, twist it."

Kirrin thought Sandor was making too big a fuss. "I only did what they did," he protested. "Anyway, then they slid into the picture in the stone on the floor. Right into it, as if it was a well. It was scary. When they were gone, Skorce went into the other chamber and I crept over to the moving picture.

"I could see Ward and the Assam man in the picture in the stone. They were in the river, and a cradle was bobbing about. There were trees sloshing about too. So I took a shiny sto... I took a crystal out of Skorce's big silver cup and put my feet over the stone and looked in. Water's horrible." Kirrin shivered. "I was scared. But they were swimming closer to the baby, so I just – I twisted the top the way they did and then jumped. It felt funny, all black and glittery, and I got a bit dizzy. I tried to get onto a tree near the cradle, but I didn't get as near as I wanted."

"Yes, translation is difficult," Sandor said. "It's never precise."

Kirrin didn't understand that. But Sandor sighed with a mixture of exasperation and admiration, and Kirrin knew the worst was over. He felt relieved that they weren't going to hang him after all.

"It was bravely done, Kirrin, bravely done. But you could have died. Or lost the crystal and never got home. You could have been stuck there."

"But they were going to kill her!" Kirrin leant in closer to the child's face. She was so good. She just lay there gazing at them.

Kirrin swivelled his head from Sandor to the dead man lying in the reeds, then back to Sandor, with dramatically arched eyebrows. "What would you have done?"

Sandor scowled but Kirrin knew it was good-natured; they understood each other.

"How did you know how to bring her back through?"

Kirrin shrugged again. "The crystal... Key thing... It wouldn't turn any further, so I twisted it the other way. I caught the top of it in my teeth and turned till I heard it click. I thought of Thorn, and you, and Aquila. I wanted to see you all again."

Aquila had been standing silent all this time. She cocked her head to one side and looked at Kirrin.

"I think she's surprised to hear that," said Sandor. "The way you play sometimes, perhaps she feels you don't appreciate her. Like when you pounce on her, or try to swat her."

"That's only a game. She knows. I just wish she could talk out loud and not only in my head."

"Just be glad you can hear her in your head." Sandor laid his hand gently on Aquila's tawny hair. "I wish I could."

Aquila's face remained impassive. She blinked.

"Well," Sandor sighed. "You were lucky. But how did she end up in the pool alone?"

Kirrin shook his head. "I don't know. It was night-time when I tried to come back. But when I woke up it was morning and I was in that tree. My head hurt – look."

He tipped his head back for Sandor to see the dried blood, though he was sure most of it must have rubbed off in his tussle with Ward.

"That'll mend," Sandor said. "Though I can't say the same for your shirt. You've done very well. But, just give me that for now." Sandor eased the chain and crystal over Kirrin's still-damp hair and put it into his tunic pocket.

"That's not fair. I want to keep it," Kirrin protested.

But Sandor was adamant. "No, I'll give it back to Skorce." His voice grew hard. "He's another with a lot of explaining to do."

Aquila began moving from one foot to the other. She turned her face to Sandor, then to the sky, then back to Sandor.

Sandor nodded. "Yes, of course. Off you go. But one more thing..." He stayed her. Already, Kirrin saw soft down rippling along her arms and shoulders, brown bars darkening paler feathers across her chest. Her face grew sharper, her eyes hardening to golden beads. He knew she was eager for the air. He heard her sharp voice in his head. "Sky. Wind."

"Light the cooking fire and give Madelaine the milk jug," Sandor said. "She'll know to warm it for our return."

Aquila's form shifted in a blur of beak and feathers. Kirrin watched her take flight, circling above them for a moment, wings beating soundlessly, a flash of brown and white against a cloudless sky. She gave a high call and soared over the autumn trees.

Kirrin saw Sandor shift his weight on his knees. He was getting cramp kneeling in the lumpy tufts of grass.

"Are you all right?" Kirrin laid his hand on Sandor's shoulder. Sandor's face was grim, but he gave a tight smile. "I'm fine. And so is she, thanks to you."

Sandor stood, careful of the baby he held. He stretched his back as if it ached. "I'm too old for this," he said. "Right, then. Enough talking. You've proved you're a good soldier, and a good soldier never leaves weapons. So, pick up that dagger, and the sword. I'll come back later and deal with the body. We must get you home and into dry clothes."

Kirrin had forgotten he was still wet. No wonder he was shivering. He followed Sandor up the tree-lined path to Thorn Rise and home. Then he thought of something else. "What's her name?"

"See those squiggles carved into the head of her cradle? That's her name. Megan."

Kirrin peered at them. They looked strange. "Megan." Kirrin liked her name. He liked putting his lips together to say it. "Megan."

He looked down. The baby was gurgling soft nonsense. He touched his knuckles to her cheek, as he had seen Sandor do. His hand was dark against her skin. At least she didn't look like wax any more; a hint of peach tinged her face now, her lips were pink. Kirrin looked up to find Sandor smiling at him.

"She's a good baby," said Kirrin. He'd heard other people say that of children and it always brought nods of agreement.

To Kirrin's delight, Sandor nodded on cue. "Yes, she is."

They walked the woodland path in companionable silence. Kirrin saw Sandor frowning at the squiggles on the cradle.

"What?" Kirrin asked. He wondered what the Assam man's sword tasted like and licked the hilt. It had a bitter metallic taste.

"It's Elandan script," Sandor said, puzzled. Then he turned to Kirrin. "Give me that before you slice your tongue off." Sandor put the cradle down. He tucked Ward's dagger under his belt, then took the sword. Kirrin picked up the cradle with both hands and kicked golden leaves up as he walked by Sandor's side. "Can I have that sword when I get home? The Assam man won't need it now."

Sandor frowned. "What is this Assam man you keep talking about?"

"Him, in the reeds. The dead one. He won't need his sword any more."

Sandor let out a bellow of a laugh. "He's an *assassin*. They kill for gain."

Kirrin didn't mind the laugh. He let Sandor tousle his damp hair without protest. "Can I have the sword?"

"No."

Kirrin tutted in annoyance so Sandor would know how unfair he was being.

"Why is the King sick? Did he fall?"

"No, he's just gravely ill."

Kirrin's mind jumped again. "What'll we feed her? Mice?"

"Milk," said Sandor.

"Milk's good. I like milk."

"And we keep her warm."

Kirrin nodded. "I know a spot by the hearth. I'll make room for her. She can sleep with me."

"No, we'll feed her and get her warm and then we must take her back where she came from."

Kirrin didn't like that idea. "But I found her! I'm keeping her."

"You can't. She doesn't belong here." Sandor didn't seem open to negotiation on this. He had on his "closed" face. Kirrin had never managed to breach it yet.

He tried anyway. "But I saved her."

"You did."

"So she's mine."

Kirrin thought he saw Sandor's mouth twitch in a smile, but it was fleeting.

"Only you are yours," said Sandor. "And the only person Megan belongs to is Megan. Remember that. You saved her once, and now we must save her again – we'll dry her, feed her and return her to her own world."

"But it's forbidden!" Kirrin felt triumphant. "You said so. We can't go back to her world. We'll be secuted." Now she would have to stay.

To Kirrin's disgust, Sandor smiled widely. "Sometimes even good rules must be broken. We'll tiptoe in and tiptoe out again. They won't even know we were there. She needs her own world. And we need Skorce and his sorcery to make sure she's five years old when we put her back there."

"But I want her in my world." Kirrin burned with the injustice of it. He was prepared to let the assassin's sword go, but not this. This was important. Megan was important. His belly ached at the thought of losing her. "I found her!"

Again, Sandor bent his frame down to Kirrin's level. He was sympathetic but unyielding. "You can never own a person as you own the mice you catch. If you care for Megan, you must do what's best for her. Now, another thing a good soldier must learn, is to obey a superior officer."

Kirrin looked straight into Sandor's eyes. "What's that?"

"Me. Now come on; we have a child to feed."

Sandor straightened and turned for the path home. Behind him, Kirrin stuck out his tongue. *One day,* he thought, *I'll be a superior officer.*

One day I'll bring her back. Just wait.

Behind them the autumn leaves continued to fall. Winter was coming.

Felicity Crentsil | Innocent Sydney

Chapter One

Start with a question, she said. Something like, How did I get here, or why do I think I need counselling? I'll go with the first one. I know the answer to that. All of this started with Gemma, the first day she turned up at my school.

Monday morning, after the register, Miss Parry came over to our table.

"Sydney and May," she said. "Could you go down to reception, please? We have someone new joining our tutor group."

May was tired, same as every morning. Her heels hammered into the silence of the empty corridors. "Who starts one week before the end of term?" she said. "I can't be bothered to be enthusiastic about school. I just want to get out of here."

I didn't mind doing it. I was curious about people who chose to come to Hertvale, when half the people who lived here couldn't wait to get out. "We'll probably just have to show her the classrooms, where to get food and where the toilets are," I said. "You can cope with that, can't you?"

"I suppose," she said. She let out a huge yawn. "Who changes schools halfway through final year, though?"

"We'll see," I said as we turned the corner into reception.

Sitting on the sofa was a pretty, blonde girl. She smiled as we walked over to her.

"Hi," I said. "I'm Sydney and this is May."

"Hey," said May.

The girl stood up. She was a few inches taller than me. And thin.

"I'm Gemma," she said. She had a sweet, almost childish voice.

We stood there for a moment, all smiles, taking each other in. Gemma was very pretty. She had green eyes, high cheekbones and a cute little nose.

"Come on then," said May, like she was about to take us for walkies.

We headed back to class.

"So you two are the safe ones around here," Gemma said.

May and I frowned. Safe. Did she mean boring?

"I mean," Gemma said, "they don't send anyone who's trouble or anything to get new girls, do they? At least, they didn't at my old school."

"So who did they send?" May asked.

"Nice girls like me," she said. She had a big grin on her face. "They used to make me show them their classes and the toilets and stuff."

I caught May's eye and we smiled.

"I appreciate what you're doing," said Gemma. "I promise I won't cling on to you for the rest of the year."

She was nice. I thought.

We got back to class and everyone looked up as we walked in. Gemma was being inspected by the guys and the girls. May and I went back to our desk, while Miss Parry pounced on Gemma and half dragged her to the board.

"Everyone," she said.

She opened her mouth to speak again and was drowned out by the bell, scraping chairs and more important conversations. May and I hung back.

"I'll introduce you after lunch," Miss Parry said to Gemma. "Do you have your timetable?"

"Yes," she said. She pulled a folder out of her bag and opened it. Double Maths in room 12G."

"Same as me," I said.

"Upper set," said May. "I'm off then. "See you at break, Syd," She was almost out the door when she turned around. "You too, Gemma."

Gemma and I walked down the main corridor. "So have you just moved here?" I said. It's what I always asked.

"Yeah," she said. "My parents didn't want to live in the city, even though they've both kept jobs there."

"Which city?" I said.

"Bristol."

It was the same old story. Bristol is forty-five minutes away. People see Hertvale as the perfect place for village life, that's still within reach of civilisation.

"My sister Audrey lives in Bristol," I said. "She's at uni there."

"Really?"

The conversation ended as we got to class, although I think we'd both run out of things to say. We were late. Everyone else was already sitting down.

"Good of you to join us, Sydney," said Miss Delaney.

She's the only teacher who never warmed to me. Cold is all she's capable of.

"Sorry, Miss," I said. "I had to go to reception to meet Gemma. She's new."

"Yes, thank you, Sydney. I am aware of who I ordinarily teach in this class."

Nobody sniggered or laughed. Sounds like that are never heard in Miss Delaney's classroom.

"Sit down, then," she said.

We took an empty desk at the front. I caught Cassie's eye and shrugged before I sat down. Cassie and I sat together in that class but I couldn't leave Gemma on her own.

We didn't speak during the lesson. No one did, unless they were asking a question. I waited outside with Gemma, once the bell rang, to catch Cassie.

"Hey," I said. "Sorry. Thanks for trying to save me a seat. This is Gemma. Gemma, this is Cassie."

"Hi," said Cassie. "Miss Delaney is pretty much the ice queen of the school, so if you survived her you'll be fine."

I spotted May heading towards us.

"See you later, Syd," said Cassie. She's seen her friends, too. "Nice to meet you, Gemma."

May and Cassie stopped to say hello, halfway down the corridor, before May caught up with us.

"Let's eat," she said. "You can get something healthy, like fruit from the hall, or there's a vending machine for crisps and chocolate." She was looking at Gemma.

"Oh, chocolate. Without question," she said.

May smiled. "I like this girl."

We all bought a packet of crisps and a chocolate bar. I couldn't help wondering how she stayed as thin as May. They were both wearing short skirts and a fitted shirt. I wore trousers. Nobody needed to see my tree trunks.

It was cold outside, so we stayed indoors and just walked around the school. May and I pointed out the hall, classrooms and, of course, the girls' loo. We laughed about it.

"Thanks for the guided tour," said Gemma.

"No problem," said May. "What have you got next?"

Gemma checked her timetable. "Geography, in 1F, so that's upstairs, right?"

"Yeah," I said. "We might as well head up there now." There were a few minutes left of break.

"Do you guys have that too?" she asked.

"No," said May. "I'm afraid you're on your own for that one."

"Cassie's in that class, though," I said.

That was how it worked. In the first week, time was spent with us and we made introductions. The girl got to know people in different classes and, by Friday, found the ones she was going to stay friends with.

"Right, okay," Gemma said. She sounded disappointed, rather than nervous.

"We can meet for lunch," I said. "Remember where the hall is?"

"Yes," she said. She was smiling again. "Next to reception, isn't it? Shall I meet you outside there?"

"Yeah, sure," said May.

The bell rang.

"See you then," I said.

I found myself worrying about Gemma during class. May was right about starting halfway through this year. It was one week until Christmas break. After that the countdown to exams would start. Gemma had been fine in Maths, but, I was thinking, it must be hard trying to step into time with every subject. No one was thinking about making friends. We were focusing on GCSEs. The ones who weren't interested in grades and were already bored might take an interest in Gemma, but I had a feeling she didn't belong with any of those groups.

Gemma seemed okay at lunch, though, when May and I asked how she was getting on.

"It's weird," she said. "The syllabus is the same but it's all different, like, the way you approach it here."

"Well, I couldn't do it," said May. "I'd be too stressed out if I had to change schools now."

"I had no choice," said Gemma. She shrugged like it was no big deal. "If I stress about it I'll just fail anyway, so I have to get on with it."

We finished eating. Gemma cleared her plate. I ate the same amount as them, but I knew only my arse would grow.

"So," said Gemma. "Who should I give Christmas cards to and who do I avoid at this place?"

"That's up to you," I said. "Give them to whoever you get on with, I suppose."

May rolled her eyes. "You'll have to excuse Sydney. She's a freak of nature, being a teenage girl who doesn't bitch."

"Ha, ha," I said.

"Don't worry, Syd, it's part of your charm," said May. She turned back to Gemma. "As you know, Sydney and I are wonderful and should be at the top of your list."

Gemma laughed. "Okay," she said.

May carried on. "I'm on the netball team and most of us are okay."

"Oh," said Gemma. "Is there room for anyone else? I played on the wing at my old school. Attack or defence."

Exercise. I'd forgotten. That's what they did different.

May and Gemma talked about the team and May gave a rundown of the various girls, groups and guys in our year.

She mentioned Ben, but not the way I felt about him.

Gemma took it all in. I gave my opinion every now and again, and by the end of break it was clear. The place Gemma belonged was with us. I liked her. A lot. So did May. That's what made everything that's happened so hard.

I think if we'd stuck to rooms, the hall and the toilets, I wouldn't be in this situation now. We didn't do that, though. We arranged to go shopping.

Chapter Two

The three of us clicked, over the rest of that week. Gemma spent time with me, May or both of us, in class and at breaks. She became friends with Cassie and a couple of other girls too. Christmas cards went out on Friday. May and I did get special ones.

"For not ditching me the first chance you got," she said.

"Thank you," I said. It was sweet of her.

"As if we would do such a thing," said May.

"Are we still on for tomorrow?" Gemma asked.

"Yeah, of course." I said. "We'll come and get you and take you on the grand tour of Hertvale."

"It'll take about ten minutes," said May, "but we can get a hot chocolate afterwards and goss about your first week here."

"It's gone so fast," said Gemma. "It's been good, though."

"I've got to go," I said. My dad was pulling up outside the school. He beeped the horn, even though I've told him not to, a million times. Gemma and May waved as I got in.

"Is that your new friend?" he asked. He said it like we were all five years old.

"Yes, Dad," I said.

"How was your day?" he said, as we drove away.

"Okay. They've given us a load of work to do over the holidays, which is a pain, so I'll have to get that out of the way."

"You should expect to work hard, Sydney," he said. "This is a very important year."

Talk about stating the obvious. "Yes, Dad," I said. I turned on the stereo to see what he was listening to. It was *Christmas Hits*. Great. I'd been listening to the songs on that album for far too many years. There's only one song that I can stand. Dad hates it. It's one of those songs that divide the nation. I turned up the volume and started to sing.

"I don't want a lot for Christmas."

"No, Sydney," said Dad.

"There is just one thing I need." I saw Dad's hands twitch. "You can't cover your ears, Dad, you'll crash the car." The sleigh bells had kicked in and I started belting out the words and dancing in my seat. Dad was laughing and cringing at the same time. I sounded bad but I didn't care. I was enjoying myself.

Dad managed to get his revenge, with Slade, before we pulled onto the driveway. I got out as fast as I could and left him drumming on the steering wheel.

I did my usual after-school routine: dumped my bag, went to the kitchen and put the kettle on. I liked to have a sandwich, a packet of crisps or some biscuits with my tea.

"Do you want anything, Dad?" I asked as he came in.

"No, thanks," he said. "Your mum is on duty until nine o'clock to-night so I thought I'd make dinner."

"Oh," I said. "What are you making?" I tried to sound enthusiastic. Dad can't cook. He likes to try, but nothing ever turns out right. By right, I mean edible.

"I thought I'd try something simple," he said. "Maybe have a go at spaghetti bolognese."

"Sounds great," I said. I made two, extra-thick, cheese and salami sandwiches and went up to my room. After I'd eaten, I got out my home-work and made a list of what I needed to do for each subject, so I could tick it off as I went along.

May thought me doing that kind of thing was sad and, to use her exact words, "so anal", but I had to do it. I'd forget or do the wrong thing otherwise. Plus, for as long as I could remember, the first thing my mum said when she got home was "Hello" and "Have you done your home-work?" The way she used to go on at Audrey, if she said "No" or "Not yet", wasn't something I ever wanted to experience.

I find Maths and Science the hardest, so I started with the Maths. It took me two hours. I had to keep checking I'd done it right, but I wouldn't know for sure until it had been marked.

I couldn't believe it, but there was actually a pleasant smell coming from the kitchen. Mum wasn't due home for another few hours, so there was still plenty of time for it to go wrong.

Six o'clock meant I was allowed to make calls on the house phone, so I rang May. She picked up straight away.

"Four more sleeps to go," she said. "I'm so excited now we're out of school."

I laughed. "You were excited anyway. You've been counting sleeps for weeks."

"Yeah, I know," she said. "It's Christmas."

May had been acting like a little kid at Christmas for far too long.

"Anyway," I said, "I wanted to ask if you're going to get Gemma a present."

"I don't know," said May. "Do you think she'll get us anything?"

"May," I said. "Does it matter?"

"Of course it does. I've done all my Christmas shopping and I'm not going out to get anything else if I don't have to. Not that she isn't lovely. I have no idea what she'd like, anyway."

"I don't know," I said. "I was thinking, we could keep an eye out tomorrow for anything she seems to like."

"Yeah, I suppose," said May.

"How about we get her a joint present? I think she'd appreciate it."

"Okay," said May. "You can buy it and I'll give you the money back. I don't understand how you can leave your shopping so late."

"And I think you're a freak for doing it so early, but there you go." We have the same conversation every year, and every year I go Christmas Eve eve shopping with my Mum and Audrey. It's a tradition.

"My mum's calling me," said May. "See you tomorrow?"

"Yeah," I said. "I'll be round at ten."

We said our goodbyes and I realised I had nothing to do until the food was ready. I tried to read and re-read our Shakespeare text, but I wasn't in the mood. I was bored. Various gatherings had been organised by people from school, to mark the end of term, but I knew there was no point going to any of them. They would all be over before they got started.

I read a book and went on the internet and almost died of boredom and starvation before I heard the front door go at last. I went downstairs and Mum was hanging her coat on the hallstand.

"Hello, Sydney," she said. "Is your homework done?"

"Yes, Mum," I said.

She let out a huge sigh. "Every year," she said. "Every single year, someone from your school thinks they can get away with under-age drinking." She took off her shoes and her badge. "This is a small village. You think they'd realise that we will find out about their parties."

I just nodded and smiled. Mum's the reason I've never done anything reckless or dangerous or fun, unlike most people my age. It's her job to stop that kind of thing happening.

"What's your father doing?" she asked.

"Cooking," I said.

She groaned and went to open the kitchen door. A strong smell cloaked us. Burning. Dad was nowhere to be seen.

"Get the takeaway menus, Syd," she said. "Three, two, one," she counted down and the loud bleep made me jump. "Turn off the smoke alarm as well, please?"

We all saw the funny side, although Dad insisted we would have had a perfect meal if he hadn't fallen asleep on the sofa. I told Mum about going shopping with May and Gemma, over our Chinese.

"So you think I should get her something?" I said.

"Yes, sweetheart," she said. "I think it's a lovely idea. Find out her family's names and we can send them a Christmas card. Make them feel welcome."

"Okay," I said.

We watched a film after dinner. Only a tiny part of me that thought it was sad to be spending a Friday night in with my parents, because it was nice.

I think that's the kind of day I'm meant to think about. I'm supposed to remember the reasons I was happy. Singing in the car. School was over. It was Christmas. Having dinner and chatting to Mum and Dad.

Mum doesn't talk to me the way she did before. Dad tries. Too hard, sometimes. I think they both need counselling too, but at least they talk to each other. About me and what I did.

It's strange the way one person, and one act, can shift so many lives.

I fell asleep that night, wondering about Gemma. What she was like and what she would want for Christmas. I was looking forward to going out with her and May the next day.

Chapter Three

Dad offered me a lift to May's in the morning, but I chose to walk. I did get some exercise. I liked to listen to my music and it was only fifteen minutes away from our house.

May opened the door looking very chic, in a red crochet hat over her bob, her black fitted winter coat and matching red gloves and scarf. I was just wearing a big black puff coat which made me look even more huge, but it was warm.

"Look at you," I said. "We're only walking up the high street."

"I'm cold," she said. "It is December, you know."

I just shook my head and laughed. I was used to May's morning grumps.

Gemma's house was another ten minutes on from May's. It was one of the terraced cottages a few roads back from the high street. It even had a quaint wooden gate leading to the path and ivy hugging the stone front wall. I'm not surprised her parents had fallen in love with it. I couldn't resist using the old brass knocker, even though there was a doorbell.

"I'll get it, I'll get it," we heard this voice call.

The front door opened and a little girl with wavy blonde hair and big green eyes stared up at us.

"Gemma, you shrank," said May.

"I'm not Gemma," she said, like May was the silliest person in the whole world. "I'm Bella," she announced.

"Nice to meet you, Bella," I said. "I'm Sydney and this is my friend May."

"Hello," she said. "I've got a friend too. Her name is Celeste."

Gemma appeared at the top of the stairs. "Bella," she said. "You could have invited them in. Go and find Mum."

"Okay," said Bella. She skipped off into another room.

Gemma came downstairs and said hi. She was wearing a pure white puff coat which didn't make her look massive at all. She'd brushed her hair all back and she slid on baby-pink earmuffs.

"Bye," she shouted and came out, without waiting for a reply. She pulled baby-pink gloves out of her pocket and put those on, too.

I was the only one who didn't look ready for a catalogue shoot. Pink earmuffs should look ridiculous on anyone, but Gemma looked like one of those models who get paid to laugh and frolic in the snow. I made a mental note to make more effort with my appearance.

"Your little sister's cute," I said.

"She's a pain," said Gemma. "All she keeps going on about is her new best friend Celeste."

"You mean you haven't been raving about me and Syd all week?" said May.

"Oh, of course I have," said Gemma. She grinned.

"Are you ready for your tour?" I asked.

"Yes, I am," she said. "I'll have a look around today and then get my presents on Christmas Eve."

"Ugh," said May. "Another one."

Gemma frowned and looked at me.

"May hates last-minute shopping," I said.

"Right," said Gemma. "I don't usually leave it so late, but I just haven't had a chance, what with moving and everything."

"Your house looks so gorgeous," I said.

"You should see the inside," said Gemma. "It's a bombsite. Bella cried yesterday because we couldn't find the boxes with the tree and the decorations."

"May would cry now if that happened to her," I said.

She didn't deny it.

We'd been walking for less than ten minutes and we were already on the high street.

"This is it," said May. "The centre of Hertvale."

It's just one straight long road with shops either side.

"We can walk up *and* down, and if you feel compelled to go in anywhere, just shout," said May.

A lot of people were coming and going, in and out of shops carrying loads of bags. They all seemed to be rushing. The three of us just strolled along.

"This is our bookshop," I said. "They sell beautiful notepads and diaries in there, as well." Gemma just nodded and we kept walking.

"A.N.A. is the best clothes shop we have," said May. "Ariadne, the owner, grew up here, went away to uni to study fashion, and when she came back Syd's dad gave her the money to open the shop."

"Your dad gave her the money?" said Gemma.

"It was a loan," I said. "He runs the branch over there." I pointed to the bank on the other side of the road.

"Oh, okay," said Gemma. She turned back to A.N.A. and looked through the window. "Can we go in here?"

"Yeah," said May.

It was busy. There was a queue at the till and at the changing rooms.

"This stuff's amazing," said Gemma. She pulled out an aquamarine vest top with silver thread stitched in waves across the chest. "Five pounds?" she said. She looked at the price tag, at us, and back at the price tag. "Is that all?"

May nodded. "It's all made by students from sixth forms and by Ariadne. Everything is one-off, which is a good thing in a place as small as this."

"I'd love to own a shop like this," said Gemma.

"You like clothes, then?" I asked. Present-buying bells were ringing.

"Unique stuff, like this, yeah," she said. "I used to have to customise most stuff I bought from The Mall or Cabot Circus."

We spent about five minutes in there before it got too hard to move and we had to go. May and I showed Gemma where to get stuff like candles, smellies and hand-made jewellery. We told her about the Sunday market for bags and May pointed out the electronics store where all the guys hover and get their computer games. Ben and his mates weren't around.

"Have you left anyone broken-hearted in Bristol?" May asked.

"No," said Gemma. "I didn't have a boyfriend."

"Well we're not exactly spoilt for choice around here, but you never know," said May.

"As you can see," I said, as we crossed to the other side of the road, "these are all the food shops. We have the butcher's, the veg shop and my personal favourite, the bakery. Sally makes the most gorgeous banana bread." I waved through the window. May and I had been waving and saying hello to various people we knew all morning.

"It's great," said Gemma. "You guys know everyone, don't you? Like, all the shop owners."

"Pretty much," said May. "Give it time, though. The novelty of local shops does wear off. My mum drives out to the supermarket once a fortnight, but don't tell anyone."

Gemma laughed. "My lips are sealed."

It was freezing cold, so we went into Georgie's Café and joined the back of the queue. All of the tables were taken, a lot of them by kids from school. I spotted a group of boys from our year at a table by the counter. My heart started pounding at my chest like it wanted to break out and go over there. In three seconds flat I went from being frozen to desperate to get out of my huge stifling coat.

That's the effect Ben had on me.

I undid my coat and wished I'd put on something a lot more exciting than a cream polo-neck jumper that morning.

I thought it was my imagination when he looked up and smiled. There had to be someone behind me it was meant for, so I didn't smile back. May and Gemma were standing next to me and I felt like such a frump compared to them.

"What are you staring at?" said May. "Oh," she said when she realised.

She couldn't have been any louder or more obvious if she'd tried. The queue was moving along and we were just a few steps from their table. We moved up right alongside them and my skin was on fire.

"Hey, Sydney."

I turned to look and Ben's best friend, Nathan, was shaking his head at me.

"Your mum is harsh," he said. "She was like Robocop, shutting everything down last night, like 'step away from the alcohol'." He put on this stupid voice and they all laughed.

I was ready to die on the spot. "Yeah, well," I said. "You lot are lucky. Try living with her."

May was ordering our drinks. "Three hot chocolates, please, with marshmallows."

"To go," I barked. I turned around and walked out.

May and Gemma came out a couple of minutes later. May handed me my drink.

"You OK?" she said.

I nodded.

"What was that about?" asked Gemma.

I thought it was kind of rude of her.

May sighed. "Syd's mum is the law around here," she said.

"What, she's a policewoman?"

"Yep," said May.

"Cool," said Gemma.

I narrowed my eyes and glared at her. "No, it isn't," I snapped. I started walking off, but I stopped a few shops down and let them catch up. My temper's more like a sparkler than dynamite. It fizzles out fast. "Sorry," I said.

"She gets a hard time for it sometimes," said May.

"Oh," said Gemma. "I'm sorry, Sydney."

"It didn't help that there was a certain special someone in there, either," May said.

"Who?"

"Ben," said May.

I wish she'd never said anything about him in front of Gemma, now that I know for sure Ben wasn't smiling at me.

"Who's Ben?" Gemma asked.

Roy Davis | Scales

Chapter One

Abra Cadabra

"Ladies and gentlemen," said Gabe, "as you can see, there is nothing in my hat." He was talking to his empty backyard.

The backyard didn't respond, of course. But if he concentrated real hard, he could imagine he was performing at the Pantages Theater. Instead of a neatly trimmed lawn surrounded by gravel, he saw a packed auditorium, with an audience all dressed up in suits and evening gowns. Chandeliers hung from the ceiling. The cool grass beneath his feet became the theater's hardwood stage, and the chirping of crickets was the excited murmur of the crowd.

He held out his top hat so his audience could inspect it. "Empty," he said. "For now. But with a little magic, even an ordinary top hat can become a doorway to another—"

The hat twitched in his hands. Marshmallow the rabbit leapt out and landed on the grass. He grabbed at her, but she was too fast. She took off across the backyard, celebrating her freedom by jumping into the air and doing little twists.

Darn it! It'd take him forever to catch her. And he couldn't ask Mom for help because he wasn't supposed to have his sister's rabbit out after dark. But when else could he practice? During the day a nosey neighbor or, worse, another student might spot him. He was in seventh grade, and seventh-graders didn't *do* magic.

"Fine," Gabe said out loud. "Nobody wants to see a stupid rabbit trick, anyway." Marshmallow stopped to chew on a blade of grass. He took a step towards her, holding out the hat. "In fact," he continued, "you're lucky I'm even practicing with you. The magicians on TV are all lighting themselves on fire and getting frozen in ice and *maybe* levitating a few cards, but hats and rabbits are so last century." He took another step. Marshmallow raised her head and stared back at him, her black eyes reflecting the porch light. He reached for her, but she darted away, heading for the safety of the bamboo plants that grew in the gravel at the back of the yard.

Maybe reverse psychology didn't work on rabbits.

He glanced at his house as he put on his top hat and fished flash paper out of his pocket. His parents didn't like him practicing with fire. If he got caught now, he'd get in double-trouble for the flash paper *and* for letting the rabbit get loose.

"A few lucky people," Gabe said, talking to his imaginary audience again, "have money to burn." With a flourish he produced his practice dollar bill, which was very crinkled and singed on one end. He held the dollar out in front of him and snapped his fingers, lighting the flash paper nestled in his palm.

The paper was supposed to send up a little ball of flame, which would distract an audience long enough for him to fold the dollar bill and hide it between his fingers. But instead the dollar bill caught fire, singeing his thumb.

He dropped the money and stuck his thumb in his mouth. "Ow, ow, ow!" He grimaced and danced around in a little circle. The dollar continued to burn, catching the grass on fire. Gabe stamped on the burning money to put it out. Then he remembered he was barefoot.

"Ow!" He said again, holding his foot. The grass was really burning now. He hopped over to the rabbit hutch, grabbed Marshmallow's water dish, and dumped the water onto the grass. The fire hissed out, sending up a big cloud of white smoke. He coughed and waved his hand in front of his face. Now there was a plate-sized black spot in his dad's perfect lawn. It smelled like wet campfire.

A bright light came on, throwing Gabe's shadow across the yard. Great, he thought, his parents were coming to yell at him. But the circle of light was too intense to be coming from the kitchen door. It was bright as a camera flash and big around as a swimming pool. And it moved. The light slid silently off of him and glided across the backyard. At the edge of the yard it illuminated the bamboo stand and one frightened rabbit, then slipped over the back fence and lit up the bonsai trees and topiary animals in his neighbor's backyard.

Another circle of light appeared on a roof three houses down, then another on the yard next door. Gabe didn't freak out—he knew what was happening. In Southern California high-speed car chases were as regular as Mondays. He looked up and tried to find the news helicopters.

City lights reflected back from LA's smog layer, making the sky glow a dull orange even at night. Four sleek, black helicopters hovered in slow circles overhead. They weren't like anything he'd seen before. They ran almost silently, with just a hushed purr from their rotors. And now that he was paying attention, he realized even the crickets in the backyard had gone quiet.

Then the porch light went out.

"C-come on, Marshmallow," he called. "Time to go in." He took a step towards the bamboo stand. The rabbit was just a little spot of white in the dark. Gabe rubbed his eyes and tried to blink away the after-image of the searchlights.

A great cracking, crunching noise, like branches snapping, sounded from down the block. He hopped over to his fence—his foot still hurt—and peered through the iron bars. But it was too dark to see anything. All the porch lights had gone out in that part of the neighborhood, too.

Closer, he heard a tremendous splash, like a huge creature hitting the water. That had to be the swimming pool three houses down.

Even closer there was an eruption of squeaking and squawking. The aviary next door! The squawking quit just as suddenly as it started, and again he was wrapped in silence.

He backed away from the fence. Maybe whatever was making all the noise had changed directions. Or maybe it had stopped to snack on the poor birds.

He took another couple steps back and slipped in the patch of burnt, wet grass. He landed painfully on his butt, his teeth snapping together. A large, sinuous shape leapt smoothly over his fence. For a moment it was silhouetted against the orange smog. The creature was big as a horse, but wider across the shoulders. It had bat-like wings and a long, spiked tail. Gabe saw a flash of blue and silver scales—scales?—and then it was towering over him.

Gabe's palms went all sweaty and his heart pounded. It didn't matter that the creature, the *dragon*, standing over him couldn't exist. His body had decided he was scared before his brain did. It was like the old, caveman part of him realized he was being hunted.

I should scream now, he thought. But when he opened his mouth the only thing that came out was a whispery "Eeee..."

He pushed himself backwards across the grass. The dragon kept pace with him, watching him curiously; its horned head cocked to the side. It looked like a cat playing with a mouse.

Gabe reached into his pocket, hoping to find something to distract the monster, but there was no more flash paper left. At the bottom of his pocket he felt a capsule shaped like an oversized vitamin. A smoke bomb! He'd ordered a bunch from a magic store in Arizona, but he'd never used one before. He hadn't even read the directions.

He threw it at the dragon. The pellet bounced off its scales and landed in the wet grass. The dragon made a surprised clicking noise with its mouth. It hopped backwards and crouched down, eyeing the smoke bomb warily.

Nothing happened. The pellet just sat there in the grass. The dragon extended its neck and sniffed. And that's when the smoke bomb began to sizzle like frying bacon. The sizzling got louder, and a big cloud of blue smoke gushed out. The cloud was so thick that it blocked the dragon from view.

Hopefully, that meant it couldn't see Gabe, either.

He struggled to his feet and started limping towards his house. He frantically checked his pockets as he went, but they were empty. He was out of tricks.

With a roar like thunder, the dragon burst through the smoke cloud. It charged straight at Gabe. It opened its mouth wide, revealing double-rows of alligator-sized teeth.

The dragon was lightning-quick; there was no time to run. Gabe closed his eyes and covered his head with his arms. Would it hurt a lot when those huge teeth clamped down on him, or would he die right away?

He waited, but the bite never came. He felt hot breath on his face. It smelled like oranges and dog food.

Gabe slowly took his arms away and opened his eyes. The dragon's head was just inches away from his. It regarded him with its blue, cat-like eyes, then it roared loud and deep like a lion. The sound thumped through Gabe's chest and tingled out along his fingers. And in that roar he could swear he heard words.

A sudden wind stung his face and the grass flattened around him.

Again he was wrapped in that blinding white light. A black helicopter was hovering right above his backyard.

The dragon glanced up at the helicopter, then lowered its head so it was eye to eye with Gabe. Its cat-like pupils contracted in the brightness. It roared once more, and this time Gabe was sure he heard words. In a voice that both thundered like a storm and purred like a lion it said, "Are you a wizard?"

"Wha...?" was all Gabe could manage.

It didn't wait for an answer. With a single leap the dragon cleared half the back yard. Another jump brought it over the fence and out of sight. Gabe watched as first one, then two, then all four of the weird helicopters aimed north in silent pursuit.

His legs gave out and he sat down hard on the grass. The backyard was dark and quiet again, as if nothing extraordinary had happened. One by one the crickets resumed their chirping. Gabe waited for his heart to slow down. His fingers and toes were all tingly with—what was it called? Adrenaline. Wasn't that stuff supposed to help you run? Fat lot of good it did him.

Something cool pressed against the back of his hand and he nearly screamed. "Marshmallow!" he said. He gathered up the rabbit. "Did you see that? Was there a...?" But he already knew the answer. He hadn't imagined it—the dragon footprint in the wet grass was proof.

No, the more important question, the one he was afraid to say out loud, was: Would it come back?

Chapter Two

Conspiracy

Classical music was coming from the dining room stereo. Gabe followed the sound. His mom sat at the dining room table, playing a game of checkers with his eleven-year-old sister, Lindsay. "Time to get ready for dinner," Mom said, without looking up. "Your father will be home any minute with Chinese."

Had she not heard anything? The roaring? The helicopters? Gabe opened his mouth, to tell her what happened, then shut it again. He knew what he must look like—sweaty and covered with grass stains. Did he have any *real* proof he'd seen a dragon? She might think he was making up stories again. That's if she even listened. In his parents' eyes he was practically invisible, and that suited Gabe just fine.

Still, he paused for a moment at the foot of the stairs. His sister looked up, black checker in one hand. He placed his top hat on his head to free his hands and in American Sign Language said, *How are you doing, Mouse?* His sister wore hearing aids. They pushed her ears forward and made her look slightly mousey.

Lindsay rolled her eyes. *Just fine, Houdini*, she signed back. *Mom's letting me win again.* She frowned. *What happened? You look terrible.*

Nothing, he signed. *I... tripped and fell.*

His mom pointed at a blank square on the checkers board and shook her head, her heavily permed curls bouncing. "Oh my," she said. "I forgot to take your king."

Gabe headed up the stairs, frowning to himself. He never let his sister win games just because he felt sorry for her. And, unlike his parents, he never had the urge to talk as he signed. When he and his sister played together, he enjoyed the quiet space that surrounded them.

Upstairs, he tossed his top hat on his bed and clicked his computer out of sleep mode. He checked the evening's news stories. Nothing. He Googled "Dragons Black Helicopters Orange County." All he got were old blogs about UFOs. Maybe the story was too new for the Internet. How could he find out what was happening right this minute?

He dug through his closet, past clothes and comics he'd grown out of, till he found his hand-crank emergency radio. It was a dusty relic from an age when he and his dad had gone camping together. After a dozen cranks the green battery light glowed weakly. He dialed through the AM stations—commercials, a stock report, the Lakers game, traffic. Then he heard:

...armed with tranquilizers are conducting a street-by-street search in north Brea and south Diamond Bar. Residents near the Chino Hills are advised to stay indoors and to call 911 immediately if they see the animal.

Zoo officials are stressing that the rhino is lost and confused, and may be dangerous. No attempt should be made to waylay the animal or draw its attention.

The LA Zoo is one of only three breeding facilities worldwide in the endangered—

"Gabe! Dinner!"

He shut off the radio and joined his family in the dining room, where he picked at his lukewarm noodles without tasting them. His body still felt strangely numb and he didn't have much of an appetite. His parents didn't notice, of course. His dad was asking Lindsay about her day at school, and Mom was translating. Dad only had a five-hundred-word sign vocabulary.

Gabe pushed his food around so it looked like he'd eaten more than he had, then asked to be excused. He rinsed his dishes in the kitchen sink and stared out the window at his now empty backyard. He kept expecting to see helicopter searchlights painting the lawn, or maybe cat-like eyes peering at him from the bamboo stand. But there was just the half-moon of grass revealed by the light of the kitchen window. Beyond that, the back yard lay in darkness.

He couldn't spend his nights like this, watching and waiting for the creature to come back. He had to do *something*; he had to find out what was going on. His only clue so far was that news report from the zoo about the rhino. A dragon and a rhino on the loose in the same neighborhood was just too big of a coincidence. Which meant they were covering up the real story—whoever *they* were.

He turned off the sink and put his dishes in the dishwasher. He thought about Carlos, a strange kid from school. He'd know about the black helicopters. But asking him meant becoming visible, and in junior high that was dangerous.

Chapter Three

Black Horizon

Gabe jogged across the sun-bleached concrete sea of his junior high. Beige, stucco classroom buildings rose from the sea like mountains of dried dirt. He passed a couple of planters—little islands of green—that held stunted palm trees and weeds.

As he ran he dodged between pairs of lumbering eighth-graders, and skirted groups of sixth-grade girls who always seemed to travel in flocks. Nobody stopped him to say "Hi," or ask about his day. Most students didn't even make eye contact with him. Sometimes he had to duck to the side at the last minute to avoid a collision.

Gabe was practically invisible at school. It wasn't a terrible existence, being invisible. At least he didn't attract the attention of the bullies. Even the teachers ignored him. Maybe it was because he was just average-sized and average-looking, with unremarkable sandy-blond hair that was a little long in front. Or maybe it was because he was the new kid in school. Again. His dad had a job in sales—something to do with plastics—and his family moved a lot, so Gabe never stayed in one school for longer than a semester.

Richland Junior High, school number seven, was the weirdest one yet. Southern California weather was so warm and boring that they built schools like outdoor malls—no internal hallways. Student lockers were stuck around the outside of the buildings. It made the passing period between classes sound different. Instead of echoing back from tile walls, the shouts and laughter of students just drifted up and into the sky. Everything sounded muted, like he had water in his ears.

Metal shop with Mr Kim was all the way at the back of the school, next to the chain link fence that separated the junior high from Albertson's. A tall Hispanic boy was leaning against the fence, fingers idly curled in the metal links. A cigarette dangled low from his lips.

Gabe ducked back around the corner of the metal shop building. This was nuts. Carlos had to be the most recognizable weirdo at school. He wore a battered army-surplus jacket, stitched with patches that read

"Military Intelligence is an Oxymoron," "The Truth is Out There," and "Searching for Intelligent Life Forms on THIS Planet." His short black hair was chopped in a vicious crew cut, and his mustache was thick enough to make Gabe believe he'd been held back a grade.

Gabe knew that if another student saw him and Carlos together, he could kiss his invisibility goodbye. He'd instantly be labeled *Friend of the Crazy Guy* or, worse, *Crazy Guy Number Two.*

He took a deep breath and checked once more to make sure the coast was clear. Then, with a half-smile plastered firmly on his face, he walked over to Carlos. Carlos tossed his cigarette and eyed him warily as he approached, like a feral dog guarding a kill.

"Carlos, right?" he asked. "I'm Gabe. Hey, can you look at something real quick? I figured if anyone recognized this helicopter it'd be you." He held out the sketch he'd worked on through his morning classes. "You got a reputation, you know, for being an expert on the weird government—"

Carlos grabbed him, his strong fingers digging into Gabe's shoulder, and pushed him against the shop building. Gabe felt warm stucco biting into his back. Carlos looked around wildly. He even looked up. Then he leant in close and whispered, "Who's been talking about me?" His breath stank of Doritos and cigarettes.

Gabe didn't try to escape. He had to play along with this psycho if he wanted information. "Don't remember who," he said casually, trying not to gag on Carlos's bad breath, "just one or two kids. They weren't talking crap about you or anything. There was, uh, some news special on military secrets and they said Carlos would know if that stuff was true."

"The news?" Carlos asked. He barked a hyena-like laugh and let go of Gabe's shoulder. "Man, the news is part of the government conspiracy. They probably made up a few weird aircraft or spaceships to draw attention away from the *real* military secrets." He leant against the shop wall and fished another cigarette out of his pocket. He put in his mouth without lighting it, then took Gabe's sketch. "Did you draw this?" he asked. "It's not bad."

"Thanks," Gabe said, resisting the urge to rub his sore shoulder. "It's what I saw over my house last night."

"You sure you got the perpendicular wings over the tail rotor right?"

Gabe nodded.

"Then you saw a ghost." When Gabe just frowned, Carlos barked another laugh. "It's a Comanche, man, a stealth helicopter. But that program was cancelled in 2004. Military decided not to make 'em after all." He studied the sketch again and grew serious. "Where do you live?"

"North Brea, up near the Chino Hills."

"Well, I'd stay inside my house if I were you. If you really saw a Comanche, then you got Black Horizon in the neighborhood. When they're around, people either disappear or wind up dead."

As if a dragon wasn't weird enough, Gabe thought. "What's Black Horizon?"

"A military branch that can get away with anything because officially they don't exist."

The final bell rang. Gabe could hear lockers slamming out in the quad. Carlos handed back the sketch.

"Thanks for your—" Gabe began, but Carlos grabbed his wrist and twisted it painfully behind his back. He shoved Gabe face-first into the wall. The hot stucco pressed into Gabe's cheek.

"That's BS about the news special," Carlos whispered from behind him, his mouth just inches away from Gabe's ear. "I'd know if something like that was on TV. Why are you lying? Who sent you?"

Gabe's heart pounded. What had he gotten himself into? He'd been so careful making sure no teachers or kids were around before he had approached Carlos. Now he had no one to call to for help.

He took a deep breath, inhaling the smells of dust and old paint. He forced his body to relax. It was just like escaping from a straitjacket, he tried to tell himself. The trick was to go all loose.

"Answer me," Carlos said, his voice low and threatening. "Who sent you?"

Gabe sidestepped and spun around, letting his arm twist painfully out of place for a moment. But then he was suddenly behind Carlos, pinning his arm. Their positions were reversed.

"Get... off of me!" Carlos said. He struggled. Gabe wouldn't be able to hold him for long. He yanked Carlos's jacket down so that it wrapped around his wrists. Then he let go and ran across the concrete, heading for the quad.

Carlos chased him for a few steps, but the jacket was messing up his balance. He stopped and tried to free his arms. "I'll get you for this!" he shouted. "If Black Horizon doesn't get you first."

Gabe ran and didn't look back.

Chapter Four

Two's a Crowd

Gabe sat at the dining room table and drew dragons in the margins of his geometry book. He'd gotten paper out for his homework, but so far it only had his name and the date on it.

The dining room was his favorite place to come and think. He liked the way the late afternoon sunlight spilled in through the living room's big window and warmed his skin. Lindsay sat next to him, frowning over an astronomy book, her tongue stuck out in concentration. She'd gone to Space Camp last summer, and ever since then she'd been reading books about planets and rockets and even algebra. She wanted to be an astronaut.

Gabe played back last night's encounter in his head and tried to match it with Carlos's information. What did secret government agencies have to do with dragons? Could the dragon be some genetically modified animal? Maybe it *had* been a rhino to start with. But if that was the case, then how could it speak? And why did it think he was a wizard?

He had to find the dragon again and ask it. It was way dangerous, but *not* knowing what was going on would drive him crazy. And, from what Carlos said, Black Horizon sounded like the bad guys. That made the dragon the good guy... didn't it?

Lindsay looked up at him. *You're messing up your book with all those dragons,* she signed.

He'd never seen her use the sign for dragon before. She snarled, and wiggled her fingers next to her mouth to represent dragon fire. The snarl was supposed to be ferocious, but on her it was cute. He laughed.

I've got dragons on the brain, he signed back, exaggerating the snarl. When she frowned, he signed, *I'm trying to figure something out.*

About what happened to you last night?

"What? Nothing happened..." he began out loud, but stopped himself. He hated to lie to his sister. Plus, he just *had* to tell someone the story.

He signed to Lindsay everything that had happened last night, as well as the encounter with Carlos at school.

I'm jealous, she signed when he finished. *You saw a real dragon.*

You don't think I'm crazy? he asked. She shook her head enthusiastically. *Fine,* he said, *then how do I find it again?*

She thought for a moment. *I think it was interested in your magic,* she signed. *Do some more tricks, and maybe it will come back.*

Was it that simple? *It thought I was a wizard,* he signed, *because a rabbit came out of my hat?*

She just gave him a "Duh!" look, then went back to reading.

• • •

The next day at school was a real test of Gabe's invisibility. As he pushed through crowds of students on his way to lunch, he was very conscious of his boots and long pants, because all the other kids were wearing shorts. Instead of a book bag, he carried his bright orange hiking backpack with its dozen straps and zippers. He probably looked like a lost deer hunter or mountain climber.

"Hey, Gabe!" a voice called.

Nobody besides a teacher had said his name in school for years. It sounded so strange in his ears that his pace faltered and he almost tripped over his own feet.

Carlos angled across the quad towards him. He wore the same camouflage jacket and faded jeans. He reminded Gabe of a cartoon character, always wearing the same outfit.

"Hey," he called again, "wait up!" It wasn't a request; it was an order. He was smiling but his eyes were dead serious.

Gabe tried to blend in with a group of students filing out of the math building. Unfortunately, they were mostly sixth-graders. It was like trying to hide behind a crowd of hobbits.

Carlos caught up with him. "What's wrong, man?" he said, shoving him in the shoulder. "Tryin' to avoid me?"

Gabe made a show of looking at a watch that he wasn't wearing. "Uh, I'm running late for lunch detention."

Carlos stared at him for a moment, then he barked a laugh. This time his smile reached his eyes. "You, detention?" he said, loudly. "Yeah, right."

A handful of students were watching them now. The first post-lunch bell had rung, and the quad was quickly filling with shouts and laughter and Gucci book bags, and with kids who might think he and Carlos were actually friends or something.

Gabe turned and ducked around the corner of the math building. There was a dusty alcove with a broken drinking fountain. He squeezed inside. Maybe Carlos would give up and...

"Man, and I thought *I* was paranoid," Carlos said. He stopped in front of the alcove, blocking any escape. He nodded at Gabe's backpack. "Planning on taking a trip?"

"It's a book bag."

"Book bag, my butt. That's for hiking, 'cause it's got one of those camel-packs for drinking water out of."

"Why do you care?" Gabe asked. "Are you going to pin my arm again and try to steal my stuff?"

"Nah, you're too slippery for that, but..." Carlos waited for a couple straggling students to pass, then said in a low voice, "Man, you lied to me yesterday. Right to my face."

Gabe blew hair out of his eyes. "Fine," he said. "There wasn't a TV special on secret military hardware. What was I supposed to say? That everyone knows about you and your... hobby?" He slipped his backpack off his shoulder. If Carlos wanted a fight, he'd give him one. It was almost a relief, actually. If other students saw them fighting, then no one would assume he was Carlos's friend.

Carlos just shook his head and pulled out a cigarette. "Honesty's the best policy, man. *They* tell us enough lies. We don't need to help 'em out by lying to each other."

"Then what do you want from me?"

Carlos barked his hyena laugh. "I'm just here to offer some friendly advice. Yesterday you're asking about stealth helicopters up near the Chino Hills. Today you got hiking gear on. Doesn't take much to put two and two together." He lit his cigarette and blew out an eye-watering cloud of blue smoke. "I warned you," he continued. "Those guys are bad news."

"You mean those Black Horizon guys?" Gabe re-shouldered his backpack. "Carlos, it's broad daylight. They wouldn't do anything in front of witnesses and stuff, even if they're as bad as you say they are." *Which they couldn't be*, Gabe thought. Could they? Were paranoid kids like Carlos sometimes right?

Carlos pressed the button on the drinking fountain. A fan whirred somewhere in its metal guts, but no water came out. "That's the problem with you people," he said, switching the cigarette from one side of his mouth to the other. "You don't take *them* seriously."

That's why I'm coming to the Hills with you."

Ollie Wright | Danny Lambert Tells All

Cast

DANNY LAMBERT - Me, your daily chronicler of my exciting life and times.

THE FLF (*Fruity Little Frodo*) - Nickname of Calvin Kendrick, best friend number one. Elijah Wood lookey-likey with much hibbity-hobbity red hair and of general Shire-ish height and build. Obsessed with the ladies.

GRINGO - Nickname of Simon Wormald, best friend number two. Quiet. A bit moody. A keen and talented archer. Has twice featured in the Sharp-shooter Spotlight section of *On Target* magazine.

Brief Glossary

LITTLE DANNY PLUFFERS - Wind, breaking of; name originated by my mother during my early days on the planet

JAMBONGERS (plural = *JAMBONGI*) - Upstairs area; female (named after a chucklesome brand of biscuits spotted by Me and Gringo on a school trip to Switzerland)

ONE-STRING BED BANJO - Downstairs area; male

KECKSTRETCHER/BANJOVIAL - A banjo salute in appreciation of the female form

Sunday 12th - 1.15am

I really hope Princess Anne shut all her windows tonight. She only lives a few miles away, and I'm worried that the wind might've carried my unfortunate midnight mini-meltdown straight over the common and right into her big house. If this is the case, I hope she wasn't holding anything expensive at the time. This isn't a boast or anything, but I really let rip with the rudies during the incident. I didn't know my mouth was capable of producing such words. Some of them are probably illegal for a 14-year-old boy such as myself to utter. But in my defence I've been very stressed lately and it was the chuffing cows that finally drove me over the edge.

I shall explain, dear diary-thief. Things haven't been particular splendid in Lambertland. My older brother Matty has been held hostage in a super-grim rehabilitation lodge for the last six months, ever since a stroke snuck up on him one afternoon at work, stealing the whole left side of his body from under his nose and leaving him in a miserable life tangle at the age of merely 27. (Countless doctors have told us how massively uncommon it is for someone so young to suffer such a thing, and they've all said it with the same slightly excited boffin expression, as if the rareness of it is something to be a bit chuffed about.)

My dad – from here on known as Rev – is a vicar and he's started smoking again. He reckons none of us know that he's taken up the filthsticks again, after a successful fifteen-year healthy hiatus, but I can certainly see through the old *just going for a walk to clear my head* ploy. Plus, he honks like a tobacconist's cat when he comes back in.

With these two things combined, my mum is currently a bit twitchy and stropulistic and her usually soothing soft tones have recently been replaced by a more serious voice, like a newsreader with really *really* bad news to relay sort of voice. Every time she speaks the theme from *Panorama* plays in my mind. Weird.

And if all this wasn't craparse enough to be going on with, there are incidental miseries floating around. I'm a bit of an insomniac at the moment, which is no fun at all. The village's broadband has died once again – at least a month to fix it this time – so I can't distract myself with the online billiards game that I treasure and adore. And despite promises from one and all that my body would start to fill out about this time I'm still built like a pipe cleaner and I don't know who to complain to about it.

Anyway, earlier on this evening, as I was preparing for a German monologue I'm supposed to deliver for Miss Allen tomorrow, my mind was suddenly invaded by all the nastiness I have just listed. I was trying so hard to push through it and concentrate, pacing up and down rather manically wearing nothing but my undercrackers. (The vicarage has under-floor heating and it's gone a bit wacky and won't turn off properly. It's boiling us alive.)

I wasn't doing too badly until the cows started with all that mooing business. There are a lot of cows in Minchbury. They wander free from the common around this time of year, taking troublemaking trips into the village centre. They enjoy noshing from window boxes and doing their flat shatners on people's doorsteps. And now they've even started scaring old people for fun. I know this because my mum sleeps over at The Cedars rest home one night a week – just in case they need an extra person in an emergency – and the cows have started gurning through the windows late at night and troubling the residents. These are proper ASBO cows I'm talking about. Mooligans, each and every one of them.

So late-night cattle chatter is not an uncommon sound around these parts, and I normally find it quite comforting. But tonight there was one strange, weirdly non-mooish moo that stuck out and started me on my funny turn. It was half-squeak and half-honk, like a foghorn playing a kazoo. The more I heard it, the more it made me angry. Just that one-off note sent me into a huge freakout and before I knew it I'd bitten into my bottom lip so hard that it sprang a stringy little leak. Strange, I know.

It got worse. I was suddenly outside in the rain, running up the vicarage path towards the field, screaming something along the lines of "NAUGHTY COWS! DO BE QUIET!", except that is the Certificate U version of what I actually said.

I was out there screaming in my kecks for a few minutes before Rev spotted me through his study window. He came racing out shouting *"What the hell are you doing?"*, which may seem a bit cheeky for a vicar but it was clearly with good reason.

I shouted one last thing at the herd, then Rev said "Enough", and marched me back inside. I went into the living room and slouched in the sofa chair whilst Rev fixed me some Ovaltine to calm me down. The telly was on with the sound turned down. Some late-night culture review talk show thing was in full swing. People with silly hairdos and even sillier glasses were waving their hands around quite a lot. It felt comforting that I wasn't the only one getting hysterical at such a late hour.

Rev came back in with the Ovaltine, and it did indeed calm me down. He said it was lucky that Mum was having a rest-home evening tonight; otherwise she would've been very cross with my rage/swear/near-nudity tantrum.

I apologised for my outburst, telling Rev that I was getting a bit overwhelmed with everything. After one of his whopper sighs, the one that sounds like a jet engine coming to rest, he said he understood. "Don't worry, Danno. Matty will be home soon and we can help him get back on his feet."

I told him I'd been having sleep troubles and, after fishing around in a drawer for ages, he gave me some herbal thingies that apparently might help me. "They're not drugs, but even so, don't tell your mother. They should do the trick."

The label defines them as sleep-promoters, which sounds quite sweet and nice. Not sure about the ingredients, though. Lettuce extract, valerian root, powdered Passiflora compound. All sounds a bit cosmic and Stonehengey to me.

Anyway, here goes.

Monday 13th

Didn't sleep much last night. Despite another, much quieter and certainly more polite request from me, the cows refused to shut up. And the promoters did chuff all but leave a horrid taste in my mouth.

I felt totally exhausted this morning, though I perked up a bit on the bus because we had an unscheduled girlyjourney. This is The FLF's invented technical term for when our usual boys-only school coach is replaced with a double-decker, which is an exciting enough event in this tweedy village, but made more so by the fact that tons of Millington High School girls get on it, too. Somehow it always happens during this event that the ladies take the top deck for themselves, with us Conville Grammar chaps on the bottom. This, we all assume, is at the secret request of Miss Marrows, the guy-despising headmistress of their school. (There's a rumour that a few years ago she got a bit tipsy at a parent–teacher evening and stood on the stage and horrified everyone by shouting "Remember girls, no c*cks 'til Cambridge!" and I doubt very much that she was referring to rules regarding keeping poultry as pets.)

There were far too many Millington types on the bus today, so some of them had no choice but to mingle against their wishes with us on the bottom level. Naturally, The FLF nearly self-combusted. He sat with his mouth appallingly wide open, looking slowly up and down the length of the coach as if he was watching an amazing game of underwater tennis.

"Wouldn't it be great if we crashed!" he squeaked to us at one point. Me and Gringo asked what the chuff he was on about. "Well, all these girls would be flying about, and for a minute it'd be like something from the *Matrix*, then we'd land and some of them might land on me. Cool!"

We informed him it was not in the slightest bit cool to wish for a crash, and would he please close his mouth as ladies were looking at us, and not at all in the good way. Gringo was especially vicious towards him, actually. His bad mood was partly down to his sister standing on his *Battlestar Galactica* season two box set last night, snapping six of his favourite episodes in half in the process. "You really need to grow up," he said to our furry friend as he peered over the edge of some imported spacegeek magazine he was trying to enjoy. "No female will ever want you if you carry on like this.'

It's all right for Gringo. He has lady interest in his life. He's been writing to a fellow sci-fi lover in Cheltenham for months now, and they're going to meet up very soon. Apparently she speaks fluent Klingon. Perhaps that's handy in Cheltenham. Plus, he looks the most grown-up and manlike out of the three of us. Hence his nickname – it relates to the impressive tash shadow that he sports. He has to shave every three days. And he's the second tallest in our year and enviously deep in the voice department. Perhaps he's some kind of Pied Piper of puberty, pinching the height and squeakless vocal capabilities from the rest of us, just to make himself cooler. Sod.

Anyway, those two carried on arguing, getting horribly louder with each insult. Gringo called FLF "Gandalf's Gimp". FLF said something I can't really repeat here, but it caused one sweet, mousey-looking Millington moppet a few seats down to shriek in horror and stick her fingers in her ears for the rest of the journey. Everyone was looking at us and I sank further into my seat, hoping I was thin enough to squish through the crack. They wore themselves out eventually, plus thankfully most people had turned their attention to their phones because the signal kicks in when the bus passes Toddington Post Office.

FLF apologised to the pair of us for being so crude. He said the lack of internet access in the village was causing him anguish. "The sauce portal is closed. What am I going to do?" he said, sounding genuinely panic-stricken. He asked me if I would be willing to go on a mission to Mr Mukherjee's newsagents/mini-market/adult entertainment emporium and procure some gentleman's literature for him. That place is very rude. A couple of dusty bags of Hula Hoops, a few racks of congealed Twixes and the biggest shelf of filth you have ever seen. It's actually sagging under the weight. It's always bustling with unsavoury-looking types reaching sheepishly for something rude, then doing a left turn and pretending to go for *Trout and Salmon Fishing* whenever Mrs Mukherjee appears from the back room. At first I rejected the FLF's grubby offer, but he kept pleading with me to help him, and he has this cheeky habit of making his eyelids go heavy and his eyes a bit bulgy and forlorn, like he's the saddest, most persecuted person alive, and I always seem to fall for it. Plus he said I looked the most grown-up and manlike out of the three of us, which made Gringo, King Teenage Hairyface, immensely pouty and jealous. So I ended up agreeing to take up the mission at some point.

'That's the spirit!' FLF said. 'And make sure you aim right. I don't want you getting confused and coming away with a banjo catalogue.'

Such gratitude. I'm really not sure why I bother with him.

Tuesday 14th

Samantha Mumba! The sleep-promoters really did their thing last night. Nine tip-top hours away from all my troubles, and one wholly bizzonkers dream about a futuristic United Kingdom. Not sure what brought it on, possibly some late-night whining I witnessed on *Newsnight Review* last week – the guests getting incredibly gesticulatey about how horrid and naff reality TV has become, and why are people so desperate to advertise their awfulness and why are the public so desperate to watch it until their eyes bleed and all that sort of stuff. Could also have been influenced by Mr Lipton forcing George Orwell's *1984* upon us in English.

So the future of our island, according to my dream, involves nobody being able to escape such awful TV stuff. The sky had been sold off to TV channels, so everywhere you looked up there, there was no dodging such reality nonsense with some silly-haired goober chuntering on about how fantastic he/she was.

I was trying to find some way of turning the sound down so I didn't have to hear it all (I reckon there was about fifty different shows going on in the skies above Minchbury) but they were all booming over the top of each other. This girl was stood next to me watching a segment – a segment which was hovering roughly above the vicarage, as it happens – about a bunch of firemen posing in their pants for a charity calendar, and every time I politely asked her about how I could turn the volume down she shushed me so hard she covered me in flob.

Suddenly there was a nasty blast from a klaxon and an announcement came out of nowhere. The announcement was in a rubbish, old-style computer voice. Imagine if Ceefax could talk and that's what it was like. "Two minutes' sun break", it said, about ten times. Then all the screens fizzled out in random bursts and in its place was a giant digital clock, counting down the time until it all came back on again. I seemed to be the only one who was dead chuffed for the break and I was clapping and dancing but everyone else was just gawping at the clock, some looking at their watches at the same time, waiting for it all to start again.

And then, as a truly odd finale to the strangest dream I've had in ages, the digital display in the sky went all wonky and was suddenly replaced by a fuzzy image of Princess Anne. She was sat at a desk stroking a fluffy white cat. Both of them wearing tiaras. *"Now look here everyone,"* she said. *"I've run out of patience will all of this. I enjoy a spot of telly watching just as much as the next gal, but all this enforced sky activity is disturbing my horses and the lack of light has killed everything in my garden. I won't do. Enough, I say!"* And then she fiddled about with something on the side of her tiara and laser beams shot out from the centre, coming out of the sky and zapping and exploding all the giant TV transmitters all around the valley. All the telly addicts were screaming and running away and I was jumping up and clapping, giving the thumbs up to the unexpected but totally cool anarchy of the Princess Royal. I think she actually winked at me and gave me the thumbs up back, but I was waking up at that point, so I'm not so sure.

It's official. Sleep-promoters rock!

Thursday 16th

Just got back from an unscheduled visit to Matty at the lodge. Was feeling a bit tired after school today, and I really didn't fancy going at all. But Rev had to go out to sort out some communion details at somebody's house in the next village, and Mum clearly wanted some company for the visit.

The place was as grim as usual. It's an old Victorian hospital, which means high roofs all over the shop, which also means echoes galore. Every sneeze, cough and snivel is repeated several times in quieter and quieter instalments. If someone is crying in there, it's absolutely horrific. There's plenty of air fresheners and bowls of potpourri dotted around, but their combined powers can't seem to chase away the main pong of the place, which is an odd mix of feet and toothpaste.

There are only twenty or so patients, and they have their own little rooms, which seem cosy enough. But most of the time they sit around in the main communal area, which is full of big, boring metal tables like we used to have at primary school and, also just like primary school, the tables are covered in a mess of glue sticks, pens, paper and that sprinkly glitter stuff. It doesn't seem fair to me. Suffering a stroke and having one side of your body pinched from you is nasty enough, but having to force the side that does work to do arts and crafts projects all day must be enough to make you blow several important brain fuses and wonder what it's all about. To be fair, it was explained to us by some of the staff that farting about with bits of coloured card and crinkle-cut scissors is apparently helpful stimulatory activity for stroke patients because it helps with focus and left/right side brain stuff. I'm sure this is true. Thinking about it Matty did indeed produce a very attractive Easter bonnet for Rev to raffle at the church fête, but Mum didn't shut the car boot properly when we left and it flew up on the drive home and the Matty hat flew out and whizzed across a field like a very dainty Frisbee.

(We did Frankenstein at school last year, and ever since Matt got ill I've had these occasional fantasies about constructing some mighty machine that can channel the power of lightning and direct it to the dead arms, legs and cheeks of stroke victims across the world and make them all function properly again. I would be able to write a book about it and possibly even walk off with the Nobel prize for services to the stroked.)

Anyhow, back to tonight's visit.

There's a chap in the lodge who I've secretly nicknamed Mr Badpasty. I call him this because he's clearly had major brain surgery due to the two thick flaps of his scalp being held together with tons of industrial-strength staples. But the flaps overlap a bit, creating a ripply ridge effect like the top of a mutant Cornish pasty. He had his wife with him tonight. He always waves whenever he spots me, and I get the feeling that he would rather talk to me than her – that is, if he could actually talk rather than make the sad gargle which is the only sound his mouth can currently manage. Physically his wife looks like one of those henpecky types on display in the medical *Carry On* films, the ones who sit and moan and groan at the bedside of their poorly, yawning hubbies. Except Badpasty's wife rarely speaks. It's as if she's found a way to moan at him through the use of ESP. The way they sit in silence makes me think of an early round of a snooker championship when there are loads of matches going on at once, so two players have to squish next to each other in a bit normally reserved for one, and they just sit there looking stern and straight ahead, pretending that their buttocks are not actually just about touching.

After me and Mum had a little natter with Nurse Super-Smiley (so named by me for the obvious reason that she is always beaming and friendly and ready to dispense fantastically strong cups of tea), we went in to Matty's room to say hello.

He was sleeping in his wheelchair in front of the window. Mum said not to wake him up, so we dimmed the lights a bit and did some tidying. Then we sat on the bed for a bit and drank our tea and ate biccies.

Finally Matty stopped snoring and realised he had company. It's amazing to see how quickly he's adapted to his (hopefully temporary) life in a wheelchair. When he first got one, trying to work it with only one functioning arm kept sending him into fruitless spins that did nothing but snare up the carpet and make him a bit dizzy. Now he's learnt to use his good foot to pull himself forward, scrunching at the carpet with his toes.

It was getting a bit dark outside and, apart from the brassy blare of *Coronation Street* theme tune coming from a room down the corridor, the rest of the lodge was in a rare moment of quiet. There was suddenly something really peaceful about the scene I was in. Mum was cuddling Matty and telling him about all the non-excitement he was missing in Minchbury, and I was feeling a bit snoozy, trying to read the back of *Autumn Temptress*, a vintage Mills & Boon novel, in the bad light. (Wimpy romance books are all the lodge seems to offer in the way of written entertainment. There are thousands of them lying around, half read, some decaying and falling apart. Seeing as it's mostly chaps in there, you'd think the lodge people could slip a few Andy McNabbish numbers around the place.)

Everything seemed still and calm. Matty was telling us how excited he was about coming home in a few weeks. His speech is getting much better. In just a few months he's gone from sounding as if he was from another planet to the sound he produces now, which resembles someone desperate to tell you something, even though they have a mouthful of atomically hot sausages.

Despite having only a few hours out of his chair a day, and even though he has little diversion in this place besides a tiny telly with dodgy reception, Matty has managed to fashion a snuggly little living space in here. But even though I'm hugely chuffed that he's coming home, it's going to be a shock going back to a place that he hasn't lived in since he was a teenager, with none of his London chummos around. One of the therapists recommended that he live in the downstairs of the house for at least a month, with a couple of test trips up the stairs every day, just to get him used to it. Rev's been sorting out his study in order to change it into a Matty rehab room. At least there will be plenty to read in there, I suppose, even if it's all Bibles and back issues of the parish magazine. Better than Mills & Boon, though.

Friday 17th

A hideous thing occurred in History today. I feel ashamed and embarrassed, but perhaps by detailing the unfortunate incident I might get what the Yankeedoodles are fond of calling *closure*.

A statue of Sir William Endelton Bellamy, Minchbury's most famous former resident, is being unveiled in the market square next week. You've probably never heard of him, so I won't bore you with all the details, but according to Mr Tinton he was ye olde explorer who had something terribly important to do with the colonising of Australia. He was also apparently kicked in the banjo area by a kangaroo, leaving him unable to have children, but this salacious detail might've been made up by Mr Tinton just to keep us awake and interested.

Anyway, to celebrate the statue's arrival Tinters started showing us a film from the eighties called *The Bounty*. It's about Fletcher Christian's mutiny against Captain Bligh, and though it has chuff all to do with Billy Bellend (which, inevitably, has become the official abbreviation for Sir William), Mr Tinton assured us it was relevant because it depicted the same era of the British Navy's dominance of the world's oceans. Mel Gibson plays Fletcher Christian in it, and Hannibal Lecter plays Bligh.

The first section of the film was a bit snoozy, to be honest. Lots of stinky pox-faced deckhands getting the business ends of great big waves landing all over them every ten seconds. The occasional menacing glance from Bligh to Christian was thrown in to stir up the promise of some decent fisticuffs later in the film. So far, so nothing. Then, twenty or so minutes in it all went a bit... well, a bit booby.

I'm aware that I'm a growing boy, but I do wish one part of me would stop growing without my permission, and at the most uncouth and inappropriate moments. Basically, as soon as Mel and Hannibal the Cannibal hit Tahiti, the lack of ladies in the movie was suddenly compensated for by the arrival of what seemed like thousands of native island women without any tops on. (By which I mean no jambonger covering device, as opposed to having no tops to their bodies entirely.)

They all came sloshing through the sea to greet the ship's arrival, waving their arms and everything else. What followed was endless slow-motion, soft-focused shots of lady native above-the-waist nudeness. Large ones, small ones, some as startlingly big as prize-winning pumpkins. *Fair enough,* I hear you think. What young chap wouldn't admit to feeling a bit banjovial when faced with such a display? Where's the crime? Even Mr Tinton had to pass comment, turning to us during that saucy sequence to say, "And I'm off to Tahiti on my next holiday!" Ho Ho Ho! It got a few nervous chuckles out of the way from the class and then everyone settled down. Everyone except me, it seemed.

A keckstrectcher of almighty power sprung into being. It was really vicious and it reminded me of that bit from *Alien* where the baby monster bursts out of that poor man's chest and runs across the room making a frightening vampire-cat sort of scream. I feared the same thing was about to happen from my trousers.

I thought of all the tricks I've heard about for taming this (perfectly natural) boy event. Flicking it on the summit with a pencil is apparently a winner, and I decided upon this option. But in my panic I seemed to lose all logic. I searched for a pencil in my pencil case but there wasn't one. I could find pens and compasses and pencil sharpeners galore, but where was an actual chuffing pencil when I most wanted one? At the time it didn't occur to me that a pen of any description would have done just as well, and the presence of lead and an eraser at the end wasn't particularly significant for the operation to work.

Then I dropped my pencil case to the floor with a bit of a clatter and a fuss. A few people turned to see what the racket was about, tutting me to be quiet. By this time my face was drunk with sweat, as if someone had sloshed a bucketload of wallpaper paste over me, and I feared that I was turning into the world's youngest sex maniac. Then I tried some thought voodoo – summoning up horrible, miserable memories in the hope that my trouser trauma might subside and lose interest. It didn't work.

I looked up, and yet another selection of suntanned sauceparts was being beamed onto the classroom wall from the projector. Up until now my discomfort was a completely private affair, but that suddenly changed as, without me even realising it, I put my hand into the air and made a grabbing movement upon one of the jambongi on display. And for extra stupidness I accompanied this action with an involuntary whine that was a twisted, hideous mix of a roar of joy and a girly shriek.

I pulled my hand down quickly and looked the other way, hoping that someone else might be thought of as the culprit due to the relative darkness in the room. But the damage was done and I had been rumbled. Everyone was looking at me like I was the filthiest person on the planet.

'Daniel, please control yourself. I'm sure you've seen it all before,' said Mr Tinton. Everyone was giggling. Never in my entire short life have I wished to disappear into the ground so much. *If only The FLF was in my History class*, I thought. I dread to think how he might've reacted in this situation, but at least it would've taken the attention off me. Probably might have made it onto the news.

Naturally, news of my attempt to fondle an imaginary breast spread very quickly through the rest of my year and much teasing and shouts of "There's the fantasy knab-grabber" ensued.

It's all so unfair and I'm never speaking to my banjo ever again. Wish I'd been born without one, in fact. Why couldn't God have given all men a Rubik's cube each instead of these stupid things. They seem to cause nothing but trouble.

Biographies

Janine Amos (p.32) has been writing for children for fifteen years. She is a successful author in the field of "special issue" non-fiction and faction. She is now concentrating on fiction and her first picture book was published in 2000. Janine lives in Bristol with her son and a cat called BeeBee, in a house full of books. *The Toothgrinder* is her first novel.

Email: janine@pickandmixanthology.com

Felicity Crentsil (p.206) is approaching her mid-twenties, has two degrees and is very happy writing and working part time. Felicity sings nursery rhymes to babies, tells stories to toddlers and helps with reading groups for primary and secondary school children at her local library. She likes being around people who appreciate books and reading, and would love to see her own novels for teenagers and younger readers picked from the shelves.

Email: felicity@pickandmixanthology.com

Roy Davis (p.222) holds an MA in English and Creative Writing from Miami University, where he acted as editor for the university's fiction magazine, *Oxmag*. Last Autumn he received an MA in Writing for Young People from Bath Spa University. He has been teaching for over eight years, everything from elementary school science to college composition and creative writing. Before teaching, he worked as an animal behaviourist, living in the mountains and counting lizards doing push-ups.

Email: roy@pickandmixanthology.com

Diana Gittins (p.166) came to the UK when she was 14 and has worked in a wide variety of jobs, including palmist, factory operative and research fellow. She has published four works of non-fiction, one collection of poetry, various essays and a short story for children. She is currently an associate lecturer in creative writing for the Open University. This is her first novel for teenagers.

Email: diana@pickandmixanthology.com

Alison Killeen (p.12) lives in Wiltshire with her husband and three children. Over the years she has worked as a barmaid, shop assistant, camera packer, teaching assistant and is currently working in a library. At the tender age of 36, Alison returned to education and it was then that she became infected with the writing bug.

Email: alison@pickandmixanthology.com

Kay Leitch (p.182) wants to live in Spain, near water and mountains. She wants to walk under a blue sky with her beautiful black dog, Dyce, then spend eight hours a day writing her next successful children's book. That's the dream. Hold it.

Email: kay@pickandmixanthology.com

Emma Ludlow (p.80) is a young journalist and copywriter with a background in corporate and consumer magazines. She penned her first story at the age of 5 and has written creatively ever since. Her favourite things are cheesecake, 1980s music and the film *If...*

Email: emma@pickandmixanthology.com

Dawn McNiff (p.60) lives in Gloucestershire with her two teenage daughters and big, bad dog, Gooner. In the past she has worked as a bereavement counsellor and an advertising copywriter, but now she works in her local children's bookshop, so she can read children's books all day. She had a short story published by Scholastic Children's Books in 2008.

Email: dawn@pickandmixanthology.com

E.C. Newman (p.40) started writing in her freshman Ancient History class. After a month, with twenty poems and a couple of stories, she did the smart thing and added a Creative Writing major to her Theatre one. She's been writing ever since, finding herself consistently stuck in high school, where she exorcises her own demons and creates new ones for her characters.

Email: e.c@pickandmixanthology.com

Jack Roberts (p.102) grew up in the Rocky Mountains of Utah, and took many of the experiences of *Indian Summer* from his own childhood. Jack loves the quest for adventure and, even though he hasn't discovered anything like the Holy Grail, his venturesome spirit has taken him to live in the villages of Puerto Rico, the townships of South Africa and even the legendary countryside of England.

Email: jack@pickandmixanthology.com

Susan Sedgwick (p.144) has been making things up all her life, mostly playing around in theatre. She's really pleased to discover that writing for young people is even more fun. This extract is from the first of Benny and Zeff's adventures aboard the Windbird. Susan enjoys writing in more than one style, and she's left the boys to follow their next story through time and space, while she's busy on a mysterious romance for teen readers.

Email: susan@pickandmixanthology.com

C.J. Skuse (p.120) spent her childhood re-enacting scenes from *Moonlighting* and roller skating down pub skittle alleys. She loves graphic novels, 1980s sitcoms, Gummy Bears and My Chemical Romance. She hates omelettes, carnivals, exaggerated sneezes and sandals – she needs to know she can run at any time. Claire lives with a psychotic brown rabbit called Sonny and plans to write in the horror genre next.

Email: c.j@pickandmixanthology.com

Ollie Wright (p.240) grew up in Lincolnshire, but that was a very long time ago and there's nothing he can do about it now. He's spent his adult working life in the front line of the British film industry, tearing cinema tickets, pointing out where the toilets are and serving popcorn to celebrities like Keanu Reeves, Thom Yorke and, most exciting of all, Maggie Philbin (give her a Google if you're under 30). *Danny Lambert Tells All* is his first book for teenagers.

Email: ollie@pickandmixanthology.com